CHRISTMAS
IN
ASPEN

Also by Anita Hughes

CHRISTMAS IN ASPEN

A Novel

ANITA HUGHES

ST. MARTIN'S GRIFFIN
NEW YORK

First published in the United States by St. Martin's Griffin, an imprint of St. Martin's Publishing Group

CHRISTMAS IN ASPEN. Copyright © 2024 by Anita Hughes. All rights reserved. Printed in the United States of America. For information, address St. Martin's Publishing Group, 120 Broadway, New York, NY 10271.

www.stmartins.com

Library of Congress Cataloging-in-Publication Data

Names: Hughes, Anita, 1963– author.
Title: Christmas in Aspen : a novel / Anita Hughes.
Description: First Edition. | New York : St. Martin's Griffin, 2024. |
Identifiers: LCCN 2024009208 | ISBN 9781250908155 (trade paperback) |
    ISBN 9781250908162 (ebook)
Subjects: LCSH: Christmas stories. | LCGFT: Romance fiction. | Novels.
Classification: LCC PS3608.U356755 C48 2024 | DDC 813/.6—dc23/
    eng/20240301
LC record available at https://lccn.loc.gov/2024009208

Our books may be purchased in bulk for promotional, educational, or business use. Please contact your local bookseller or the Macmillan Corporate and Premium Sales Department at 1-800-221-7945, extension 5442, or by email at MacmillanSpecialMarkets@macmillan.com.

First Edition: 2024

1   3   5   7   9   10   8   6   4   2

To my mother

CHRISTMAS
IN
ASPEN

Chapter One

Caroline Holt was supposed to be in London, having a hot holiday romance with Brad, an attractive British editor she'd met in the spring at the London Book Fair. Instead, she was driving to upstate New York, to spend Christmas at the family cabin in Hudson, with her younger sister, Daphne.

Caroline had always loved her mother's cabin, nestled in a forest of pine trees. When she was young, she adored Christmas in the Hudson Valley. The winter walk in town, with the shop windows all lit up and the lampposts decorated with huge red bows. The evenings always ended with hot chocolate and reindeer-shaped cinnamon cookies.

But this year she was dreading the holidays; it had been the worst year of her life. A few months ago, her mother, Anne, died from breast cancer. In November, Jack Barret, the guy she was having a fling with, did not take it well when she'd ended their relationship, and she had to change the locks in her apartment. Jack was an attorney for celebrity book contracts, and he was handsome and confident. But after she told him they couldn't see each other anymore, he wouldn't leave her alone.

Anne had been a successful agent at the House of Books, a prestigious New York City literary agency. Caroline's childhood revolved around books. Once a month, Anne hosted a literary salon at the apartment, and in the summers, authors sometimes stayed at the cabin.

When Caroline landed her first job as an editorial assistant at a publishing house, she couldn't believe she was being paid to do what she loved. She had grown up around books and had dreamed of a career in publishing for as long as she could remember. And her passion only grew over the years. She adored every aspect of being an editor—from the initial thrill of falling head over heels for a manuscript to removing the dust jacket of the printed book and smelling the spine as if it were a bouquet of flowers.

But for the past several months, she'd felt burned out. She couldn't get excited enough about the submissions sent to her by agents. She didn't agree with the marketing team on several strategies, and when one of her authors panicked a few weeks before publication, she was too exhausted to give her usual pep talk to cheer her up.

At first, she attributed it to her mother's diagnosis, and to inheriting extra books when another editor quit. But then her mother went into remission, and the publisher hired a new editor, and she felt the same. The problem was with her, and she didn't know how to fix it.

Two days ago, the publisher, Claudia Kennedy, called Caroline into her office. Claudia was in her mid-forties. Her dark hair was worn in a sleek bob, and she wore a beige turtleneck and a red wool sweater.

"Caroline, please sit down." Claudia motioned to the chair. "Would you like a gingerbread cookie?"

A gift box of Christmas cookies from the *New York Times* bestselling author Aaron Robertson sat on the desk. Caroline smiled in spite of herself.

"I hate having this talk so close to the holidays, but this can't wait," Claudia said when Caroline accepted the cookie. "I think you know what it's about."

Claudia had been the publisher for five years. She knew how hard Caroline worked from her editorial-assistant days when they worked together at a different house.

"I don't know why Greta Egan's book didn't do better, it had fantastic word of mouth," Caroline blurted out. "And I know my edit notes for Samantha Wong took longer to reach her than usual, but she turned in a hundred and fifty thousand words. The book she delivered before that was eighty K."

"It's not about one particular book," Claudia cut in. "You hardly participate at meetings, and lately you've been canceling lunches with agents. I got a concerned call from one of your mother's close friends at the House of Books. You won't acquire new books unless you're out there, talking to people. It could help you too."

Caroline put down the cookie. Every editor was expected to buy a certain number of books per year. This was the first year that Caroline hadn't come close to reaching her goal.

"I've been feeling down, and I didn't want anyone to see," she admitted. "I know it will pass." She put on her most professional smile. "A week at my mother's cabin will help. Daphne and I are going to spend all day in pajamas, drinking clove tea and reading by the fireplace."

"I can't imagine how hard it's been without Anne, the whole

publishing world loved her," Claudia said kindly. "But I have to think about the company. I can tell your heart isn't in your work. You haven't bought any new books since the fall. If you don't bring something to an acquisition meeting by the end of the winter, I will have to answer to our CEO, who noticed you didn't have books to present at last season's sales conference."

Caroline tried to swallow. No matter how exhausted she felt, she couldn't imagine having any other job. But where would she find a book, when every manuscript she received left her feeling numb?

"I promise, I'll find one, I won't let you down," Caroline said.

"I want to believe you," Claudia sighed. "I'll tell you what. If you prove yourself at the winter sales meeting, we can revisit this in your spring job review."

Caroline's breathing relaxed. She stood up. "I know the manuscript is out there, I just need a lucky break. Thank you for the cookie, I should go."

Caroline had gone home and canceled her trip to London. Claudia was giving her another chance and she couldn't spend the holidays browsing in Harrods' luxury Christmas ornament department or sitting in a pub drinking mulled wine when she needed to discover a new author. Brad was an editor too, he would understand. She texted him that she wasn't coming, and asked for a rain check for the following year. Then, this afternoon, she loaded her iPad and overnight bag into her car and headed for the cabin. At first, she felt excited about her decision. She and Daphne had barely seen each other since their mother died. They could ski at Mohonk in New Paltz. Stock up on eggnog and waffle mix at Cold Spring General Store. But the closer she got to the cabin, the more she doubted herself. Memories of Anne would be everywhere. At least in London with Brad, she could have distracted herself by listening to him talk about the British publishing industry with that sexy upper-crust accent.

As she pulled up, Daphne flung open the front door. Daphne's blond hair was pulled into a ponytail, and she wore jeans and a cable-knit sweater.

When they were growing up, no one thought they were related. Daphne looked exactly like Anne. They both had blue eyes and that all-American style that looked best in casual clothes. Caroline must have taken after her father. She was too tall, and her hair was wavy, even when she straightened it. Her best feature was her smile. Brad said it reminded him of Julia Roberts in *Notting Hill.*

"I'm so glad you came." Daphne hugged her. "I thought you'd be eating plum pudding and drinking Buck's fizzes at an estate in the English countryside."

Daphne worked at a public relations company in Boston. Unlike Caroline, she wasn't interested in a job in the literary world, and she loved to travel. The walls in her apartment were covered with posters of canals in Amsterdam, and churches in Prague.

Caroline told her about her meeting with Claudia.

"I wouldn't have been good company for Brad," Caroline sighed. "I'm going to spend the week glued to my iPad."

"You can spend the week any way you like." Daphne slipped her arm through Caroline's. "First, I have a big surprise."

A man stood near the fireplace in the living room. He had sandy-blond hair and wide shoulders. His eyes were a deep blue and there was a cleft in his chin.

"This is my boyfriend, Luke," Daphne said. "Luke, this is the sister I've been gushing about."

Daphne hadn't dated anyone seriously in over a year. And she never had little flings like Caroline. Daphne preferred spending her time visiting travel bookstores and cooking foreign dishes.

"Your boyfriend?" Caroline repeated.

"Not exactly." Daphne looked as fresh-faced and eager as she had as a little girl. She stuck out her left hand. "Luke isn't my boyfriend, he's my fiancé."

A round, clear diamond sat on a platinum band.

He held out his hand. "Luke Harper. I know this must come as a surprise, and I hate to intrude on your Christmas." He gave her a winning smile. "But Daphne said you'd be pleased."

Luke was definitely good-looking and he seemed nice. But engaged! She wondered why Daphne hadn't told her. It was probably Caroline's fault. Since Daphne moved to Boston a few months ago, they had barely seen each other. Caroline kept promising to come to Boston to see Daphne's new apartment, but she never had. And when Daphne suggested she come to New York, Caroline had put her off. She was so weighed down by her own grief over their mother's death, she couldn't take on Daphne's as well. Now she wished she had made the trip to Boston, or had Daphne visit her. Even though she was five years older than Daphne, they had always confided in each other, and she hated that she didn't know about this important person in her life.

"So, tell me how you met," Caroline said when they settled on the sofa.

Luke took Daphne's hand, and she curled her fingers around his.

"It was about two months ago, I came down here for the weekend," Daphne began. "I was walking Truffles in the woods, and he got free from his collar. Luke brought him back for me."

"He wouldn't have gone far," Luke volunteered. "I've never seen a dog so attached to his owner."

Daphne had always been wonderful with dogs. The few times they had a dog when they were growing up, it always became Daphne's. Anne was busy at work, and Caroline didn't have the patience to walk the dog early in the morning. The dog slept curled up on Daphne's bed, and Daphne tossed a ball with him for hours.

"We talked for a while, then I invited Luke to come over for dinner," Daphne continued. "I was cooking paella and I always make too much. It's nicer to have someone to share it with."

Caroline never invited men to dinner at her apartment. It was one of her rules. Never let a guy see where you live. The most important rule was never to date a guy for more than a month. It was the only way to not get her heart broken, and make sure she always took care of herself.

She and Jack had lasted three weeks. One night, it started raining when they met for dinner after work. She lived close by, so she broke her own rule and invited him to her apartment for pizza instead. If she hadn't, he wouldn't have been able to spend the week after she broke up with him pacing up and down in front of her building.

"Daphne is a wonderful cook." Luke beamed. "I told her if she ever quits the PR firm, she should be the chef at my restaurant."

"Luke opened a restaurant in Hudson," Daphne piped up. "It's on Warren Street in one of those old clapboard houses. There's even an apartment above, where he lives."

"But your job is in Boston," Caroline said to Daphne. "Where will you live?"

"We'll figure it out." Daphne waved her hand. "I can work remotely, or we can spend part of our time in Boston. The important thing is that we love each other and want to be together."

Anne had been one of those fiercely committed New Yorkers and Caroline was the same. It was one thing to be able to escape to the cabin during the summer and on holidays, but she couldn't imagine living anywhere besides Manhattan.

Daphne cut into her thoughts. "Just think—if Truffles had behaved himself, it never would have happened."

Luke placed his arm around Daphne. "I'm going to spend my life making you happy."

Caroline glanced at the diamond ring again. It really was beautiful. Simple and classic and elegant. "When did that happen, and why didn't you tell me?"

"It was about two weeks ago. I tried to call you," Daphne said. "Your phone was always off. Then I thought it would be better to surprise you." She gave a little laugh. "It worked. You should have seen your face when you saw the ring."

After Jack started stalking her, Caroline got in the habit of turning off her phone. A new wave of guilt washed over her. She should have been there for Daphne. But she had been so consumed with work and the grief over Anne's death, it had been easier to keep to herself.

"You've only known each other a few weeks," Caroline said. "Was there any reason to . . ."

"I'm not pregnant," Daphne assured her. She leaned against the cushions and sighed. "There was no reason to wait. We both knew we wanted to be together forever."

"Daphne isn't saying it quite right," Luke interjected. "I had to convince her that I was serious. I bought out every florist in Hyde Park and had the flowers delivered to the restaurant. Then I arranged for the chef to prepare a special dinner."

"Five courses with wine pairings from my favorite countries," Daphne said. "The dessert was a French croquembouche. The ring was perched on top."

Caroline had tried croquembouche once. It was a pyramid of chocolate pastry balls threaded with caramel and dusted with powdered sugar.

"I had to wipe off the sugar before I slipped it on her finger," Luke laughed.

"It was the most romantic thing I've ever seen," Daphne said. "We're going to have a croquembouche wedding cake."

Caroline felt a small twinge, as if she'd gotten a splinter that wouldn't come out. She wondered if she was jealous. Daphne seemed so happy, as if she'd found the one thing she'd been searching for her whole life.

But she was being silly. Stephen Cross, the first guy she dated after college, or Aiden Gray, who worked out at the same gym, would have proposed to Caroline over the years, if she had let them get close. But she had seen too many friends huddled on their sofas, sobbing into a blanket and going through a box of tissues. There were so many other things in life to care about. Her family and career.

Daphne was twenty-five, she was too young to get married. She wondered if Daphne was reacting to their mother's death. She had to talk to her. But Daphne could be stubborn; it was another thing she got from Anne.

"I'm going to take a bath and go to bed." Caroline stood up. "I haven't been sleeping well."

"It's only eight." Daphne frowned. "We're about to make dinner. We're going to try out a recipe from the restaurant."

"I'm not really hungry." Caroline turned to Luke. "It was so nice meeting you. We will talk a lot more tomorrow."

The upstairs of the cabin was just two bedrooms and a bathroom. Daphne's room was downstairs, behind the kitchen. Anne's bedroom looked exactly the same. The four-poster king-size bed that was too big for the cramped space. Tiffany-blue bedside lamps and a Lucite desk. Cashmere sweaters arranged in shades of the same color in the closet, next to Lilly Pulitzer summer dresses and rows of loafers and Anne's favorite driving shoes.

Anne worked hard for her money and she had been determined to enjoy it.

Caroline never knew her father. Anne's relationship with him had been a college romance, in Aix-en-Provence, in France. Anne never talked about him, and Caroline at some point stopped asking. A few years ago, she tried to find him, but there were thousands of Michael Palmers from Detroit. Caroline searched Facebook and LinkedIn but came up with nothing. Eventually, she had to give up.

Anne managed to finish college while raising Caroline, and by the time she met Walter Greene, in the elevator of her new apartment building, she was a rising star at the House of Books literary agency. Walter was ten years older, and he adored her. Anne was thrilled to meet a man who seemed to love Caroline as much as she did, and who didn't mind that Anne had a career. They got married six weeks later. It was supposed to be Anne's housewarming party, but it turned into the wedding reception instead.

Caroline was four years old when they got married, and she remembered worrying what it would be like to have a man in the house. But from the beginning, Anne made it clear that being Caroline's mother was her top priority. A year later when Daphne was born, Caroline welcomed her little sister. It was fun to play with Daphne when she was sweet-smelling after a bath, and to read to her from the Beatrix Potter books on their shared bookshelf.

Anne and Walter had been complete opposites. Anne loved eating at fashionable New York restaurants, attending gallery openings, and traveling. Walter enjoyed fishing and quiet evenings at home, playing board games. But they had been happy. Then, five years ago, Walter died from a brain aneurysm. Anne spent more time at the cabin. Daphne and Caroline drove up on weekends and they'd make Belgian waffles and walk through the woods.

A pile of mail sat on the desk. Daphne must have brought it in from the mailbox. Her mother still received the occasional letter.

There were some Christmas cards and invitations to holiday parties. Toward the bottom was a red envelope. The return address was Santa's Little Red Mailbox, Main Street, Aspen.

Caroline opened it. It was dated June 30.

My dear Anne,

I just left you at the hotel. I couldn't help slipping back to the gift shop on Main Street and buying an envelope to put in Santa's Little Red Mailbox. You were so charmed by the tradition and I admit, it sounds endearing. People write letters to their loved ones and buy special envelopes at the gift shop. After they finish the letter, the sender drops the envelope in Santa's Little Red Mailbox. The Aspen post office delivers the mail to the address on the envelope, but the return address is Santa's workshop in the North Pole. That's one of the things I love about you. You're a romantic at heart.

We've been together in Aspen a short time, but it feels like we've been here forever.

What I've learned more than anything is that I want to be together. I can't imagine having anyone in my life who is more beautiful, more accomplished, and kinder than you.

Last night you asked what I wished for. The answer is to welcome the new year with you, here in Aspen where we've been so happy. I'll be waiting in front of Santa's Little Red Mailbox at seven p.m. on New Year's Eve.

With all my love,

Caroline wondered why the letter wasn't signed. Perhaps this man was afraid Anne would see him writing the letter. He had slipped it into his pocket and hurried down to the mailbox.

She turned over the cheery red envelope. The stamps had pictures of Santa Claus and Mrs. Claus. There was a lump in Caroline's throat. Her mother should have been here to receive it.

Anne had been so excited about the trip to Aspen last June. It was the annual Aspen writers' conference and writers and editors attended from all over the world. In the past, she had served on various panels, and she had worried that she would be too sick to attend this time. When the doctor finally gave her approval, Anne practically glowed with anticipation.

Afterward, Anne never said much about it. Now Caroline understood why. Anne hated to lie, and she would have had to mention that she was there with a man. But why had she kept him a secret? And did he know that she had cancer, or had that been a secret too?

What if he waited for Anne at the Little Red Mailbox on New Year's Eve and she never showed up? Caroline had to find out who he was. Then she could contact him and tell him.

She opened her mother's computer and clicked on her credit card statements. There it was, in June. Fourteen nights at the Aspen Inn, 66 Main Street, Aspen.

The photos on the hotel's website looked lovely. Guest rooms with beamed ceilings and roaring fireplaces. A restaurant called the Silver Nickel, with pictures of cozy booths, and smiling couples drinking colorful cocktails.

Caroline tapped the number into her phone.

"I'm calling about a reservation last June," Caroline said when the concierge answered. "The name was Anne Holt."

Caroline told the man what she needed.

"I'm sorry," the man replied. "We can't give out information about our guests."

"Please, it's terribly important," Caroline urged. "My mother is dead; I need to find out who she was staying with."

"I'm sorry, I wish I could help you." The man was apologetic. "We must maintain our guests' privacy, I'm sure you understand."

Caroline hung up. An empty feeling settled over her. He would never know why her mother didn't come, and Caroline would never meet the man who had been in love with her. At that moment, nothing seemed more important. Here was her chance to get a window into her mother's thoughts a few months before her death. Had she been in love with this man? Who was he? Had he made her feel vibrant and alive, even for a short time?

Suddenly she had an idea. She did a quick search on the computer. Then she took out her credit card and entered her information.

She'd go to Aspen and wait for the man in front of Santa's Little Red Mailbox. It wouldn't bring her mother back, but it would be something. And she could read manuscripts on the plane.

The flights might book up if she didn't reserve her ticket, but she couldn't go to Aspen without discussing it with her sister. It was their first Christmas since their mother died, and Caroline didn't want to do anything without Daphne's approval.

Outside the bedroom window, the stars reflected on the tips of pine trees, like the brightest Christmas lights. Perhaps there were a few miracles still out there, and perhaps Christmas wouldn't be a complete disaster.

Chapter Two

When Caroline woke up the next day, it was already midmorning. Her flight wasn't until this evening and she was tempted to curl up with her iPad and stay in bed. But she couldn't do anything without her first cup of coffee. In New York, her drip coffee maker brewed her first cup of blond roast coffee before she got out of the shower.

Her mother had bought the cabin twenty years earlier, when one of her books was turned into a feature film. Walter offered to split the cost, but Anne wanted to buy it on her own. Walter didn't come up as often; he was an ophthalmologist and was often on call during the weekends. Anne rarely missed a weekend in the spring and fall, and she spent the month of August and Christmas at the cabin.

Anne was passionate about New York, but the cabin was the one place she could truly relax. She almost never wore makeup except for her signature orange-red lipstick, and she lived in sandals and loafers. She seldom socialized with the other New Yorkers who owned second homes. Her days were spent reading and walking, and being with Caroline and Daphne when they were there.

The floor creaked as Caroline walked to the closet. The creak had always been there, along with the slightly warped closet door. Anne bought the cabin from a writer who wrote his first novel there at the age of fifty, and Anne refused to change anything. The walls were paneled in teak, and the kitchen had an avocado-green-colored oven.

Caroline's bedroom had the same furnishings it had since Caroline was in high school. A bed with a wooden headboard and a floral comforter. An armchair sat under the window, and there was a desk and a bookcase. The roof was sloped and a paisley rug covered the oak floor.

When she went downstairs, it was quiet. Daphne and Luke must have gone out. She made a cup of coffee and entered her mother's study.

A maple desk took up almost the entire space. On the walls, there were framed covers of some of her mother's books, and a few family photos. Daphne on her way to summer camp, Caroline at her high school graduation. All four of them on a gondola in Venice.

Caroline recalled the previous year, when she discovered her mother was sick. Anne was sitting at the desk, paying bills. Caroline hadn't seen her mother in a while. Anne usually wore her ash-blond hair in a smooth bob, but she was letting it grow out. Caroline liked it that way—it made her face appear softer.

Caroline placed her mother's cup of clove tea on the desk. She noticed the check her mother was writing. It was made out to NewYork-Presbyterian Hospital for ten thousand dollars.

"That's a generous donation," Caroline commented, sitting in the chair opposite her.

At fifty-two, Anne was still a beautiful woman. She had the

same blue eyes as Daphne. Her skin was almost unlined and she had high cheekbones.

"It's not a donation," Anne said. "It's for an experimental cancer treatment."

Caroline wondered which of her mother's friends was sick. Anne was so generous with the people she was close to. Once, she took a recently divorced friend on a cruise and paid for the whole trip. The friend said it was the nicest thing anyone had ever done.

"I hope the treatment is working," Caroline said.

Anne took a long sip of her tea.

"The doctors don't know yet, but they're hopeful," she said, looking at Caroline.

There was something about Anne's expression that made Caroline's heart pound. Anne wasn't talking about a friend. She was talking about herself.

"Do you have cancer?"

"Breast cancer. They found it a couple of months ago, at my routine exam." Her voice was steady. "I missed last year's scan, I was on tour with an author. My doctor suggested this treatment and it seems to be working."

It was impossible. Her mother was the strongest, most capable person she knew. Whenever something broke at the cabin, she fixed it herself. She could put on her own snow tires, and one summer she drove the girls across the country to see the Grand Canyon and the Golden Gate Bridge.

"You found out two months ago and you didn't tell us?"

"I was going to tell you sometime. You've both had a busy fall," Anne admitted.

Caroline tried to think what she had been busy with. Approving promotional copy for the catalog at work, accompanying an author on an out-of-town tour. She was always busy; that didn't excuse her mother from not telling them.

"Is that why you grew out your hair?" Caroline demanded. "Because you're worried soon you won't have any."

"It's easier to maintain this way. No more monthly appointments to keep it at the right length." Anne's expression faltered. "I didn't mean to keep it a secret. The more people I tell, the more real it becomes."

"Does anyone know?" Caroline asked.

Anne's parents were dead, and since Walter died, her mother rarely dated.

"Just the doctors and other members of the treatment group." She shook her head. "Some of them have such interesting stories, they'd make a wonderful book."

Caroline turned away so her mother couldn't see her tears. Caroline almost never cried. It was another one of her rules. Crying didn't help anything.

Caroline remembered the last Christmas she and Anne and Daphne spent together at the cabin. On Christmas morning, they opened presents and made eggnog waffles. After breakfast they did a mother-daughter hike to Kaaterskill Falls and then read in front of the living room fireplace. At night, they dressed up for dinner and set the table with Anne's holiday china. Anne and Daphne made glazed ham, and green beans with pecans. For dessert, Daphne baked a strawberry meringue Pavlova she discovered on a trip to New Zealand.

In the spring, Anne seemed better, and in June she announced she was in remission. She was so happy to attend the Aspen writers' conference, even if she wasn't on a panel. After Anne died,

Caroline wondered if she'd had a feeling that it would be the last time she would be well enough to travel.

Caroline sorted through some of her mother's files, and then went to the kitchen for a second cup of coffee.

Daphne was standing at the counter, unloading groceries. She looked beautiful without any makeup. Her blue turtleneck brought out her eyes, and she wore faded jeans tucked into boots.

"You're awake!" Daphne greeted her. "You look much better. You looked awful last night. Even Luke commented that you looked tired, and he's never met you before."

Caroline grimaced. She walked over to the coffee maker. "I'd had a long day. All I needed was a good night's sleep."

"I'm glad you slept in," Daphne said chirpily. "We left the Christmas tree outside because we didn't want to wake you. Luke went to get some supplies."

"The Christmas tree?"

They never bought the Christmas tree until Christmas Eve. It was a tradition. Anne and Caroline and Daphne would pile into the car on Christmas Eve and drive to BJ's Christmas Tree Farm. After they chose the tree, they'd drink hot chocolate and buy a new ornament at the gift shop.

"We picked one out early this year, Luke was afraid there wouldn't be any left," Daphne explained. "He was right. I had my heart set on a white tree and there were only a few to choose from."

Caroline glanced out the window. A tall white Christmas tree lay on the porch. They'd never had a white tree before. It resembled something out of a C. S. Lewis book. And it would look stunning when it was decorated.

"I've never heard you say you want a white tree," Caroline said.

Daphne set the carton of eggs on the counter.

"Mom always wanted the biggest fir tree on the lot." Daphne shrugged. She frowned at Caroline. "Is this about Luke? You can tell me if you don't like him."

"Of course I like him," Caroline said slowly. "He's good-looking and polite and he's obviously in love with you. But you've only known each other for two months, why rush into marriage?"

"Plenty of couples get engaged when they haven't known each other very long," Daphne insisted.

Caroline tried again. "You're twenty-five and you have a wonderful career. What if you get offered a job in Paris or London? Luke is tied to his restaurant, you couldn't go."

"We haven't thought that far ahead."

"That's what I mean, you haven't thought this through," Caroline urged. "You might not want to live in Hudson. Or you might discover things about each other that are impossible to live with."

"Mom and Walter only knew each other for six weeks before they got married. They were happy for twenty years."

"That was different. Mom already had me," Caroline said.

"Are you saying that Mom married Walter because she wanted you to have a father?" Daphne asked in surprise.

"Of course not. She didn't even let Walter officially adopt me, she was perfectly capable of raising me by herself," Caroline corrected. "But she didn't have the same opportunities as you do. You're free, you can do anything you please."

Daphne put the milk carton in the fridge. "I've never felt this way about anyone before. Luke makes everything fun. I save up things to tell him throughout the day, and I never want to be apart."

"There's more to love than enjoying each other's company," Caroline persisted.

"Maybe if you dated a guy for more than a month, you'd know what love felt like." Daphne placed her hands on her hips. "I'm not like you. I don't want to end up alone when I'm forty because I'm afraid to take a chance now."

Caroline tried not to feel hurt. Daphne had always been stubborn. When Daphne was ten, she wore her favorite yellow dress to school for five days in a row. Caroline gently explained that the other girls would make fun of her if she always wore the same clothes. Daphne retorted that she wasn't dressing for the other girls. As long as the dress was washed and hanging in her closet every morning, she put it on.

"I don't want to talk about Luke any more," Daphne said. "I'm going to the attic to get down the Christmas ornaments. Then Luke and I are going to the confectionery to buy some last-minute gifts. You should join us."

Vasilow's Confectionery had been a Hudson institution for one hundred years. Anne often gave their Grand Marnier truffles and legendary cinnamon squares as Christmas presents. The scarlet-colored gift boxes tied with gold ribbons were so like Anne. Elegant and unexpected.

Caroline's expression softened. It was almost Christmas. She didn't want to fight with Daphne.

"I'd love to join you, but I don't think I can. I want to talk to you about something. I might not be here for Christmas. I'm considering flying to Aspen tonight."

Caroline showed her the letter addressed to Anne. She told Daphne that the hotel concierge wouldn't give her any information.

"Maybe if I ask in person, they'll give me his name," she said, finishing the story. "At least I can go to Santa's Little Red Mailbox on New Year's Eve and wait for him to show up."

Daphne read the letter for herself, the tears welling in her eyes. Daphne was the opposite of Caroline; Daphne cried at everything. But a few minutes later her tears would dry up and she'd be smiling, like a puddle after a summer thundershower.

"How could she not tell us?" Daphne demanded, grabbing a tissue from the counter.

"She didn't tell us everything," Caroline reminded her. "We didn't know the cancer returned until she was in the hospital."

"She could have told us about this." Daphne waved the envelope. "You can't go to Aspen yet. You have to stay and have Christmas with Luke and me first."

Caroline shook her head. "I checked and there aren't any available flights after Christmas. I want time to ask around and see if anyone remembers them together. I didn't want to miss out so I booked the flight and ten days at the hotel where they stayed."

"Then I'll go with you," Daphne suggested. "Luke will understand."

"I thought about that. I'd love you to come. Nothing would make me happier than if we did this together. But what if it's a wild-goose chase? I'd blame myself if you missed your first Christmas with Luke and I'm wrong."

"I suppose you have a point," Daphne agreed. "Luke and I are going to spend the week planning our wedding. I always imagined a destination wedding, a beach in Mexico or a villa in Tuscany. It might be nice to have it here, with a reception in the garden. You know, in honor of Mom."

Caroline hugged Daphne. She pushed back her own tears.

"Wherever you get married, Mom will be there with you. I'm

sorry for what I said earlier. Luke is the luckiest man, and you're going to be a beautiful bride."

Caroline took her cup of coffee into the study and sorted through boxes on the floor. The boxes had been sitting there since Caroline cleared out Anne's office at the literary agency. Advance copies of books, royalty statements bound with elastic bands, a box of manuscripts from hopeful authors. Caroline had to smile. Earlier in her mother's career, authors had to go to the post office and mail off their novels to prospective agents. These days, all the submissions were made online.

There was a stack of typewritten letters, tied with a ribbon. The name at the bottom of the page sounded familiar.

Caroline untied the ribbon and read the first letter.

Dear Anne,

I've decided I owe you a letter. It was wonderful of you to meet with me when you're so busy. I do have to laugh at myself for showing up at the restaurant in a long, black coat and hat. As if anyone would recognize a seventy-five-year-old female writer who wrote a couple of bestsellers forty years ago! I can see why clients love you. You were wonderful for indulging me, you even remembered my favorite cocktail—a pink lady with two maraschino cherries—from an article you read about me in *The New Yorker*.

Anne, I do want you to represent me. But I can't expect you to approach editors without telling you the full story of why I stopped writing and where I've been for the last forty

years. So, I've decided to write it all down in letters. I can
see you frowning. I'm supposed to be spending the next few
months working on my new novel. I promise to do that too.
But you know how authors love to procrastinate. Writing
these letters will be better than replanting my window box
or lining my kitchen cabinets while I think about the new
book.

Say hello for me to those darling little girls in the
photographs. You're so lucky to have them.

Regards,
Nina Buckley

Caroline remembered reading Nina's obituary in *The New
York Times*. She had been quite well-known in the mid-1970s. Her
novels were at the forefront of the women's lib movement. Then
she disappeared. There were rumors that she was in Morocco with
the Rolling Stones, or holed up in a bedsit in Paris. But she never
resurfaced, and until that obituary ran a few years ago when she'd
died in New York, everyone had forgotten about her.

Her mother had never said she represented Nina. And there
had never been another novel.

Caroline set the letters aside. She didn't have time to read them
now, so she'd take them to Aspen. She carried her coffee cup into
the kitchen, and went to help Daphne with the Christmas ornaments.

Chapter Three

Later that evening, Caroline's flight started its descent into Aspen airport. She almost wished she had flown into Denver and taken a shuttle the extra four hours instead. Even in the dark, the airstrip looked like it belonged in a toy store, next to the model train sets. But when the plane landed and she entered the terminal, she was glad she'd flown straight to Aspen. The terminal resembled a ski lodge, with timbered walls and a beamed ceiling. A giant Christmas tree had been erected, and everyone was happy and smiling.

It only took a few minutes to drive into town. Caroline kept her face pressed to the Uber's window. When she caught sight of Main Street—lit up with more lights than she thought possible—she almost forgot why she came. It was the most magical place she'd ever seen.

Aspen trees thick with snow lined the sidewalk, benches were piled with fresh snow. A Christmas tree stood at one end, and at the other there was an ice-skating rink and a pergola with a red sleigh.

It was the lights that took her breath away. Even the Christmas tree at Rockefeller Center didn't make her feel the same way. As if she were gazing through a telescope at thousands of twinkling stars. Gold lights were wrapped around tree trunks, and every branch was strung with gold and silver lights.

The only things brighter than the trees were the shops themselves. Every window was decorated with colored lights. Frosted letters saying MERRY CHRISTMAS and HAPPY HOLIDAYS were sprayed on the glass, and Caroline could see cashmere sweaters and fleece-lined jackets and winter boots. One window had a Victorian dollhouse, another had snowflake-shaped boxes of chocolates.

The Uber dropped her off at a redbrick building tucked between a gift shop and a clothing boutique. She rolled her suitcase up the driveway and entered the lobby.

Inside, the lobby resembled a high-class Western saloon. The walls were paneled and the ceiling was hung with glass chandeliers. Cowhide sofas were arranged around a glass coffee table, and a stone fireplace took up an entire wall. A Christmas tree stood in the corner, and there was a rolltop desk complete with a quill pen.

Caroline gave the man at the front desk her name.

"Welcome to the Aspen Inn, Miss Holt. You called yesterday." He glanced at his computer. "It must be a Christmas miracle. We hardly ever have rooms available over the holidays."

"My mother stayed here during the summer, Anne Holt," Caroline said. "I wonder if I could have the same room."

The man clicked through his screen.

"Ms. Holt was in the Silver Rush suite on the second floor. I'm afraid that's not available. We have you in a lovely Copper room with a view of the slopes."

Caroline wanted to ask him questions. Did her mother have anyone else in the suite? Did she make any special requests or book an activity? Perhaps she asked the hotel kitchen to prepare a picnic for hot-air ballooning, or she reserved a couple's massage at the hotel spa. But the man kept talking.

"You're here during the Twelve Days of Aspen celebration. It goes through New Year's. There are concerts and caroling. The Hotel Jerome next door has a gingerbread-house-making contest for children, and the Silver Circle ice-skating rink offers free ice-skating. Many of the shops give out hot chocolate, and you can reserve a horse and carriage for a romantic moonlit ride through the forest. All the information is on our website."

Caroline sighed. She didn't have anyone to share a romantic horse and carriage ride with, and she had never been a good ice-skater. Right now, she was tired and hungry.

"It sounds wonderful," Caroline said, accepting the room key. "I haven't eaten in hours. Is there anywhere I could get a burger and a salad?"

She almost never craved red meat. But somehow standing there, with antlers on the walls and a pair of cowboy boots displayed on a side table, she desperately wanted a burger.

The man smiled. "You're in Aspen, we have over eighty restaurants. Why don't you start with our own bar and grill. We serve the best Angus beef in town."

Caroline first wanted to change her clothes. The Western theme continued in her guest room. The bed had a dark wood headboard and there was a striped upholstered armchair. A brass chest took the place of a coffee table. Next to the window was a velvet daybed that would have looked at home in a brothel.

Caroline wondered if her mother's suite had been furnished in the same way. Anne had loved period furniture. She said it transported you to another time and place, like the pages of a novel.

The hotel restaurant was called the Silver Nickel. It was in the back of the hotel, facing the mountain. Caroline entered through swinging doors. The bar was lined with bottles, and there was a long mirror. Leather booths were scattered around the space, and Caroline caught sight of a kitchen with a brick oven.

Everything on the menu sounded delicious. Cauliflower gratin and braised Brussels sprouts as appetizers. Cheeseburgers with local cheddar cheeses, and sirloin steaks with truffle fries as main courses. She counted fifteen different cocktails. A drink called an Aspen Mule was vodka and ginger beer with golden bitters. Another was a hot toddy and was made with gin and honey and chai tea.

"You have to try the sausage fennel pizza," a male voice said. "And an Earl Grey old-fashioned. Rye whiskey and Earl Grey syrup stirred in the glass. With a dash of walnut bitters and an orange zest for garnish."

Caroline thought the voice belonged to the waiter or the bartender, but instead it came from a man sitting at the bar. He was in his early thirties and very handsome. His light brown hair was worn short, and he had hazel eyes. He had the kind of chiseled features that belonged in an ad for men's cologne, and white, straight teeth. He wore a green sweater over a turtleneck.

"Thank you, but I'm going to have the cheeseburger, and I don't drink whiskey."

"You can get a cheeseburger anywhere in Aspen. The hotel chef here worked at a ski resort in the Italian Alps, his pizza is renowned. And the rye whiskey isn't like other whiskey. This brand is made right here in Aspen. It uses only locally grown grains and potatoes."

Caroline went back to her menu.

"Thank you for the suggestions, I'll order the pizza another time."

"At least try the old-fashioned, you'd be doing me a favor."

"A favor?" Caroline repeated.

"I own the distillery that makes the rye whiskey. If you like it, you can tell the bartender and they'll keep stocking it."

Something about the way he asked was endearing, rather than pushy. It reminded Caroline of when she and Daphne were teenagers. Daphne would ask Caroline to sample a sauce she was making for a spaghetti dinner at school, or brownies she had baked for a new boyfriend.

"All right, I'll have an old-fashioned," Caroline conceded.

The man's eyes danced. "Do you mind if I join you? I'll order the pizza and you can try a slice. I promise you won't be disappointed."

She had planned on pulling out her iPad and reading. She'd scrolled through several manuscripts on the plane. A few had well-thought-out plots and interesting characters. But she'd been an editor long enough to know that wasn't sufficient. A book she acquired had to make her feel like she had discovered new friends when she finished reading it. If the manuscript was really good, she'd go back to the beginning and read it again.

But her eyes were tired, and she didn't feel like being alone. It was almost Christmas and she was in Aspen.

"If that's your usual pickup line, it's not the kind most women go for," she said with a laugh.

"I almost never pick up women at bars. Especially not bars that sell my whiskey—that would be mixing business with pleasure." He walked over to her and held out his hand. "Max Carpenter. If you'd like, this time I can make an exception."

Caroline was used to this type of back-and-forth. It was how many of her flings started. But somehow, this felt different. Max's smile was wider and more honest than the smiles of most of the men she met, and he wasn't afraid to say he was worried about his job.

"Caroline Holt. I'm not in the market for romance," she said evenly. "But you're welcome to join me."

Max had been right; the pizza was the best she ever had. Sausage with melted mozzarella cheese, sprinkled with fennel. But the burger was even better. Just one bite of juicy beef on toasted brioche made her wonder why she didn't eat burgers more often.

"Do you live in Aspen?" she asked.

"I moved here two years ago to get the distillery up and running," he answered. "I grew up in Santa Barbara but my mother's family has always owned a house in Aspen. Her ancestor was one of the miners during the silver rush."

Max told her about the silver rush that brought miners to Aspen a hundred and fifty years earlier. Aspen was called Ute City then and consisted of a mining camp and a few shops. The miners struck silver and the area became the biggest producer of silver in the United States.

"At the turn of the nineteenth century, there was the Great Panic and the mines started running out of silver." Max sipped his cocktail. "Most of the miners left. My ancestors stayed and the next generation persuaded investors to fund the first ski resort." He grinned. "I'm trying to create a completely sustainable distillery. You might say I have the pioneering spirit in my blood."

The ryecorn for Max's distillery was locally grown. The copper pots used to distill the whiskey were fueled with cooking oil from local restaurants. The spent mash was fed to cows, and the wastewater was recycled and used on the next crop.

Caroline couldn't help but be impressed.

"I was a biology major in college. When I started the distillery, I was lucky enough to hire a foreman who is an expert in the field," Max finished. "We're still in the early stages. If people don't buy the whiskey, all the time and money will be wasted."

They talked about publishing and Caroline's love of books. She didn't tell him the things that were troubling her. Her mother's death, the constant feeling of career burnout, Claudia's ultimatum about whether she'd keep her job. And now her new worries: Daphne's engagement to Luke, and finding the sender of the letter from Santa's Little Red Mailbox.

It was getting late. A few diners were finishing their desserts.

"My mother is hosting an open house tomorrow night, you should come," Max suggested.

Max was good-looking, and she admired how passionate he was about the distillery. But if she wanted a fling she would be in London with Brad.

She shook her head. "I'm not in Aspen long enough to date."

He took a pen from his pocket and wrote an address and phone number on a napkin.

"Who said anything about a date? My parents own one of the Queen Anne houses on Walnut Street. It's beautifully lit, almost everyone in Aspen stops by."

"I'll think about it." She tucked the napkin in her purse.

Max stood up and held out his hand.

"Even if you don't come, I'm glad we met." His smile was as bright as the lights wrapped around the bar. "It's not often I get to spend the evening with an attractive woman and drink my whiskey at the same time."

* * *

Caroline went up to her room and texted Daphne that she had arrived. By the time she had taken a bath, she was too tired to read another manuscript. But for some reason, she was wide awake.

She remembered the letters she found in her mother's study. She dug them out of her suitcase and read the next one.

Dear Anne,

It was so kind of you to invite me to Thanksgiving with your family. I almost said yes—a proper Thanksgiving in one of those wonderful, prewar Fifth Avenue apartments with a doorman! It reminds me of the dinners I attended during the short and glorious period of my success. I'll have to tell you about those dinners someday. Being invited into the homes of my publisher and other writers. I'd slip into their libraries and spend the whole party drooling over the books. Then I'd walk back to my apartment, drunk with the knowledge that my little book sat on the same shelves.

But I couldn't intrude on your family, and I don't mind spending Thanksgiving alone. It will give me time to work. Writing is tricky. Sometimes I write as fast as a racehorse in the last lap of the Kentucky Derby, other times I feel like a workhorse one step away from the glue factory.

But I'm not writing these letters to complain, only to explain why I disappeared. It all started with Laura Carter, the writer of the *Women's World Monthly* column that ran for a few years in the 1970s. The column was hugely successful. It was called How an Upper East Side Society Girl Escaped to a Maple Syrup Farm in Vermont.

I was twenty-eight and my first two novels had been

published. The reviews of my books were glowing, and I was compared to the best feminist writers of the day—women who wrote about their career goals instead of men and heartbreak. But I was still broke financially, so I kept my job as a copy editor at *Women's World Monthly.*

One day in December, the lifestyle editor, Margaret Baker, called me into her office. We started at the magazine at the same time. Now Margaret occupied a corner office on the seventh floor with her own secretary.

"I hope you invited me here to share some of your Christmas loot," I said to Margaret, eyeing the plates of cookies on the sideboard. There were two wrapped fruit loaves, and a bottle of champagne with a silver ribbon.

Margaret followed my gaze. "Harry sent the champagne to make up for all the times he's been away this year. I don't know why I stay with him, he even missed my birthday," she sighed. "If he doesn't propose soon, we're finished."

Margaret was involved in a long romance with a travel editor. She'd been trying to get him to propose for ages, but he kept running off to exotic locations.

"At least it's expensive champagne." I picked up the bottle. "I didn't know travel editors made that much money."

"They don't, they get free gifts like the rest of us," Margaret said. "You should see the kinds of presents I receive. One reader sent me an eggbeater, as if I spend all my time in the kitchen. I doubt any of the male editors received hammers or screwdrivers."

I hid my smile. Margaret was one of those 1970s women

who wore slacks all the time, because wearing a dress was "giving in." She subscribed to men's magazines like *Esquire* and *GQ,* and she had taught herself to change a tire so she wasn't dependent on a man.

"I wouldn't mind taking the fruit loaf," I said. "I can't afford to fly home this year, and I have to cook my own Christmas dinner."

"Two bestselling books and you still can't treat yourself to an airline ticket." Margaret frowned. "I wonder if the male authors on the list have the same kind of problems."

"It's the *New York Times* list, it doesn't mean anything financially." I shrugged. "The only authors who make money are the ones whose books sell at supermarkets and airports. My publisher thinks my books are too literary to be released in paperback."

"What if I told you that you didn't have to spend Christmas in New York," Margaret said. "Instead, you'd have a free week at a maple syrup farm in Vermont, with a fully stocked fridge and a traditional Christmas dinner. Stuffed Cornish hens, mashed potatoes, and pecan pie."

Margaret handed me a copy of *Women's World Monthly.* There was a photo of a farmhouse with a white picket fence. The living room had a huge fireplace and beamed ceiling. There was a kitchen with an old-fashioned stove, and a bedroom with a four-poster bed and a quilted comforter.

"This is Laura Carter's column."

Laura Carter was a thirty-year-old former New York socialite. A couple of years earlier she had left behind the nightclubs and dinner parties in Manhattan and moved to Vermont. She wrote a wildly successful column about living on a farm. She collected firewood to heat the farmhouse, and sold maple syrup from a roadside stall.

"Those are the only photos of the farmhouse, we've never had a photographer up there before," Margaret said.

"What does it have to do with me?" I asked.

"Archie had the brilliant idea to hold a nationwide contest inviting readers to share their perfect Christmas getaway. The winner will spend Christmas week with Laura at the cabin."

Archie owned *Women's World Monthly* and a few other magazines. I'd only met him once, at a company Christmas party. He liked to believe he was very involved, even though he spent most of his time playing golf and eating at his private clubs.

"The thing is, Laura Carter is actually Betty Shapiro and she's a seventy-year-old retiree living in Florida," Margaret continued. "I was hoping you could pretend to be Laura Carter for the week."

I was horrified. For one thing, I was a terrible liar. I could never pretend to be someone I wasn't. And I was from New Jersey. I'd never lived in the country. I didn't know what to do with firewood. The only time I'd used a match was to light a cigarette.

Margaret piled on the compliments. I could hold a conversation with anyone. I was a feminist, I could do anything if I set my mind to it.

"What if the winner recognizes me?" I asked.

"There might be a few photos of you in the style section of *The New York Times* but you're hardly a celebrity. Your photo isn't even on your book jackets."

That had been a decision made by my agent and publisher. I was attractive—light brown hair, brown eyes, curves in the right places. They didn't want my looks to overshadow my books' message. I agreed with them. I wanted my words to speak for themselves.

"I'll pay you five hundred dollars, from my own petty cash. You can never tell anyone," Margaret warned. "Even Archie thinks Laura Carter is a young socialite from the Upper East Side."

I asked how Margaret could hide the truth from the publisher. She explained that Betty had been a friend of Margaret's mother's and the column was meant to be a one-time thing. It became so popular that Betty was able to sell her studio apartment and move to a luxurious retirement community in Florida. Betty didn't want the column to end and neither did *Women's World Monthly.*

"All you have to do is spend one week with the contest winner. Then Betty can go back to telling readers how to watch for bears in Vermont, from her screened-in porch in Palm Beach."

Five hundred dollars would pay off my charge cards, and allow me to buy a new winter coat. There was another reason I wanted to get away. I had just broken up with my fiancé, Teddy, and I didn't want to spend my first Christmas without him in New York.

"All right, I'll do it," I agreed. "But you have to make sure no photographers show up."

"Scout's honor." She wrote out a check and handed it to me. "One more thing: your fiancé has to be there. Laura Carter got engaged in her last column."

"What did you say?" My mouth dropped open.

Apparently, Laura's boyfriend had recently proposed. It was a very romantic proposal. He served Laura a candlelit dinner. The diamond ring was hidden in the maple pudding they ate for dessert.

"What's her fiancé's name?"

"That's the thing. Laura has kept it secret. Her fiancé is supposed to be very private. So Teddy can just be himself."

I was already holding the check. The promise of staying warm all winter was too good to pass up. I had the subway trip home to figure out how I was going to ask the man whose suits I had tossed out the window of my building to join me for Christmas in Vermont.

Authors have an old trick. Always finish the day's writing in the middle of a character's dilemma. Then the next day, it's easier to pick up where one left off. So, I'll stop here and go back to rewriting the first chapter of my new book. I promise, I'm making progress. It's like building a house. It doesn't have any walls yet, or even a roof, but I've laid the first bricks.

Regards,
Nina

Caroline placed the letter back on the stack of papers. Outside the window a soft snow was falling. The hotel room was bright and warm. She turned off the lights and crawled under the covers.

Chapter Four

The next morning, Caroline woke up early. She lay in bed, wishing it were the previous Christmas and she was in her bedroom at the cabin. Her mother and Daphne would be downstairs making waffles while Christmas music played in the background. Anne had loved all kinds of Christmas music. The classics, and Mariah Carey, and whatever was trending on Spotify.

But then she pulled back the shades, and her heart made a small leap. It had snowed overnight, and everything was white. Skiers trudged over deep powder, and the roof of the ski gondola was blanketed with a layer of snow. The branches of the aspen trees were white, and the frozen creek outside her room was the blue-white of a diamond.

Caroline dressed warmly in a wool coat and suede boots. She grabbed a bagel and a cup of coffee from the hotel restaurant and approached the reception desk. A different man stood behind the counter.

"How can I help you, Miss Holt?" he asked when she told him her name. "We have ski rentals on the property. And I'd be happy to make dinner reservations. Aspen gets so busy at Christmas, it's better to plan ahead."

Caroline didn't have time to go skiing. And she didn't have anyone to eat dinner with. She was there to find Anne's lover. She explained about her mother's stay in June.

"Did my mother make any special requests?" Caroline asked. "Perhaps she rented fat-tire bicycles or booked one of the horseback-riding tours."

The man scrolled down his computer screen.

"I'm afraid not. I do see newspapers delivered to the room. *The New York Times* and *The Philadelphia Inquirer.*"

Anne couldn't live without her *New York Times*. Caroline had encouraged her to read it online. Anne could read it on her phone on the way to work or during lunchtime. But she refused. She usually walked the six blocks to the House of Books instead of taking the subway, and her lunch hours were spent taking editors and authors to lunch.

The Philadelphia Inquirer didn't tell Caroline anything. If it had been a small-town newspaper, it might have been a clue. But over a million people lived in Philadelphia.

Caroline thanked him and walked on to Main Street. The sidewalk was filled with people enjoying the crisp morning air. Women wearing parkas carried designer shopping bags, and children bundled in ski suits clutched hot chocolates. Several men had toddlers perched on their shoulders, and a young couple held a small paper bag that Caroline guessed was from a bakery.

She couldn't resist entering a women's clothing boutique called Odd Molly. The inn's website said it had been an Aspen favorite for years. She picked out a snowflake-patterned sweater for Daphne and a wool scarf for herself. Then she went to a men's store and bought a pair of wool gloves for Luke. As she left, something on the opposite sidewalk caught her attention. It was Santa's Little Red Mailbox.

Of course—why hadn't she thought of it sooner?

Anne's lover could have visited the gift shop next to Santa's Little Red Mailbox to buy the envelope. Maybe someone there would remember him.

She hurried across the street. The mailbox looked just like in the photos when she searched it online. LETTERS FROM SANTA was printed in white capitals. Below that, it read "This mailbox will be emptied on the first of December."

That was why it took six months for Anne's letter to arrive.

The interior wasn't anything like the trendy gift shops in Hudson with their glass shelves of scented candles and bath soaps. And it wasn't like Cold Spring General Store and its metal racks of Christmas cards and slightly dusty board games. Instead, it resembled the parlor of a Victorian mansion. Tables were arranged with porcelain dolls, and there was a bookshelf with leather-bound books. Christmas ornaments were everywhere—on top of the books, on the cash register, in the windows of a large gingerbread house.

"Excuse me." Caroline addressed the girl behind the counter. "This is a long shot, but I'm looking for a man who bought a Letter from Santa envelope last June. It's important that I find him."

"I'm sorry. I didn't work here during the summer." The girl shrugged.

"No, of course not," Caroline sighed. She was about to leave but the girl stopped her.

"You could ask the owner, Beth. She remembers practically every face."

Caroline turned around. "She does?"

"If I had her memory, I would have aced my college classes," the girl said cheerfully. "She's owned this shop for decades. She knows everyone in Aspen."

For the first time since she started her search, Caroline felt hopeful.

"Will she be here soon?"

"She's going to visit her daughter in Denver, she'll be back after New Year's."

"Oh, I see." Caroline's face fell.

Caroline would have to wait until New Year's Eve. But what if Anne's lover didn't show up because he hadn't heard from her?

"Beth might be at the Carpenters' open house tonight, before going to Denver tomorrow," the girl volunteered. "You could try her there."

"The Carpenters?" Caroline repeated, wondering why the name sounded familiar.

"They own one of the Queen Anne mansions on Walnut Street. They hold an open house every year."

It was Max's parents' house! Max had given her the address.

The girl went back to arranging ornaments on the counter. "Wait until you see the houses on Walnut Street. It's like Disney's Magic Kingdom during the holidays."

By the time Caroline returned to the hotel, it was late afternoon. The maids had left a pot of cinnamon tea and a plate of spiced shortbread. She was tempted to call Max and say that she was coming. But she didn't want him to get the wrong idea. The only reason she was going was to talk to Beth.

Then she took out her iPad, and curled up in the armchair, hoping desperately that the next manuscript she clicked on would be the one she couldn't live without acquiring.

* * *

The girl at the gift shop had been right. Every house on Walnut Street was strung with colored lights. Most of them had elaborate displays on the front lawns. At one house, there was a Christmas nativity scene, with three wise men carrying sacks of gold. At another, Santa's sleigh was pulled by life-size reindeer. The display on Max's parents' lawn was the best. A dozen elves wearing red caps worked in Santa's workshop. There was a model train set, and a conveyor belt for their tools. She took a photo to show Daphne; she'd never seen anything like it before.

Caroline wore a black velvet dress paired with ankle-high boots. This year, the trend at Manhattan holiday parties had been loungewear and plaid. Caroline's boss, Claudia, wore red silk pajamas to the company Christmas party, and her assistant, Darcy, showed up in a plaid jacket that she never took off. Caroline usually wore the same thing: a variation of the little black cocktail dress with a pair of heels. She learned that from her mother. Anne wasn't going to spend her commission on a dress that would be out of style by the following Christmas.

But when Caroline peered through the window of Max's parents' house, the women were dressed casually in slacks and sweaters. She debated going back to the hotel to change, but the front door was already open.

"Please come in," a woman greeted her. She was in her mid-thirties, with light brown hair and hazel eyes. She reminded Caroline of Max. Caroline wondered if she was his sister.

"I'm Caroline Holt," Caroline said, introducing herself. "Max invited me."

"I'm Helen." The woman shook her hand. "I'd go and find

Max, but my daughter just discovered the punch bowl. Last year, she got a goldfish for Christmas. She's always wanted another goldfish, I don't want to remind her." Helen pointed down the hallway. "Everyone's in the kitchen. You could look for him there."

The kitchen was like a scene from one of those Nancy Meyers movies, where the kitchens always had white marble counters, and tile backsplashes, and copper range hoods. People stood around talking about movies and books while someone passed around glasses of wine and tossed the salad.

Caroline had loved watching those movies with her mother and Daphne. Anne and Daphne would drool over the fancy cookware, and Caroline would write down the names of the books that were being discussed.

"Please join us, I'm Pamela." A woman in her fifties approached her. Her light brown hair was cut to her chin. She had brown eyes and high cheekbones. "There's still plenty to do. You can cut the bread. It just came out of the oven."

Caroline was about to introduce herself when Max appeared. He looked even more handsome than the previous day. He wore a wool sweater and navy slacks. His hair was brushed to the side, and he was smiling.

"If you had called, I would have told you the dress code. I'm afraid we're quite casual," he said, laughing. "But I'm glad you came."

Caroline's cheeks turned red.

"I wasn't sure until this afternoon that I was coming," she admitted.

"That dress is much too pretty for my mother to put you to work." Max took her arm. "Why don't we get out of here and find you a drink."

They walked back to the living room, and Max poured two glasses of punch.

"You better check the bowl for a goldfish." Caroline smiled. She told him about Helen and her daughter.

"Helen is my sister and Lily is my niece," Max said. "Helen and her husband and Lily live in Los Angeles."

The living room was furnished in the Queen Anne style. A marble fireplace was protected by an old-fashioned grille, and rose-colored love seats faced a coffee table. In the corner, there was a round table where Caroline imagined women played bridge while they waited for their husbands to return from the mines. The ceiling had an ornate fresco, and the walls were papered with green velvet wallpaper.

"My mother loved old houses," Caroline reflected. "She was a literary agent, she said every house told a story."

Caroline realized she hadn't told Max anything about her mother.

"My mother died two months ago, she's the reason why I came to Aspen."

Max handed her a glass of punch.

"I'm very sorry. It sounds like you and your mother had a lot in common," he said. "When you didn't call, I thought I'd never see you again." He nursed his glass. "So, I took Lily's advice and made a deal with one of Santa Claus's elves."

"With an elf?" Caroline repeated, puzzled.

"I said the elf could have all the candy I receive for Christmas, as long as you called." Max tried to keep a serious expression. "Lily swore that it works. Last year, she gave him her candy and in return she got the goldfish for Christmas."

"I'm glad I'm as important as the goldfish," Caroline laughed.

She was about to ask Max more about himself when his mother appeared.

"There you are, I came to apologize. I thought you were a friend of Helen's and you knew that everyone helps with dinner." Pamela held out her hand. "I'm Max and Helen's mother."

Caroline shook hands. She told Pamela that she was a book editor in New York.

"I can't live without my books. My husband says we'll never move from our house in Santa Barbara, because no moving company would transport so many books," Pamela laughed. "I love my library in this house even more. You'll have to take a look."

"My mother is vice-president of the Aspen cultural board and the literary foundation," Max explained ruefully.

"That's what's wonderful about Aspen. Even if you don't ski, you never run out of things to do," Pamela continued. "We have author events and music recitals and gallery openings throughout the year."

Caroline wished she had gone to Aspen with Anne the previous June. They could have visited art galleries, and taken in an outdoor concert. It was suddenly hard to swallow. She missed her mother so much.

"I have to go and check on the pecan pie." Pamela's eyes sparkled. "Max hardly ever invites a girl to our open house. I'm very glad you came."

Pamela drifted off and Caroline and Max were left alone.

"I'd ask if you wanted another drink, but we should wait until dinner," Max said with a smile.

"Your mother is lovely," Caroline assured him.

"She is, as long as she's not trying to marry me off," Max chuckled.

"My sister and her husband have busy careers. It's up to me to give my mother more grandchildren."

Anne had never pushed Caroline or Daphne to get married. Daphne dreamed of having three or four children, and a dog. Caroline hadn't been so sure. She loved her job, and she worried that she wouldn't give a child enough attention. Lately, she felt so burned out, she didn't know what she wanted.

"What about you?" Caroline asked Max. "What do you want?"

"I love being an uncle, I see the world through Lily's eyes. That's enough for now." His voice became teasing. "What about you? Is there some fiancé or serious boyfriend waiting in New York?"

Caroline told him about her one-month dating rule.

"So let me get this straight," Max said. "You get up to thirty days of stimulating conversation and great sex with someone you're interested in, then you both walk away?"

Caroline blushed. No one had ever put it in those words.

"It's better than risking a broken heart," she said stiffly. "What if I put all my energy into a relationship and it doesn't work out?"

Max gazed at her thoughtfully. He looked so handsome. His shoulders were broad under his sweater, and he had long, muscular legs.

"I see your point. That's how I've felt since I started the distillery." He nodded. "I'll do anything to make it a success. Most women wouldn't understand that."

Caroline felt a little shiver. It was stronger than she had felt with Brad, and different than she had experienced with Jack. It felt like when the subway stopped abruptly and she had to regain her balance.

"I would understand." She flashed him a smile. "I feel exactly the same way."

Dinner was served at round tables set up in the dining room. Caroline was seated next to Helen. They talked about books that Lily loved, and the yoga studio that Helen had opened in Santa Monica.

The meal started with pumpkin soup, followed by sirloin tips and guinea fowl. For vegetarians there was cauliflower steak and potatoes baked in their jackets. Each table had bottles of wine and champagne. The desserts were pecan pie and a fruit loaf served with butter rum ice cream.

Max was seated at another table. Every now and then he glanced over at her. He smiled as if they shared some kind of secret, and she smiled back.

After dinner, everyone moved to the living room for games. Caroline waited for Beth, the owner of the gift shop, but she never arrived.

"I had a lovely time, but I should go," Caroline said when the guests were beginning to leave.

"I'll walk back with you to the hotel," Max offered.

Caroline had drunk three glasses of champagne. She was just tipsy enough to let something happen between them. It had been such a pleasant evening, but she wasn't ready for things between her and Max to progress further.

"No, thank you, I already called an Uber." She shook her head.

It had started snowing as the Uber pulled up in front of the Aspen Inn. Couples strolled hand in hand down Main Street, the air smelled of fresh snow. For a moment, she wished she had let Max take her to the inn. They could have gone ice-skating or drunk hot toddies in the lobby. But she didn't want Max to end up in her hotel room. There would be the usual awkwardness of their first time. Should Max spend the night, and would they have breakfast together? What if he wanted to use her toothbrush, or he could only sleep with the heat on?

She still wasn't sure she was ready to have a fling. It was better to take things slowly.

She was about to take out her phone to text him that she had gotten there safely when she heard a familiar voice.

Daphne stood on the front steps of the inn. She wore a long green jacket. Her hair was tucked under a wool hat and she wore black gloves.

"You're here!" Daphne exclaimed. "I've been calling your phone for ages."

Caroline's mouth dropped open.

"I left my phone in my coat," Caroline apologized. "What are you doing in Aspen?"

"I'll tell you, but it's freezing out here." Daphne looped her arm through Caroline's. They entered the lobby. "Luke went to get sandwiches and coffee. We're so lucky to have gotten a room here. Luke called, and there was a last-minute cancelation. The hotel restaurant is closed and we're starving. They hardly fed us anything on the plane."

They sat on chairs in the lobby. Daphne explained that she felt terrible after Caroline left.

"Christmas morning wouldn't be the same if you weren't there to open presents," Daphne said.

"What did Luke say? You were going to spend Christmas week planning the wedding," Caroline said.

"That's the thing." Daphne's eyes grew bright. "We spent all day yesterday talking about dates and venues. Spring and summer are the restaurant's busy seasons and I travel for work in the fall.

Luke was raised on a farm in Wisconsin. His grandparents are too old to travel, but I doubt my friends would like to attend a wedding there."

"Weddings can be complicated," Caroline agreed. "Maybe you and Luke should wait."

"That's when it dawned on me," Daphne continued eagerly. "Why have a big wedding when we can elope instead?"

Caroline's stomach tightened.

"You eloped?" she repeated.

"I wanted to. I told Luke we could drive to Niagara Falls, it's magical at this time of year," Daphne said dreamily. "He convinced me that I couldn't get married without you." Her smile widened. "So, we decided we're going to get married in Aspen on New Year's Day."

Caroline's face paled. Daphne couldn't get married so soon. Caroline still believed the engagement was rushed, and they should wait. Now she wouldn't have a chance to change Daphne's mind.

"You're going to get married in a week?" Caroline gasped.

"It will be so much fun," Daphne gushed. "You and I can shop for dresses. I called the hotel in advance, they're going to make a croquembouche wedding cake. And I found the sweetest church."

"Are you sure about this?" Caroline asked anxiously.

"Surer than I've been about anything." Daphne nodded. "You're the one who said Mom would be with me, wherever I got married. But somehow, I feel like she's here. This is the last place that she was happy."

Caroline glanced at her sister. They were different in so many ways. Often Daphne seemed young for her age and impulsive, but sometimes she surprised her.

"You're right," Caroline admitted, glancing around the lobby. It was so festive and it smelled of nutmeg and cloves. "I think she was happy here too."

Chapter Five

Caroline couldn't fall asleep. When she finally drifted off, she was awoken by the hiss of the heater. She propped herself against the headboard and pulled out her iPad. One romance kept her interested until the last chapter, but then the love interest was killed off. Caroline had to discard it. Romance novels required a happily-ever-after ending, it was one of the rules of publishing.

When the morning sun filtered through the window, she debated texting Daphne and asking if she wanted to go for a walk. But Daphne had always been a late riser. As a teenager Caroline had envied Daphne's ability to sleep in. On Sundays, Daphne never appeared until noon. She'd enter in the kitchen while Anne was making lunch and wolf down a sandwich and a glass of orange juice. Her skin would be smooth and she'd be smiling. No matter how late Caroline stayed up the night before, she was awake by 9:00 a.m. She could never stomach more than a piece of toast, and she was often grumpy.

Anne used to laugh and say wait until they were adults. There was nothing wrong with getting up early, and a strong cup of coffee cured anything.

Caroline reached for the next letter from Nina.

Dear Anne,

I hope you and your family had a wonderful Thanksgiving.
I watched the Macy's Thanksgiving Parade for the first time
in forty years. Afterward, I walked through the Central
Park Zoo. I thought about your darling girls. That's one of
the things I miss about never having children of my own.
The joy on a child's face when he sees an elephant pick up a
peanut with his trunk is as good as reading my first review
in *The New York Times*.

My apologies, I sound like a lonely, bitter writer again,
and that isn't my intention. But it's good to be back in New
York. I didn't realize how much I missed it. I treated myself
to Thanksgiving dinner at Porter House Bar and Grill. It
blew my monthly budget, but a juicy steak at my age is as
impossible to resist as sex when I was young.

I didn't start this letter to talk about my life now in New
York. I'm trying to explain why you should represent me
and what you should say to editors. Authors don't give up
writing for forty years without a reason. It's as necessary
to our well-being as breathing. But when you're young, you
make all sorts of mistakes. Especially when it comes to love.
Even in the 1970s, when we women were so focused on our
careers, love could find a way to derail us. That's the human
condition. If love didn't exist, we wouldn't have literature.

Which leads me back to my story. I wasn't thinking
about love or my career after I had accepted Margaret's
request to be Laura Carter. I was too worried about how to
tell Teddy that he was going to spend Christmas week with
me in Vermont, after I had demanded he get his things out

of my apartment and told him I never wanted to see him again.

Teddy and I had met almost two years earlier at the office. Teddy Chandler III looked exactly like his name sounded. Blond hair, blue eyes, and a smile that could light up a skyscraper during a blackout.

Every woman at *Women's World Monthly* fell in love with him. I was determined to be the exception. Even before I published my first novel, I was consumed by the feminist movement. I wasn't going to let a man, especially not a man who knew his own sex appeal, get in the way of my career.

Teddy was an account executive for Palmolive soap. It didn't sound like a glamorous job, but Teddy made it one. His days were spent being taken to lunch by magazine editors and television producers who wanted Palmolive's advertising dollars. In the evenings he frequented fashionable clubs and restaurants like the Copacabana and the Oak Room, usually with a secretary or an account assistant on his arm. Once, a rumor went around that he was seeing Glenda, the married head of human resources. It wasn't true. Teddy was too clever to get involved with a married woman.

The first year after college, I worked for a wonderful female boss, but she was promoted and I had a new boss. He worked under Margaret as well and I was his direct secretary. He was about forty and his name was Gus Drummond. One evening, as I was about to leave, Gus called the office. It was the start of the Labor Day weekend and he had forgotten the short stories on his desk.

Teddy walked out of the elevator. He was carrying a bouquet of roses.

"Everyone's gone home. Whoever those are for, they're going to wilt," I said to Teddy.

"The roses won't look worse than I feel." He wiped his brow. "New York in August is unbearable. Everyone I know is headed to Long Island but that's not much better. It's like taking a crowded party and moving it to a new location. If I could be anywhere in the world, it would be on top of a mountain."

Even with sweat on his forehead, Teddy was the most handsome man I ever met. He wore a white V-neck vest and pleated trousers. The only thing he was wearing that wasn't white was his shoes. Scuffed brown loafers, no socks.

"You won't find any women on top of a mountain." I pointed to the roses.

His smile grew even wider. "You're right. That's the problem with love, it beats common sense every time."

"Are you in love?" I inquired.

I wondered which of the women on that floor was the object of his feelings.

"I'm always in love but it never lasts." He shrugged.

"That sounds like a terrible waste of time."

"On the contrary, life would be dull without it." He walked to where I was standing. "Love is like the Picasso exhibit at the Guggenheim. I don't understand his paintings but they're amusing to look at. They have all that color and energy."

I was quite certain that the woman receiving the flowers felt differently. Many women in their twenties then still dreamed of diamond rings and long, white dresses. If they didn't crave a house in the suburbs, they at least wanted to share a New York co-op with a handsome man.

"Well, everyone but me has left for the long weekend. So, you'll have to keep the flowers until Tuesday."

"Why are you still here?" he wondered.

I explained that my boss asked me to bring the short stories to him on my way home.

"You're meeting him at the White Horse Tavern?" Teddy asked.

The White Horse Tavern was a popular bar in the West Village. I lived close by. The neighborhood was too bohemian for my tastes—I wasn't interested in tie-dyed shirts, or men with long, flowing hair—but the rent was cheap and my bedroom had a window.

"I'm not having a drink with him, if that's what you're thinking." I gathered my purse. "He needs them tonight. He's driving out tomorrow morning to join his family in the Hamptons."

When I arrived at the bar, Gus was sitting in a table in the back. He was a tall man with dark hair and brown eyes behind glasses. He had taken off his suit jacket, and he was wearing a white shirt and red tie.

"Sit down and have something cool to drink," he suggested. "It's too hot to be outside."

I wondered if men talked with women about anything except the weather.

"No, thank you. I'm only a few blocks from here."

"Then at least let me give you subway fare and a little extra." He reached into his pocket. "I would have had to pay a courier to pick these up."

Gus only had a twenty-dollar bill. He gave it to the waiter; I had no choice but to wait for the change.

Suddenly Teddy appeared. He walked right up to me and kissed me on the cheek.

"I'm sorry to keep you waiting, holiday traffic is murder." He placed his arm around me.

I was so shocked, my mouth dropped open.

Teddy pretended not to notice my surprise. He turned to Gus and held out his hand.

"Teddy Chandler the Third. It's nice to meet you."

"Gus Drummond." Gus shook his hand. His face had a peculiar expression, but I wasn't experienced enough with men to know what it meant.

"I was talking about you the other day with Edgar, the head of your department," Teddy said to Gus. "You're new at the company, but Edgar has big things in store for you."

"You were talking to Edgar?" Gus repeated.

"Edgar loves to take me to lunch at the Carlyle. He thinks a plate of oysters and a few cocktails will win him Palmolive's advertising dollars."

"Teddy is the account executive for Palmolive soap," I volunteered.

Gus's cheeks turned red. He pulled at his shirt collar.

"At the moment I'm the very late boyfriend of this beautiful young lady." Teddy drew me closer. "It was nice to meet you, Gus. I'm sure we'll see each other again."

"What was that about?" I demanded when we were outside.

"I thought I'd at least get a thank-you," Teddy said.

I replied that I had no idea what I was thanking him for.

"I'll explain over a couple of martinis." He still held my arm. He was guiding me into a restaurant.

I stopped on the sidewalk. "What makes you think I'll have a drink with you?"

"Because you're not going home until Gus walks out of the tavern and gets into a taxi," Teddy said.

I was too flustered to argue. We sat in a booth and Teddy ordered two vodka martinis and a club sandwich.

"Hot weather makes me hungry." He offered me half the club sandwich.

By then, I was fuming. I should have been home, working on my novel. Instead, I was sitting with a man I barely knew, watching him eat turkey and mayonnaise.

"Gus forgot those short stories on purpose. It was a ploy to get you to have a drink with him." He wiped mayonnaise from his mouth. "Afterward, he'd offer to walk you home. He'd say he needed to call his wife and ask if he could come up and use your phone. The next thing you'd know, his tongue would be in your mouth and his hands would be on your dress."

I shifted uncomfortably at the image of Gus putting his hands on me.

"How do you know?" I demanded.

"He's done it before. The last time was uptown because the girl lived on the Upper West Side. Gus happened to be at a bar near her apartment."

I didn't believe him. All sorts of rumors circulated around *Women's World Monthly.*

"It isn't a rumor, I heard it from the woman herself," he insisted.

Suddenly it dawned on me.

"Is she the same woman who was supposed to receive your bouquet of roses?" I asked.

Teddy nodded. "I can't tell you her name, it wouldn't be the gentlemanly thing to do."

"Why didn't you warn me before I left the office?" I asked, puzzled.

"You might not have believed me. Gus is your boss and we just met." He shrugged. "Gus didn't need change from the waiter. It was an excuse to keep you there."

I had thought it odd that the waiter took so long to return with the change. Suddenly I needed the martini very badly.

"I hope your friend didn't get into trouble," I sighed.

"Don't worry about her," he said. "You can thank me by going out to dinner with me tomorrow."

I raised my eyebrows. "What will the recipient of the roses say?"

"There was a note on her desk saying she went to the Hamptons. She's decided she wants to see other men."

I didn't ask why; it was none of my business. Secretly I was pleased. Teddy was worldly and charming. I wanted to see him again.

I started this letter to explain how I broke the news to Teddy about Vermont, and I've written six pages on how we met! I can see you with a red pen, slashing through sentences and demanding that I come to the point.

I'm afraid it's going to have to wait until the next letter.

I have a ticket to a Broadway play and I can't be late. Theater is another thing I missed so much about New York.

Regards,
Nina

Caroline set the letter aside. She wondered whether Nina ever finished a new book. Surely the manuscript would have been somewhere in her mother's boxes. Why had Anne kept the letters? And why had she never mentioned them?

She was about to reach for the next letter when her phone pinged. It was a text from Daphne accompanied by a smile emoji.

"Eating breakfast at the hotel restaurant. I can't believe we're in Aspen! Come join us, they make the best Western-style omelet."

Caroline got dressed, hoping she'd feel half as chirpy as Daphne's text after a cup of coffee.

When she entered the restaurant, Daphne and Luke were seated at a table near the fireplace. Their heads were bowed together and there was that look about them, as if they were the only two people in the world.

Daphne glanced up and waved. She wore a white turtleneck that accentuated her blond hair, and blue jeans.

"You have to try the hotel breakfast." Daphne waved at her plate. "Omelets and bacon, and homemade muffins with strawberry jam."

"I'm not hungry, I'll stick with coffee," Caroline said.

She didn't want to tell Daphne about Max's open house. Daphne would ask too many questions.

"The wedding is so soon and there's so much to do!" Daphne squeezed Luke's hand. "Luke is going to pick out the rings."

"Daphne wants the rings to be a surprise," Luke offered.

"Most couples choose their wedding bands together, but this will make it more special," Daphne gushed to Caroline. "I want to show you the church. I saw pictures online, it's like something in a fairy tale."

"Aren't your parents disappointed that they're going to miss the wedding?" Caroline asked Luke.

If Daphne wouldn't listen to her, maybe she could persuade Luke to postpone the wedding.

Luke sprinkled salt on his omelet. "I offered to pay for their plane tickets, but my father is about to have back surgery. We're going to FaceTime them during the ceremony." He glanced at Daphne. "It's better this way. Since Daphne doesn't have anyone to walk her down the aisle."

After Walter died, Anne often said the happiest days of her life would be when she walked her daughters down the aisle. Luke had a point. How would Daphne feel if Luke's parents were at the wedding and all Daphne had was Caroline?

"Luke's best friend is going to be the best man. He's flying in on New Year's Eve," Daphne piped up.

"Eric works in finance, he just moved to New York," Luke said.

Daphne ate a bite of her muffin. She smiled at Caroline. "Who knows, maybe you and Eric will fall in love and we'll have a double reception next summer."

From the outside, the church reminded Caroline of a Christmas postcard taken in Switzerland or Germany. It was a few blocks from Main Street, nestled between tall aspen trees. The walls were thick timber, and it had a sloped roof and a small steeple. Inside, several rows of pews faced a wooden altar. There was an organ, and there were stained-glass windows.

"I googled the oldest churches in Aspen, and this was on the list," Daphne said. "There was only one church in Aspen when it was first settled, and the miners and their wives got married here in this church. We're carrying on a tradition that's been going on for a hundred and fifty years."

"How did you manage to get it on such short notice?" Caroline asked.

Daphne had told the woman on the phone about the man waiting in front of Santa's Little Red Mailbox. And that she and her fiancé wanted to get married at the same time.

"She thought it was the most romantic thing she'd ever heard," Daphne finished.

"The wedding still seems so rushed," Caroline said. "You always dreamed of wearing a beautiful wedding dress."

Whenever they passed a bridal boutique in New York, Daphne made them go inside to see the new styles.

"Maybe I've grown up," Daphne replied, sticking out her chin. "The dress isn't the most important thing."

"You don't want to start your new life by giving up the things you love," Caroline said carefully. "You might grow to resent Luke."

"It was my idea to elope," Daphne reminded her. "And you're wrong. Love and marriage are about compromise."

"As long as you agree on the important things." Caroline had to make Daphne see how complicated marriage could be. "For instance, how many children does Luke want?"

Daphne avoided Caroline's eyes. "I don't know, we haven't talked about children."

"That should have been your first conversation!"

"It's not the thing you discuss on a first date. Somehow after that, it never came up." Daphne twisted her diamond ring. "Luke is great with kids, he'll be a wonderful father."

"If he wants children," Caroline persisted. "Restaurant owners keep terrible hours, and a commuter marriage is even worse. You'll have to get help, or quit your job."

Daphne sat down in a pew. When she looked up, her eyes were rimmed with tears.

"I don't know why you keep doing this. Don't you want me to be happy?"

Caroline slid in beside her. "Of course I do. But with Mom gone, it's my job to look out for you."

"I don't need you to tell me what to do. I'm an adult, I can make my own decisions."

Caroline ran her hand over the front of the pew.

"Mom would say the same thing. Marriage is a huge step. It's hard to know if you've made the right decision," she ventured.

"My feelings for Luke keep growing stronger. He's so supportive, he's doing everything I suggest." Daphne wiped her eyes. "He even agreed to wear a bow tie, and he hates ties. It's one of the reasons he doesn't have a corporate job."

Nothing would change Daphne's mind. If Caroline kept pushing, Daphne would object even more.

"All right," Caroline agreed. "But do you promise you'll talk to Luke about children?"

The smile came back to Daphne's expression. Caroline was reminded of the fights they had when they were children. Daphne would always stop being angry first. Her pout would dissolve, and her smile would be as bright as the sun.

"I promise, and we'll talk about pets too," Daphne said with a laugh. "During college, Luke had a pet lizard. I could never live with a reptile."

After they left church, they strolled along Main Street. It was almost noon when they reached the inn. The concierge approached them. He held a bouquet of roses.

"Miss Holt, these came for you, here's the card." He set the bouquet down and handed her an envelope.

The card was from Max.

Caroline. It seems a shame to waste such a promising beginning. I'm happy to play by your rules. Are you free this afternoon? Regards, Max

"Who in Aspen would send you flowers?" Daphne asked.

"Just a guy I met, it's not important."

The card fell on the floor. Daphne picked it up. She read it and handed it to Caroline.

Daphne's eyes flickered. "You didn't say you met a man. You're never going to change."

"I don't know what you mean." Caroline glanced around the lobby to see if anyone was listening. The concierge had returned to his desk, the space was almost empty.

"When you drove up to the cabin instead of going to London to see Brad, I thought maybe you were done with your flings. I even hoped that Luke and I might inspire you to find the right guy and settle down." She waved at the card. "You've been in Aspen for two days and you're already getting involved. I bet he's like the others. Sexy and charming, and someone you couldn't have a future with because he lives far away," she raged. "Well, you can stop looking out for me. I'm never going to take your advice. I couldn't be like you, and I wouldn't want to try."

Daphne stormed onto the street. Caroline was left in the lobby with the bouquet of roses, and feeling completely alone.

Chapter Six

Caroline ran after Daphne, but she had disappeared. A light snow was falling on the sidewalk. She slipped her hands into her pockets and started walking. She should have told Daphne about Max. But there was nothing to tell. The reason she had gone to dinner was to try to find out something about Anne's lover.

These days, most of Caroline's friends' social media posts were filled with photos of weddings and baby showers. Caroline wanted a husband and children. But it had always been part of a distant future. Like buying a house or investing in serious furniture. Until now, she'd preferred to focus on her career.

She stopped in front of the skating rink. She noticed a little girl with long braids. Her father was skating beside her. They both had dark hair, and wore matching red scarves and gloves.

Caroline recalled the first Christmas that she worried about not having a father. It was in third grade. The teacher asked them to write down everyone on their Christmas list. Caroline made a column with her mother and Walter, and her little sister, Daphne.

"Who's Walter?" the girl sitting next to her, Jenny, had asked.

"Walter is my stepfather," Caroline replied. "He and my mom got married a couple of years ago."

"You should put down your own father too," Jenny said knowledgeably. "I know, my parents are divorced."

"I don't have a father."

"Everyone has a father," Jenny persisted. "Even if your parents aren't married anymore."

Caroline explained that she never knew her father. Her parents never married, and her mother didn't talk about him. Jenny gasped in astonishment.

"It doesn't matter," Caroline said uncomfortably. She consulted her list. "I have plenty of people to give presents to."

"That's too bad." Jenny went back to her own list. "Extra fathers come in handy at Christmas. I get double the number of presents, my parents are always trying to outdo each other."

Caroline remembered the stuck feeling in her throat. As if she were eating a peanut butter sandwich and the peanut butter on it was too thick and she couldn't swallow.

Walter had been kind and generous, and Anne was the best mother she could have asked for. She introduced Caroline and Daphne to fashion and cooking and books. But Caroline wondered whether if she'd had a father she would be more like Daphne. Secure and trusting when it came to love.

She stopped to buy a warm pretzel and then went back to the inn and pulled out her iPad. After a while she gave up trying to find a manuscript that hooked her. But she couldn't shake the burned-out feeling. If she didn't come up with something soon, she'd have to evaluate whether she could continue her career as an editor.

The first time in the past months that she'd felt like herself was when she had been with Max. Maybe a romance with an attractive man was just what she needed to lighten her mood.

Before she could talk herself out of it, she picked up her phone. Max answered on the first ring.

"Caroline, hello," he greeted her. He paused and then his voice came over the line. "You saved me from buying a life-size stuffed giraffe."

"How did I do that?"

The salesgirl had convinced him that eight-year-old girls loved stuffed zoo animals.

"I told her I had to take this phone call."

"I'm glad I could help." Caroline smiled at the image of Max holding a stuffed giraffe. "I have some free time and I haven't explored Aspen."

"We'll start this afternoon with a snowcat tour," Max suggested. "There's no better way to see the backwoods than from the cabin of a snowcat."

Caroline needed to have some fun.

"That sounds perfect," she agreed.

"I'll pick you up at three, and dress warmly. The snowcats aren't enclosed."

Two hours later, Max was waiting by the fireplace in the lobby. He wore a fleece jacket and wool slacks.

"I told my mother what we were doing and she lent you this." He handed her a hooded jacket.

"But I have a coat." Caroline was holding the knee-length coat that she wore in New York.

"This is a thermal parka," Max said with a smile. "She'll be furious with me if you catch cold on your holiday."

Caroline slipped on the jacket over her coat. It was deliciously warm, like stepping into a heated bath. She pulled on her gloves and followed Max onto Main Street.

The clouds had cleared and the sky was blue. The snowcat picked them up at the foot of the mountain. It was painted yellow and had huge rubber tracks.

"The snowcat goes further up the mountain than snowplows, it has to handle all kinds of terrain," Max said when he had helped her into the cabin.

Caroline had ridden the gondolas at ski resorts in New York and Vermont. But the gondolas had been warm and insulated. The cabin of the snowcat was open; even in the jacket and with a blanket on her lap, it was cold.

"It will feel warmer once we start moving." Max noticed her expression. "I promise it will be worth it."

Max gave her a quick history of snowcats. They were invented eighty years earlier to explore mountain terrain. They were always painted bright colors, usually orange or yellow or red, so they could be seen from far away.

For a while, they rode through a forest. Then the snowcat veered vertically and climbed up the mountain. When the gears creaked to a stop, Caroline turned and gazed at the view. She had never seen anything so spectacular. All around them were craggy mountain peaks, thick with snow. Skiers were toy figures, and Aspen resembled a Monopoly board with tiny houses and matchbox-size cars.

"We're at the top of Elk Mountain, the pride of the Rockies," Max said.

They climbed out of the snowcat. Caroline imagined what it must be like during the summer. Velvety grass, fields full of wildflowers, lakes that were a brilliant aquamarine. She wished again that she had joined her mother at the Aspen writers' conference.

"What are you thinking?" Max wondered.

Caroline pulled her mind back to the present.

"My mother loved Aspen, she came in June for the last time."

Suddenly Caroline wanted to tell Max about the letter from Santa, and the man who would be waiting at the Little Red Mailbox.

"So that's why you're in Aspen," Max said when she finished.

"It's silly. My mom is gone, it doesn't matter anymore." Caroline gulped. "I couldn't let him show up and wonder why she wasn't there."

"It doesn't sound silly," Max said seriously. "For someone with so many dating rules, it's incredibly romantic."

"I believe in love." Caroline frowned. "Sometimes it's not worth the effort."

"What do you mean?" Max asked.

"Never mind," she replied.

She wanted to say that the only way to not get one's heart broken was not to open it for love. But she and Max had just met. It wasn't any of his business.

They got back in the snowcat and the driver plowed through a cluster of aspen trees. At the end was a timber hut.

"I couldn't drag you up the mountain and not feed you." Max grinned. "The restaurant is owned by the Little Nell hotel. It serves Swiss-style fondue, but that's not the best thing about it."

"What's the best thing?"

"You can only reach it by snowcat." He hopped down and helped her out. "We're almost guaranteed not to have too much company."

Inside, there were benches and long wooden tables. The windows had views of the entire valley, and there was a potbellied stove.

Everything on the menu was Swiss. Fondues and raclette, which was a variety of cheeses melted over ham and potatoes. For dessert there was apple strudel, and to drink, coffee mixed with schnapps, and a wine called glühwein that the Swiss drank at Christmas.

"You really know Aspen," Caroline said. "I thought we'd just browse in the shops on Main Street, or ride a gondola."

"I've been coming to Aspen at Christmas for years. My father is often traveling, but my mother never misses it."

The waiter set down their plates. Max speared a piece of bread to dip in the pot of hot cheese and looked at Caroline.

"I don't get it. You've got everything, looks and intelligence and a great career. Why don't you want a boyfriend? I thought most women your age wanted to settle down."

Caroline sipped her coffee. She'd been asked the same thing before.

"Men aren't asked that question. Women who reach thirty without having an engagement ring are considered a failure."

"My mother is always bugging me to join a dating site," Max sighed. "Not ones like Tinder, but the type that guarantees to find your forever soulmate."

"What if we don't have soulmates?" Caroline demanded. "That's why I invented my dating rules. I never have to rely on anyone but myself."

"So, you never have a guy over to your place?"

Caroline recalled Jack stalking her apartment. "Definitely not. It's too easy for someone to slip into an apartment building. Then I'd have to change the locks."

"But you're allowed to spend the night at his place?"

"I always leave before I've had my morning coffee," Caroline clarified. "There's nothing more awkward than standing around a coffeepot with nothing to say."

Max took out his phone. He clicked on the notes.

"What are you doing?" she asked, puzzled.

"Taking notes." His eyes danced and he was smiling. "I don't want to get anything wrong."

They finished their fondue and talked about Daphne and Luke's decision to elope in Aspen.

"I take it you don't approve," Max said.

"Luke is a great guy, but they hardly know each other," Caroline ventured. "It's my job to watch out for Daphne. What if she's making a mistake?"

Max grew thoughtful. His brow furrowed, and he played with his fork.

"We all make mistakes. Life is about figuring them out, and then moving on."

Caroline was intrigued, and she wanted to ask more questions. But that would be breaking her rules. The whole point was not to get involved with someone.

Instead, she said playfully, "Somehow, I don't see Max Carpenter making mistakes. You grew up on the beach in California, now you're running your distillery in Aspen."

Max leaned back in his chair.

"You're right, but I might be making my first mistake now."

"What kind of mistake?"

His gaze held hers. His eyes were the color of honey.

"It would be a mistake to tell you." He touched her hand. "We'll have to wait and see."

After they finished their desserts, they rode the snowcat back to Aspen. Max suggested they stop at a bookstore.

The shop was called Explore Booksellers, and it was housed in a Victorian mansion. Inside, there were velvet easy chairs and walls of bookshelves lined with books. It reminded Caroline of her mother's apartment on the Upper East Side.

The apartment had always been filled with books. There was a bookshelf in the entry. Sometimes Anne brought home so many books, she couldn't carry them into the living room. There was even a bookshelf in the kitchen. Anne loved to sit at the kitchen table with a book while a meat loaf warmed in the oven or spaghetti boiled on the stove.

Caroline sipped the free hot chocolate and browsed through the fiction table. Her phone buzzed as she was waiting to pay for a book.

The text was from Daphne. "We're at the inn. Luke fell ice-skating. He might have a concussion."

All thoughts of spending the rest of the evening with Max disappeared. She showed him the text. "I have to go, Daphne needs me."

Max put his books back on the counter. "I'll come with you."

Chapter Seven

When they reached the inn, Daphne was standing at the front desk. She turned to greet Caroline. Her eyes were as big as saucers.

"Luke is upstairs in the room. The concierge was trying to reach a doctor, but he can't find one." Daphne bit her lip.

Her sweater was tied around her waist; her hair had slipped from its ponytail and fell in her face.

"How is he?" Caroline asked.

Luke had fallen and hit his head on the ice. He said he was fine, but he had a huge bump.

"You know what a head injury is like." Daphne's voice wobbled. "Luke might think he's okay, but that doesn't mean anything."

"I'm sure he's fine," Max piped in. He took out his phone. "I'll call our family doctor and ask him to check him out."

Half an hour later, a man strode into the lobby, carrying a doctor's bag. Daphne went upstairs with him, and Caroline and Max waited in the lobby. Caroline was too nervous to make small talk. She had rarely seen Daphne so frightened.

"Luke is going to be fine," Daphne said when she finally

reappeared. "The doctor is with him, writing a list of instructions." She smiled nervously. "Luke didn't want me to miss out on bob-sledding. I don't care if we spend the next few days sitting in a dark room, as long as he's okay."

Max turned to Caroline. "I'm glad he's okay. I should go and let you be together."

After Max left, Caroline and Daphne sat in the lobby.

"Life is so fragile. One minute, Luke was teasing me that he was a faster skater, the next minute he was lying on his back on the ice," Daphne said worriedly.

"He's fine now," Caroline reminded her.

"Thanks to Max." Daphne nodded. "I shouldn't have said any-thing to you about Max. He's a good guy. And your love life is your own business."

Caroline adored her sister. She didn't want to argue anymore.

"And I should stop telling you when to get married." Caroline recalled the times their mother had used Santa Claus to end Caro-line and Daphne's squabbles. "Santa Claus won't bring us presents unless we make up."

Daphne leaned forward and hugged her.

"I remember when I stopped believing in Santa Claus," Daphne said with a laugh. "I thought Mom's threat wouldn't work any-more, but every year it did."

Daphne went to her room to join Luke. Caroline debated calling Max. He really was perfect for her. He had just the right amount of sexiness, and he was kind at the same time.

But she didn't want to seem eager. She'd wait for him to make the next move.

Instead of calling, she went to her room and took a bath. Afterward, she put on a robe and sat up in bed. It was still early, and she wasn't ready to go to sleep. She took the next letter from the stack and started reading.

Dear Anne,

I hope you are having a wonderful December. I went to the Christmas tree lighting at Rockefeller Center. I've missed it, I felt like such a New Yorker again.

I always marvel at the things that writers notice. The television camera operator who kept checking his watch, as if he was late for a date. The children eating cinnamon buns and placing their sticky fingers all over their mothers' winter coats.

I can almost hear you say that I'm procrastinating. I should be working on my novel. But one can't be a writer without experiencing life. In some ways, that's every writer's tragedy. If she's successful, she's chained to her desk and doesn't go anywhere. If she's a failure, it doesn't matter what she experiences, no one will ever read her words.

And so, I return to my story. I realized after my last letter, I can't tell you why I broke off my engagement to Teddy without saying how it happened in the first place. It would be like starting a novel with the epilogue and then going back to the beginning. I suppose a clever writer might manage it, but I believe in straight storytelling. It's not the story that's important. It's the characters. We have to care about them from the beginning.

Teddy took me to dinner eight times before I let him see

my apartment. My roommate, Joan, counted, because every time we went to dinner, I put a dollar in our cookie jar. We agreed to use the money I saved on food to buy things for our apartment.

When Teddy did come over, it was only because I was late coming home from work and he didn't wait downstairs while I changed.

"My roommate isn't home," I said when we entered. I did a quick check for embarrassing objects. A box of tampons, the diet powder Joan stirred into her morning coffee even though she was thin as a rake.

"Women in Manhattan must have some kind of telepathy with their roommates," Teddy said, sinking into the sofa.

The sofa was the most expensive piece in our apartment. It was gold with velvet tassels. Joan's mother bought it because she was horrified by the secondhand sofa Joan and I found at a thrift shop. Men would never stay for coffee if they were forced to sit on a worn sofa.

I stepped behind the curtain I used to change clothes, and took off my blouse.

"What do you mean?" I asked.

"Whenever a guy shows up at a woman's apartment, the roommate isn't home. You send each other smoke signals saying the coast is clear."

I poked my head out from behind the curtain. Teddy was walking around, inspecting the place.

"If you think I told Joan to leave because I wanted us to be alone, you're wrong," I snapped. "Joan goes to dinner at her boyfriend's parents' house every Friday. They're Jewish and he wants her to convert."

Joan had nothing against Judaism. But she didn't want to give up her own faith because she happened to be in love.

Teddy's face broke into a dazzling smile. "You should have told me that sooner. I could have saved a few dollars and we could have ordered Chinese to eat here."

"I'm not asking you to dinner." I yanked back the curtain. I had changed into a navy knit dress.

"Why not?" His voice became slightly peevish. "Just because I can afford to take you to dinner doesn't mean I don't enjoy a home-cooked meal."

I pretended to be looking for something in my purse but I was stalling. I hadn't told Teddy that I was a virgin. I wasn't opposed to sex before marriage. Women's magazines were full of articles about women claiming their orgasms. I hadn't had the opportunity. But Teddy prided himself on being a gentleman. If he knew, he'd stop seeing me. He didn't want to be my first lover.

"I don't have men over, and I don't know how to cook."

Teddy glanced at the pull-out bed in the wall.

"I suppose that's wise. That contraption doesn't look very romantic. You're better off at men's apartments."

Teddy was between apartments so he hadn't asked me over. At the moment he was staying with a friend on the Upper West Side.

"I don't go to men's apartments either."

"Then how do you . . ." He stopped.

He looked at me curiously. Then his expression turned to horror. I could tell what he was thinking.

"I don't." I sat on the sofa. "I mean I haven't." For

a writer, my tongue was tied in knots. "I want to, I just haven't had the chance."

"You're a working woman in New York." His voice rose as if I were some kind of criminal. "Unless you're holding out for something. Jewelry or a mink coat."

I was getting angry. "Sex isn't something to be bartered, like a basket of strawberries at the fruit stand," I retorted. "There've been a few men, but it never got that far."

He sank on the sofa. "No wonder the women at the office call you an ice queen. I bet you deprive yourself of everything. I thought they were jealous, but they're right."

I jumped up and strode to the refrigerator.

"I don't deprive myself." I opened the freezer. "Look, I've got chocolate ice cream and frozen éclairs and even a bottle of tequila because it lasts longer in the freezer. I like sweet things and I quite like to get tipsy. But I'm not going to climb in bed with just anyone."

Teddy rubbed his forehead.

"We'll talk about this later. I just remembered I have a dentist appointment."

"A dentist appointment at six p.m. on a Friday?"

"Dr. Fineman is booked up for months. I convinced him to see me tonight."

I didn't believe him. A Jewish dentist would never see patients on Shabbat.

"I'll go with you," I said sweetly. "We'll have dinner afterward."

"I'll be numb for hours." Teddy stood up and kissed me. "I'm flying to Detroit tomorrow on business, we'll have dinner when I return."

I didn't see him for a month. He stopped coming by the office. He called a few times, but it was always from an airport or from a pay phone. I knew from a few people at work that editors still took him to lunch. He met them at the restaurant instead.

I was willing to wait, it gave me time to work on my novel. Then the novel was finally in the hands of my agent, and my nights were free.

I came up with a plan. I accepted a dinner invitation from a guy named Miles Burbank. Miles was the creative director at *Women's World Monthly* and a notorious womanizer. He kept a little black book on his desk of the women he'd slept with. Models and fashion designers. He never hid it, he was proud of it.

And I made sure Teddy knew about my date. Miles's secretary sent me flowers with Miles's name on the card, and I displayed them prominently on my desk in case Teddy stopped by the office. And I told all the women and even my boss, Gus, where we were going. Thank God for the *Women's World Monthly* gossip mill! It never failed.

Miles took me to a nightclub called the Gallery. I was overdressed in a knockoff Pucci dress, but I didn't care. I wasn't there to impress Miles or anyone in the club. I wanted to see Teddy's face when he walked in the door.

Teddy showed up as Miles and I were finishing our third round of Singapore Slings. I didn't want to drink too much but Miles was a fast drinker. I had no choice but to keep up with him.

Teddy marched over to our table. He looked furious.

I picked up my glass. "Teddy, what a surprise. This is

Miles Burbank. He's the creative genius at *Women's World Monthly*."

"I know who he is." Teddy nodded at Miles. He looked at me. "Now get your coat."

I ignored his demand. "Miles just finished writing a novel. It's so nice to be with another writer. Miles is the only person I know who's read everything by Faulkner."

I knew that would get to Teddy. I'd read everything; Teddy's knowledge of American literature didn't extend beyond Tom Sawyer and Huck Finn.

"Then you can start a book club," Teddy said. "We're late. We have dinner reservations at the Four Seasons."

Teddy never took me to expensive restaurants. He didn't make that much money, and he was frugal.

"We already ate."

He glanced contemptuously at the other diners, who were eating burgers and chili.

"This place doesn't serve anything that doesn't need to be washed down with a cocktail." He took my arm. "Thank Miles for the drinks and come with me."

I didn't like the way Teddy bossed me around, but I'd talk about that with him later. For now, my plan had worked.

Teddy hailed a taxi and we drove in silence to the Four Seasons. It really was glamorous. Waiters pushed around silver bread carts, and the chef made Baked Alaska right at the table.

We ordered oysters on the half shell, and prime rib.

Teddy waited until the waiter left and then he reached into his pocket.

"When I heard you were out with Miles, I stopped by my mother's and got this." He presented me with a small velvet box.

I opened it. Inside was an emerald ring, flanked by two diamonds.

"What is it?"

"It's my grandmother's engagement ring. I've been working on a design for your engagement ring with my dentist's brother, Ken, but it won't be ready for days. Their father died and the family is sitting shiva."

"You're asking me to marry you!" I said, shocked. I only wanted to keep dating, I hadn't considered marriage.

"We can't stop seeing each other, and we can't have sex without a plan for the future."

"I don't need a plan," I said stiffly. "I'm quite happy to go to bed with you."

"If you think I'm going to pave the way for some future . . ." He stopped.

I almost laughed. But Teddy looked so serious and he had gone to so much effort.

I tried again. "I don't even know if I want to get married. My agent thinks my book will sell, and I have an idea for the next one."

"I'm not expecting you to turn into a housewife." He took a sip of his wine. "I've had time to think, and I've discovered that I'm in love with you."

"You're in love with me," I repeated. My heart started to hammer, and my throat was dry.

"It's the emotion that usually precedes a marriage proposal." His voice became brisk. "Now, why don't you do the normal thing and accept, so the waiter can replace this wine with the expensive champagne that I ordered."

I had so many thoughts. Teddy was so sure of himself that he had already ordered the champagne. He really did have a Jewish dentist named Dr. Fineman. But I kept those to myself.

I held out my hand.

"Yes, I'll marry you. And I'm in love with you too."

I'll stop there for now, I don't want to miss the department store sales. I hope you don't mind if I buy presents for your daughters. That's one thing I miss about never having children, there's no one to spoil at Christmas.

Regards,
Nina

Caroline set the letter on the stack. She wondered whether she'd ever met Nina. Dozens of authors visited her mother's apartment over the years. She couldn't remember.

Chapter Eight

When Caroline woke up the next morning, she had that special feeling of anticipation she only felt on Christmas Eve.

In some ways, Christmas Eve had always been more special than Christmas.

On Christmas morning, all the joy and excitement had been almost over. She and Daphne would run downstairs and open presents. After breakfast, there would be the long, yawning gap during the day until dinner. At night, Anne and Walter would take them caroling or ice-skating in Hudson, but after that, there would be nothing to do except wait for next year.

But on Christmas Eve, everything had been before her. She and Daphne would finish decorating the Christmas tree, and bake cookies for Santa Claus and his reindeer. At night, the whole family would make s'mores and attend midnight services.

Caroline pulled on a turtleneck and slacks and went to check on Daphne and Luke.

Luke was sitting up in bed, and Daphne was pouring two cups of coffee.

"Come in," Daphne greeted her. "The front desk staff have

been so sweet. They sent up breakfast and didn't charge us. Help yourself."

Caroline took a pumpkin muffin from the sideboard.

"I told Daphne I could go down to breakfast, but she won't let me get out of bed," Luke said cheerfully.

"It hasn't been twenty-four hours since he hit his head." Daphne sat cross-legged on the bed. "Anyway, we've been busy. Wait until I tell you about our honeymoon."

Daphne had found a company online called Where Are the Bride and Groom. Daphne and Luke each wrote down what they were looking for in a vacation and submitted it to the website without telling each other. The company studied their choices and picked their destination. A week before their departure, they'd receive an email telling them how to pack. But they wouldn't find out where they'd be going until the day before they left.

"You can't be serious," Caroline said when Daphne finished. "What if you both want something completely different? You've never traveled together."

"I don't care where we go," Daphne remarked. "As long as we're together."

"What if you choose Thailand and Luke is allergic to some kind of spicy food? Or he picks a place to scuba dive and you don't want to go?"

"Have you ever been scuba diving?" Luke asked Daphne.

Daphne shook her head. "No, but I'm sure I'd love it if you do."

Caroline wanted to tell them to slow down planning the wedding and honeymoon and get to know each other first. But she had promised Daphne she'd stop interfering.

"The honeymoon is often a couple's first experience being

together for a long time," Caroline tried again. "Isn't it better to go somewhere you both love?"

Luke took Daphne's hand.

"I agree with Daphne. I'll be happy anywhere together," he said. "This way, we'll learn new things about each other."

Caroline didn't argue. They talked about Christmas in Aspen, and details for the wedding.

"I was about to go Christmas shopping." Caroline turned to Daphne. "Would you like to come?"

Daphne had always loved shopping in quaint boutiques. Besides travel and cooking, it was her favorite thing to do.

"You should go," Luke insisted. "I'll text if my headache gets worse."

The first store they entered was called Aspen Hatter, which made custom Western hats. Caroline and Daphne tried them on, and Daphne ordered one for Luke to wear at the wedding. Daphne bought a pair of jeans at a women's consignment store called the Little Bird, and Caroline was tempted to splurge on a pashmina at Bandana Aspen. At the last minute, she reminded herself she might be out of a job soon, and put it back.

"I adore Aspen," Daphne sighed, swinging her shopping bag. "Maybe it's not such a bad idea for you to date Max. Aspen and New York aren't that far from each other, there's no reason why you couldn't keep seeing each other once you go home. And I can tell that he likes you."

"He hasn't even called." Caroline took out her phone. She had turned it off when she and Daphne started shopping.

"Your phone isn't even on. Anyway, he's perfect for you. Why wouldn't you go out with him?"

Caroline pictured Max's wide shoulders under his ski sweater, his hazel eyes.

"I'm not thinking about Max, I've got other things to worry about."

She still wanted to search for clues to Anne's lover before New Year's Eve, and she had to bring in more potential acquisitions at work.

"If I were you, I'd make time for him." Daphne's blue eyes sparkled. "Handsome, available men don't come along often."

They browsed in art galleries, and spent an hour in a boutique called the Aspen Emporium, which sold everything from silver jewelry to hula hoops and all-natural dog biscuits.

Caroline suggested they get something hot to drink. They sat in a booth at the Spring Café. Caroline ordered two cinnamon teas and Daphne wanted to share an apple pie.

The apple pie was served with whipped cream. Caroline was reminded of the apple pies her mother used to bake on Christmas Eve. Anne always let Caroline and Daphne eat the first slices, golden and fresh from the oven.

For a moment, she found it hard to swallow. They should be at the cabin with their mother. They'd laugh and bring up memories of Christmases when they were children. The Christmas when Daphne got a new puppy and he pulled the plate of brownies onto the kitchen floor.

Instead, they were in Aspen and Anne was gone. Daphne and Luke were getting married at the end of the week, and Caroline might find herself out of a job.

"I'm glad that Luke's restaurant is in Hudson," Daphne said, interrupting Caroline's thoughts. "Living in Boston still feels so foreign, being in Hudson is like coming home."

"How did Luke end up there from Wisconsin?" Caroline wondered.

Daphne shrugged. "I guess he went to college in New York."

Caroline's eyes widened. "You don't know where he went to college?"

"Neither of us ask that many questions," Daphne said absently.

"Even dating sites ask for basic information." Caroline frowned.

"You're doing it again. You still think we don't know each other well enough to get married." Daphne bristled. "I know all I need to. Luke is kind and caring and makes me happy."

Caroline had never seen Daphne so content. Like a kitten, warming herself in the sun.

"You do look happy," Caroline conceded.

Daphne played with her spoon. "There is one thing, I'm sure it's nothing."

Daphne had called Luke's parents from his phone to tell them about his concussion. His mother answered and said they were in Paris. She'd call back when it was morning in France.

"What's wrong with his parents being in Paris?" Caroline asked.

"Nothing really, and she congratulated me on the upcoming wedding." Daphne sipped her cinnamon tea. "Luke grew up in Wisconsin, it didn't sound like he has the kind of parents who go to Paris. And he said they weren't coming to the wedding because his father was going to have back surgery."

"The surgery could be scheduled for when they return. And you don't have to be wealthy to go to Paris. Maybe they're retired and they've been saving for the trip for years."

Daphne's expression brightened. "You're right, I'm worrying

about nothing. I guess I don't want anything to interfere with the wedding."

Since Anne died, Daphne had started worrying about things for no reason. When she was transferred to Boston with a promotion and a raise, she worried that she wouldn't do a good job and she'd be let go.

"Good things are allowed to happen to you," Caroline said gently.

"Sometimes, that's hard to remember since Mom died." Daphne's voice became quiet.

Caroline finished her cinnamon tea.

"Mom loved us and it's our first Christmas without her," she said. "We owe it to her to make it the best Christmas possible."

Daphne went back to the inn. Caroline decided to go to the bookstore that she and Max had visited the day before.

The shop was filled with people buying last-minute gifts. Christmas music played and there were trays of snowflake cookies.

A salesgirl approached Caroline. "Can I help you find something?"

Caroline asked the girl what she would recommend. She loved getting the advice of booksellers.

"Try this one." The girl handed her a book. "The author is a local writer."

Caroline flipped to the back of the book. The book had been published by a small press. Small presses didn't pay advances like the bigger publishers; it was almost impossible for authors to make money.

"I'll try it." Caroline handed it back to the salesgirl so she could pay for it.

Her phone buzzed as she walked onto Main Street.

"I'm sorry I didn't call earlier," Max said when she answered. "We always deliver a Christmas tree to the Boys and Girls Club on Christmas Eve."

Max asked about Luke, and they talked about Christmas shopping in Aspen.

"I wondered if you'd have dinner with me tonight," Max said.

Caroline was surprised. She'd expected that Max would spend Christmas Eve with his family.

"My dad is traveling, and my mother was invited to a dinner party." Max paused. "Unless you have other plans."

Daphne and Luke would probably stay at the inn, and Caroline didn't want to be alone.

"I'd love to have dinner with you."

"Why don't you meet me there. I'll text you the address."

Caroline took a bath and dressed in a long skirt and a scoop-neck sweater. The sweater was from a designer sample sale and made her feel sexy and sophisticated. Her hair fell smoothly to her shoulders, and she finished the outfit with ankle-high suede boots.

It was already dark when the Uber picked her up. It drove out of Aspen and stopped in front of a long, timber building. Plate-glass windows twinkled with Christmas lights, and a giant wreath hung on the front door.

Max was waiting inside. He wore navy corduroys and a wool jacket.

"Welcome to Mad Finn Distillery," he greeted her.

"We're having Christmas Eve dinner at your distillery?" Caroline asked.

She had expected Max to take her to a romantic restaurant. Afterward, they'd wander into an intimate bar on Main Street. They'd get a little tipsy on hot toddies, and Max would lean over and kiss her. She'd kiss him back and feel the thrill of a new relationship. Then she'd try to decide whether she wanted to go to bed with him, or whether she should let the anticipation build.

"Come inside," he said, interrupting her thoughts. "I'll show you around."

The space had paneled walls and a wood floor. A few tables were scattered around the room, and there was a bar with a copper counter. Framed posters of Aspen hung behind the bar, and a spiral staircase led to the second floor.

"This is going to be the distillery's tasting area," Max said. "We'll serve the typical foods you find at distilleries, hot wings and jalapeño poppers."

Most distilleries served spicy food because the foods made people want to drink more. Max was also going to serve dishes made with potatoes they grew themselves. As a completely sustainable distillery, he didn't want anything to go to waste.

He led her to the staircase. "A manager will run the tasting area, and my favorite part is up here."

Caroline had never visited a distillery before. Four giant copper vats stood next to each other. On the other side, barrels were stacked against the wall. There was a table with a selection of glass bottles.

"The different types of rye whiskey are blended in the vats," Max said. "Then each whiskey is aged for two years in the barrels. When the whiskey is ready, we add different finishes and blend it again before it's bottled."

This was the first batch of whiskey to turn a profit. If Max failed, he couldn't afford to keep going.

"Everyone thought I was crazy to move from Santa Barbara to the mountains to open a distillery. I called it Mad Finn Whiskey after my ancestor Finn Steele," Max said. "People called him Mad Finn because he stayed in Aspen during the Great Panic when the other miners fled."

They went back downstairs to have dinner. Max had set a table with a white tablecloth, candles, and his mother's good china. He confessed that he had ordered the food—parsley and pear soup for starters, followed by rack of lamb and parmesan popovers—from the kitchen at Hotel Jerome.

After they finished eating, they went back upstairs and he explained the different varieties of rye whiskey.

"Rye whiskey is about four things. Aroma, taste, finish, and aging process." He handed her a glass. "This one is a hundred and twenty proof. The aroma is of baking bread with a hint of honey and bananas. It starts with a sweet taste, but mid-palate it changes to tobacco and dark-chocolate notes. The finish is clean with a peppery bite."

They sampled another rye whiskey, which Max loved for its cherry flavor and leathery finish, and a third that changed mid-palate from an orange-rind taste to one of maple syrup.

Caroline loved Max's enthusiasm. It reminded her of how much she adored every stage of book publishing. The rounds of book covers from the illustrator, followed by advance copies of the book sent to reviewers, and finally boxes of the finished book. She kept copies of every book that she had edited on a shelf in her office. Now she wondered when there would be a new book to add to the shelf, and if she'd have an office at all.

It was getting late. She wanted to go back to the hotel and check on Daphne and Luke.

"It's been a wonderful Christmas Eve, but I think I should get back."

Max drove her back into Aspen in his Jeep. Instead of pulling up in front of the Aspen Inn, he stopped at a Victorian mansion at the other end of Main Street.

"What are you doing?" Caroline asked.

"A buddy of mine rents an apartment on the first floor. He's traveling, so we can use his place."

"Use his place for what?"

Max turned off the engine.

"I figured you wouldn't want me to come to your hotel room, and I'm staying at my parents' . . ." His voice broke off.

Caroline's cheeks turned red. It was her fault, Max was only following her rules. Usually, she wouldn't mind. With Jack, they dated for a week and a half before she decided to sleep with him, but with Brad the attraction had been immediate. They both realized she'd only be in London for a short while and didn't want to waste time.

So why did this feel different?

Max noticed her expression.

"We can go somewhere else," he said awkwardly. "Drink hot toddies at the Limelight Hotel, or watch the torch parade."

She didn't feel like drinking more whiskey, and it was too cold to watch the parade.

"I want to check on Daphne and Luke. I think I'll go back to the hotel."

Max started the car. "I'll go with you."

Max was handsome and fun. She had wondered all night when he was going to kiss her. But the strange feeling wouldn't go away.

Max might be offended, but she didn't know what else to do. She opened the car door.

"Thank you again for a wonderful evening, but I'm going to walk from here."

Chapter Nine

Caroline was furious with herself.

Max had gone to so much trouble making the distillery feel warm and inviting. Bringing over his mother's good china, and ordering a delicious Christmas Eve dinner. He gave her the tour of the distillery, and explained about different rye whiskeys. She couldn't remember a man being so thoughtful.

Then he pulled up in front of his friend's apartment and she froze. She could have said that she wasn't ready to sleep with him. They still could have had espresso martinis at the Limelight Hotel, or strolled along Main Street and admired the Christmas lights. Instead, she jumped out of the car like a frightened rabbit avoiding a group of hunters.

Now she sat in her room, staring at the twinkling lights on the mountain. She remembered Christmas two years ago, before her mother was diagnosed with cancer. It was one of the best Christmases she'd ever had.

After they delivered meals to the women's shelter, they stopped at Country Living Home and Garden store in Hudson. Anne hardly ever bought things for the cabin. But she picked out a ceramic Santa

Claus cookie jar, and an antique candelabra with clove-scented candles. Sitting at the dining table that night, inhaling the scent of clove mixed with the buttery smell of mashed potatoes, Caroline felt like she had everything in the world.

Then last Christmas, Caroline had been so worried about her mother. All through midnight services, she kept glancing over at her. Anne looked paler than she had at Thanksgiving. She had lost more weight, her blouse hung on her, her cheeks were narrow.

This year, Caroline knew that she should be grateful that she and Daphne were together. But even seeing Daphne with Luke didn't reassure her that Daphne knew what she was doing. And Caroline was worried about her own career.

Now there was Max to think about. All she had wanted was a little fling. A few days of interesting conversation and great sex with an attractive man.

So, what had stopped her from going inside with him, when he had only been following her rules?

It was 11:00 p.m., she guessed he was still awake. She sent a text thanking him for a lovely evening. She waited for the little bubbles to appear, but he didn't reply.

After changing into a robe and slippers, she curled up in bed and opened the book the bookseller had recommended. The copy on the back cover wasn't promising. It was a love story, told from the point of view of the guy. Caroline knew from experience that first-time male authors weren't usually good at writing romantic fiction.

She'd try a few chapters. If she didn't like it, she'd leave it in the room for the next guest to read when she checked out.

The next time she looked up from the book, it was well past midnight. Her neck had a crick and her eyes were tired from reading. She had been wrong. It was the best book she'd read in months.

Caroline knew editors who insisted that they could tell within the first ten pages if a book was going to be a bestseller. It was all about pacing and the author's voice. She disagreed. Many books took a while to find their footing. The characters weren't fully formed, or the action didn't start until later. And yet, by the end she was captivated.

This time, Caroline knew what they meant. From the opening paragraph, she was swept away.

The book was set on a ranch in Colorado. It was about a guy and a girl who were wrong for each other, but couldn't let the other go. The action traveled to Europe and back to the ranch, where they came back together before splitting apart for good.

The writing needed work. The heroine could be softer, the guy's feelings weren't fleshed out. But that would come in the editing. For now, Caroline had to find the author.

She made herself close her eyes and try to sleep. When she woke up, the wintry morning light filtered through the window. She heard the cranking of the ski gondola, jumped out of bed, and pulled on slacks and a sweater.

When she stepped outside, snowcats were grooming the mountain. She had almost forgotten it was Christmas Day. In a few hours, everyone in Aspen would swarm to the ski lifts and spend a gleeful day on the slopes. In the evening, they'd return to their hotels, giddy with the sunshine and perfect ski conditions, and eat Christmas dinners of turkey with stuffing, and pecan pie.

She sent a text to Daphne saying that she'd be back soon, and then she hurried along Main Street.

The lights in the bookshop were on, but the door was locked. She didn't know what she'd been thinking. None of the shops were open. She'd have to wait until after Christmas.

She was about to go back to the inn when she noticed a young woman carrying a mug of coffee.

"You work in the bookstore." Caroline approached her. "You recommended a book to me."

"My name is Sarah," the girl said. "Can I help you with something?"

Caroline held up the book.

"I was wondering if you knew the author of this book. I'm an editor at a publishing house in New York. I need to talk to him."

"Nick Harris works at the Limelight Hotel."

"He's here in Aspen?" Caroline asked eagerly.

"He's worked there since the summer. I see him around town."

Caroline thanked her. The girl was about to cross the street.

"I'm glad you found me." She turned around. "Nick deserves a break, I've never known anyone who wanted something so badly."

The Limelight Hotel was a two-story brick building near the ski gondola. The front of the hotel was decorated with Christmas lights. On the side there was a giant Christmas tree, and a swimming pool that would be a glorious place to sit in summer.

Caroline walked straight to the concierge desk.

"I'm looking for an employee, his name is Nick Harris," she said to the man behind the desk.

"I'm sorry," the man answered. "We don't give out information about our employees."

"Please, I know it's unusual. I promise he'll be glad you did."

The man shook his head. "I'm sorry, company policy."

Caroline couldn't leave without talking to Nick.

"When you were a child, did you ever want something so badly for Christmas, you were afraid to open your presents?" she asked.

The man looked at her, puzzled. "I beg your pardon."

"When I was ten, I wanted a clock I'd seen in a shop window," Caroline continued. "It was a miniature grandfather clock, white with yellow flowers. I wrote to Santa Claus, and even had my sister, Daphne, draw a picture because I was hopeless at drawing. I was afraid to open my presents. I thought the elves couldn't make the same clock. It was the last present that I opened, tucked under the tree.

"That's how Nick probably feels now. Wanting something so badly, but afraid he can't have it. He wrote a wonderful novel. It's published by a tiny press, every copy is probably at the bookstore on Main Street. I work for a New York publisher. I can get Nick's novel into bookstores everywhere, if you tell me where to find him."

Caroline couldn't remember the last time she had given such a long speech.

The man hesitated. He clicked through his computer screen.

"Nick is in banquets. His shift ends at three p.m."

Her face broke into a smile. "I don't know how to thank you."

"My daughter is twelve, she wants to be a writer," the man said. "I told her she needs to choose a practical profession. Maybe I was wrong. No one comes in here looking for a computer programmer to tell him that she can make his dreams come true."

The hotel dining room was being set up for Christmas dinner. A gingerbread house stood in the corner. The roof was made of graham crackers, and covered with white frosting. The walls were different-colored jelly beans, and there was a picket fence made of gumdrops, and a red-licorice chimney.

Caroline approached a young woman wearing a waitress uniform.

"Excuse me, I'm looking for Nick Harris."

The woman pointed to a man in his late twenties. He was sitting at a table, folding napkins. He was tall, with long legs and a narrow build. He had dark curly hair, and brown eyes.

Caroline walked over to him.

"Excuse me." She held out her hand. "My name is Caroline Holt."

He looked up from the napkins he was folding.

"Nick Harris. Can I help you?"

Caroline smiled to herself. Not many men who were close to thirty worked at hotels, folding napkins. But writers took all sorts of jobs so they could keep writing. Caroline knew an author who performed magic tricks at children's birthday parties, and another who spent a year working on a cruise ship for the free room and board.

"I read your book. I'm a book editor in New York, I think I can get it published."

"No, thank you. It's already published."

"By a small press. I looked them up, they don't even have a website."

"How did you read it?"

"The salesgirl at the bookstore on Main Street recommended it, I bet it isn't carried anywhere else. If my publisher agrees to publish it, it will be in bookstores everywhere."

For a few moments, Nick didn't say anything.

"I wrote the book for myself. If other people read it, that's great." He went back to folding napkins. "Excuse me, I have to work."

"You can't be serious. Most writers dream of this opportunity."

"I'm not most writers. Like I said, it's already published." Nick stood up and started walking. "It's Christmas and I'm sure you have somewhere else to be."

Caroline didn't know why she felt so angry. She couldn't let him walk away.

"It's the simplest story. Boy meets girl, they fall in love, and overcome a dozen obstacles to stay together. But somehow, your writing makes it brand new. The ending is one of the best I've read. At first, I was angry at you for separating the lovers, but it couldn't have ended any other way."

Nick stopped walking. He turned around, and his brown eyes were full of anguish.

"I tried different endings. I wanted them to be happy: get married, start a family. But it wouldn't have worked. Maggie was too independent, she hurt Josh too much."

Caroline nodded. "I love Maggie, but she's a free spirit. Josh has this quiet dignity. You think he doesn't care, but really he keeps his feelings bottled inside."

Nick was about to say something, but stopped. His brow furrowed.

"I'm glad you understood the book, but I'm not interested in a publisher. Unless you want to get me fired on Christmas Day, you should go."

Caroline scribbled her full name, address, and phone number on a piece of paper and handed it to Nick.

"All right, but if you change your mind, you can text me."

When she left the hotel, the snow was beginning to fall. There was a text from Daphne saying that she and Luke were going on a dogsled ride, and they'd be back for Christmas dinner.

Caroline turned onto Main Street and stopped in front of the bookstore. The lights were on, and the salesgirl Sarah was standing at the counter.

Caroline tapped on the glass.

"I didn't think you'd be open," she said when Sarah opened the door.

"We're not, I'm here to restock the shelves. Tomorrow everyone will come in to exchange the books they didn't like." She gave a small smile. "You'd be surprised how many married couples don't know each other's tastes. Or the grandparents who buy a book for a middle schooler, when their grandchild is in third grade."

Caroline grinned. One summer, she worked at a bookstore in New York. Almost every parent thought their child read above their reading level.

"At least they're buying books," Caroline reasoned.

"The owner is thrilled with our sales for last week, I'm getting a bonus."

Caroline told her what happened with Nick. "I wondered how well you know him."

"During the summer, he walked dogs for hotel guests. I used to put a water bowl in front of the store, and we'd chat. At first, he was really excited about his book. The Aspen writers' conference was happening, and he was sure he'd find a publisher. It didn't pan out, so he went with a local press."

That sort of thing happened all the time at writers' conferences. Aspiring authors met editors and agents and got excited. Then they'd learn how publishing worked. The editorial board had to fall in love with the book as much as the acquiring editor; the sales and marketing teams could veto the deal if they didn't know how to position the book. By the end of the conference, the writer often felt disillusioned about the whole process. It sounded almost impossible to get their story out into the world. Most likely, their dreams would end up like scrunched-up paper, tossed in the garbage.

Sarah shrugged. "After that, Nick stopped talking about the book altogether."

Caroline bought a few books and walked back to the inn. Snowflakes covered the benches and settled on the branches of the aspen trees. Two boys were having a snowball fight while their parents ate cinnamon rolls.

Caroline had been so certain about Nick's book. She had already made a few edit notes, and was rehearsing how to present it to the editorial board. If she didn't find something to show Claudia by the winter sales meeting, it was very likely that she would lose her job.

When she entered the inn, Nick was standing in front of the concierge desk. He walked over to her.

"I was hoping you'd be here, I need to talk to you."

Caroline glanced at her phone. "You didn't call or text."

Nick fidgeted with his jacket. "I was pretty rude. I was afraid you wouldn't talk to me."

Caroline gave her brightest smile. "I'm in publishing, I'm used to anxious writers. Why don't we sit by the fireplace and you can tell me the whole story."

Caroline ordered two hot apple ciders and Nick let it pour out.

He grew up on a dude ranch nearby. He never liked horses and he wasn't good at sports, so he spent most of his time at the library. He got a scholarship to a college in Denver. It wasn't New York or Boston, but it was a city with history and culture.

The summer before his senior year, his parents asked him to work at the dude ranch. There was a new ranch hand. Her name was Savannah. She had strawberry-blond hair and a Southern accent. They fell in love. At the end of the summer, Savannah said she was going to stay at the dude ranch and not go back to college. Nick took a semester off, and then a whole year. They talked about getting married. Then one morning, he came down to breakfast and she was gone. Eventually, he tracked her down. She was in Greece, on an archaeological dig. Over one choppy international call, she explained that it was a pattern she couldn't break. She'd fall in love with a place and a way of life. Then one day the feeling would disappear, and she'd move on.

Nick's scholarship ran out and he couldn't go back to school. So, he wrote the novel. It took five years to write. At first, he worked at the dude ranch. But his parents pestered him to take on more responsibilities, or get a proper job. He couldn't do either so he moved in with a friend in Aspen and worked at the Limelight Hotel.

"I finished the book in April and started emailing agents and publishers. Some of them loved the manuscript. But I'd never been published and I didn't have a social media platform so they wouldn't take me on." Nick nursed his glass. "Then I met an agent at the Aspen writers' conference. She read the book in one night. Afterward, we sat for hours, and she told me all the things she wanted me to change. She gave me her email address, and asked me to send the revised manuscript.

"I worked on it for three months. I sent it to her in September and waited." His brow furrowed. "Every morning I refreshed my emails, certain that her email had slipped past me." He fished a business card out of his pocket and handed it to Caroline. "Her name was Anne Holt. I never heard from her again."

It was the same business card Anne had used for years. Caroline often teased her mother. People didn't use business cards anymore, they exchanged contact information on their phones. But Anne insisted. A business card was something you could hold, like a hardback book.

"Anne told me that her daughter was an editor. When I read

the piece of paper you gave me, I realized that she was your mother. I trusted her. The least she could have done was say that she wasn't interested."

Caroline's eyes filled with tears. She glanced up at Nick.

"She didn't answer because in September she was in the hospital. She died in October, she had breast cancer."

Nick's face paled. He stared at his hands.

"I'm sorry, I didn't know."

"She was diagnosed last winter. But she went into remission over the summer. She adored discovering new writers, I'm sure meeting you made her happy."

Nick smiled ruefully. "You must hate me. I wasn't just rude, I was a complete jerk."

"A lot of agents promise new writers the world. Their book will be a bestseller, they'll get a six-figure advance and a movie deal. My mother believed that managing an author's expectations was more important than anything. She wouldn't have been so passionate about your book if she didn't believe it would be a success."

"I loved talking to her about it. She understood the characters better than I did."

"Send me the latest manuscript and I can work with you on a final round of edits while I'm here," Caroline offered. "I can't promise my publisher will buy it, but I've got the same feeling about it my mother must have had."

Caroline found she was holding her breath. She hadn't realized how much she wanted Nick's book.

"I'll be hard to work with," Nick warned. "I'm an insomniac and once I get an idea, I don't stop until I get it down on paper. And I can argue about the silliest things. Whether a period should go at the end of a thought, or a semicolon. Why the character's eyes have to be aquamarine, because I want to imagine the ocean when I think of her."

A shiver ran down Caroline's spine. For the first time since her mother died, she felt excited and alive.

"There's nothing wrong with arguing about a period and a semicolon. A period is the end of something, a semicolon is the door to a new beginning."

Nick shook her hand, and Caroline's heart lifted. It was finally beginning to feel like Christmas.

Chapter Ten

After Nick left, Caroline went up to her room. The maid had left a plate of gingerbread cookies. There was a box wrapped in silver foil with a note from the concierge, wishing Caroline a happy Christmas. Inside the box was an ornament of the Aspen Inn.

She had that bubbly feeling she used to experience after a long day at the office. Too tired to go running or to the gym, but too energized to sit and watch Netflix. She debated sending a text to Max. It would be nice to sit by the fireplace in the lobby and drink eggnog. But he hadn't responded to her previous text and she wasn't going to disturb him on Christmas Day.

Daphne and Luke wouldn't be back for a few hours. She curled up in an armchair and picked up the next letter from Nina.

Dear Anne,

I'm sitting at the writing desk in my apartment. I can see you letting out a cheer, I'm finally going to work on the novel. I promise I will, I even made a deal with myself. If I meet my word count, I'm going to read one of the novels I bought at the Strand bookstore.

But it isn't my discipline that put me in my chair, it's today's snowstorm. I love snowstorms in New York. The streets turn white and the whole city goes to sleep. Snowstorms are the best thing for a writer. I can sit for hours without feeling I'm missing out on something: a reading at the New York Public Library, or a sale at Macy's.

Snow is different outside the city. That was the only thing that pleased me about Margaret's insistence that Teddy accompany me to Vermont. Teddy had gone to college at Cornell in Ithaca, he was used to snow. He could dig the car out, or fix the boiler if it broke.

I went home from my meeting with Margaret and called him. He was living in an apartment a few blocks away from me, in the West Village.

He answered on the second ring.

"If you're calling to tell me that you found more of my clothes and they're sitting in front of your building, you could have saved yourself the effort," Teddy said. "I visited my tailor last week. I used my bonus and bought a new wardrobe."

I deserved that. I felt terribly guilty. Not for calling off the engagement. That was the right thing to do. But for the way I behaved. It wasn't right to toss Teddy's suits out the window.

"I'm inviting you over for dinner," I offered.

Teddy's voice was cautious. "Why would you do that? Unless you've added food poisoning to the ways you want to get back at me."

I tried to think of a way to entice him.

"On the contrary, Joan is taking a cordon bleu cooking

course. She brought home a coq au vin, dauphinoise potatoes, and apricot crème brûlée. She's out of town for three days. If it sits here, it's going to go bad."

"Wrap it up and take it to work for lunch," Teddy suggested.

I was getting angry again. Teddy could be so infuriating.

"All right. The truth is I want to discuss something with you."

"You should have said so," Teddy remarked. I could hear the triumph in his voice. He probably thought I was going to beg him to get back together.

"I'll be there at seven," he said before I could answer. "And I'll bring a chardonnay. The food sounds delicious, and you're too cheap to spring for a good wine."

I spent the next hour cleaning the apartment. Joan and I had moved from the apartment we occupied when Teddy and I met. We were still in the West Village, but I had my own bedroom.

Teddy looked handsome in a tan turtleneck and brown slacks. Since we broke up, his good looks irritated me. Everything would have been easier if he was ordinary-looking.

"Things haven't changed around here." He picked up a bag of books that I had left on the counter. "You're still spending too much of your salary on books, and Joan is still dating Saul."

"Authors have to support each other, and how do you know Joan is dating Saul?"

"You have a bottle of Manischewitz wine." He pointed to the kitchen counter. "I guess Joan finally converted."

Teddy was right, Joan and Saul were engaged. Saul wanted to raise their children to be Jewish and Joan had agreed. She had spent the last year studying Judaism and had decided to convert after all.

"Why should anything change? It's only been a few weeks since we broke up," I said through gritted teeth.

Teddy glanced at me with an innocent expression.

"Is that all? It feels like a lifetime. I guess that happens, when one is released from prison. I've attended so many dinner parties, I'm afraid I'll get fat. And I'm going to the Saint Kitts after New Year's Day." His voice was level. "Gwendolyn's parents have a villa there. They invited my mother and me. Dolly wants me to go and I need the suntan. A good tan takes pounds off one's figure, that's why they shoot models on the beach."

"You just said you're going to stop attending dinner parties, why do you need a suntan too?" I blurted out before I could stop myself.

I turned away so Teddy couldn't see my expression. Gwendolyn Arthur was the cause of our breakup. But our troubles didn't start with Gwendolyn. They started with Dolly Chandler, Teddy's mother.

The first few months after Teddy proposed were the happiest I'd ever experienced. Teddy moved into his own apartment and I slept over almost every night. We didn't have sex right away. After he gave me the engagement ring, there were still a few weeks of petting on his couch. But when he finally took my virginity, we couldn't stop. It's the oldest cliché and the truest. Every new couple thinks they invented sex.

I'd be sitting at my desk, typing an article, and recall how he whispered in my ear. I never felt so alive! We rarely went out to dinner. We ordered takeout but we were so eager to go to bed, even that didn't get eaten. Instead, we consumed big breakfasts: eggs and bacon and buttered toast.

Then the first flush of romance eased and real life intruded. By "real life" I mean Dolly. It's not that Dolly didn't like me. She thought I was pretty, and she admired my career. But Teddy was her only child, and she insisted we have a large society wedding. I refused. My first book had come out the previous winter, followed by the second novel during the summer. I was one of the voices of the women's lib movement. Being photographed in a white, pouffy dress for the *New York Times* society pages would be terrible for my image.

Besides, I didn't like big weddings and I wasn't comfortable around Teddy's friends. Hardly any of the women worked, and the men said crass things about women when they thought no one was listening.

Teddy wanted me to be happy but he wanted to please his mother too. We remained at an impasse for months, then six weeks before Margaret cast me as Laura Carter, it broke.

Dolly was giving a dinner party. I had an author event in Philadelphia and couldn't go. I encouraged Teddy to attend. Between working at *Women's World Monthly* and writing, I rarely had time to socialize and Teddy didn't like to go alone.

By the time I returned from Philadelphia the night of the dinner party, Teddy was in bed. I didn't think about it again until I read the Sunday *New York Times.* Teddy and Gwendolyn's photo was splashed in the society column with the caption *Is Gwendolyn Arthur the reason that Teddy Chandler III hasn't tied the knot with his fiancée?* It went on to say that Gwendolyn was new on the New York social scene. Her father owned a shoe empire and she worked for Ralph Lauren.

I threw down the paper, furious. I was angry at Dolly for inviting Gwendolyn when she knew I couldn't come. And I was mad at Teddy, of course. Even if it had been innocent, he should have warned me that the photo would be in the newspaper.

Teddy had every excuse. He didn't have anything to do with the seating arrangements. The photographer snapped photos of everyone.

The next day, a dozen red roses waited for me at the office. I decided to forgive Teddy. But a few days later, I was at his apartment and there was a delivery from Cartier. I assumed it was for me. Teddy thought I was still angry and wanted to make me happy.

Teddy wasn't home and I opened it. Inside was a sapphire bracelet. Immediately I was suspicious. I didn't wear bracelets, they got in the way of the typewriter. And I didn't like expensive jewelry. I could barely make myself wear my engagement ring.

When Teddy got home, I showed him the bracelet. He said it was Gwendolyn's bracelet. The clasp broke and Dolly discovered it under the dining table. She took it to Cartier to get repaired and asked Teddy to pick it up and return it to Gwendolyn. Teddy didn't want to see

Gwendolyn. So, he asked Cartier to deliver it to her. The delivery man must have mixed up the addresses and sent it to him instead.

I listened to his story. Even if Teddy was telling the truth, I didn't want to spend my life stuck between Teddy and Dolly, like layers in a sponge cake.

I took off my engagement ring and handed it to Teddy.

Teddy begged me to reconsider. But I was too wound up. I stormed out the door and went home. I wasn't satisfied until I had dumped his suits out the window.

You can see why Teddy hadn't wanted to come to my apartment for dinner. And why I didn't look forward to telling him about Vermont.

"I had the most interesting conversation with Margaret this afternoon," I said as I served the crème brûlée. "It's about Laura Carter's column."

"If she wants Palmolive to advertise, she could have asked me herself," Teddy said. "The column has terrific numbers, I'd be happy to do it."

"It's not that." I explained Margaret's request.

"Let me get this straight. Laura Carter is a Jewish grandmother living in Florida, and you're going to impersonate her for a week."

"Not impersonate exactly."

"Pretending to be Laura Carter to some Midwest matron who wins the contest sounds like impersonating to me."

"There is no Laura Carter," I said impatiently. "I'm taking over the role for a week. What harm am I doing? The contest winner gets a free vacation."

"Thank you for the invitation, but I decline. I'd much

rather spend New Year's Eve at the Rainbow Room at Rockefeller Center."

"The plan doesn't work unless you're at the farm too. I can't say no to Margaret." I played with my fork. "Besides, I need the money."

Teddy's voice was quiet. "You could have kept the engagement ring."

"An engagement ring is part of a commitment," I snapped.

Teddy's eyes found mine. "I'm willing to keep the commitment."

For one moment, I was as soft and pliable as the dessert in front of me. Then I thought of Gwendolyn and her parents' villa in Saint Kitts.

"Well, I'm not." I glowered. "Will you do it?"

Teddy made a point of scraping up every crumb before he answered.

"I'm only doing it because of the bears."

"Bears?" I repeated, puzzled.

"Black bears. I'm not worried about you. You can take care of yourself," he said. "It's the bears I'm concerned about. If they rummage through your garbage, you'll shoot them."

I'll stop there. A good writer ends the chapter with a cliffhanger.

Regards,
Nina

Caroline set the letter back on the stack. Somehow, she felt closer to her mother when she was reading them. She still wished she knew why her mother had kept them in a box, and whether Nina ever finished her novel.

Her phone pinged. It was a text from Daphne.

"Luke and I are on our way back from the dogsled ride. Meet you in the lobby for Christmas dinner after we get showered and changed?"

Caroline went into the bathroom to get ready.

Chapter Eleven

Daphne and Luke had picked Prospect at Hotel Jerome for Christmas dinner.

The moment Caroline walked through the wooden doors of the hotel, she knew it was perfect. It was like stepping into the library of a century-old mansion. The walls were lined with bookshelves and filled with leather-bound books. Hand-stitched armchairs faced a fireplace and there were framed photos of Aspen during the silver rush.

Caroline entered the restaurant and saw Daphne and Luke sitting at a table near the window. Luke wore a red blazer with a shirt and tie. Daphne was glamorous in a red sequined evening gown. Her hair was scooped into a knot with blond ringlets framing her face.

"You look stunning," Caroline said, giving Daphne a hug.

"Mom loved dressing up at Christmas, and she always wanted us to wear red."

Every Christmas when they were children, Anne would take them to Macy's to buy red Christmas dresses. And she adored dressing up for Christmas dinner. She said it was like preparing for the ballet or opera. It made the meal so festive, even if it was just the three of them and Walter when he was alive, eating at the cabin.

Caroline ordered a Silver Queen cocktail and they chose a four-course Christmas tasting menu.

"We had the best day," Daphne gushed after the waiter brought the first course—seared scallops and a celery root soup. "The dog-sled ride took us to the foot of the Maroon Bells mountains. The snow had fresh footprints of squirrels and it was so quiet." She sighed happily. "Luke and I decided that next time we come to Aspen, we'll bring Truffles. She would have loved to run in the snow with the other dogs.

"We saw a herd of elk and some moose. Afterward we went back to the inn and listened to the carolers. They were having Teddy Bear Story Hour at the same time. It was so sweet. The children are given teddy bears to hold while someone reads 'The Night Before Christmas.'"

Caroline was going to tell them about Nick and his novel, but Daphne kept talking.

"We're crazy about Aspen. Luke is thinking of opening an-other restaurant here. Similar to the one in Hudson, but with fish caught in mountain streams and locally grown, organic meats."

"Luke can't be in two places at once," Caroline said in alarm.

It was bad enough if Daphne worked in Boston and Luke was in Hudson. Their marriage might not survive if he had to spend time in Colorado too.

"He wouldn't be doing it alone," Daphne said. "I'd quit the PR company and we'd run the restaurants together."

Caroline put down her soup spoon. "You can't do that! You just moved to Boston, and you love your job."

"Public relations is about selling something. Why should I work on other people's projects when I can work on our own?" Daphne smiled at Luke. "It will be more fun if it's ours."

"I told Daphne we'll have to be cautious," Luke cut in. "She'd be great in the restaurant business. Her ideas are so creative and people love her."

Daphne had that stubborn look again. She was furiously cutting her scallops. Caroline knew she should back down, but she couldn't help herself.

"You should slow down. You're not married yet."

Daphne's mouth formed a small pout. "It's Christmas and you're acting like the Grinch. You never change. When I was in college, you told me not to take a summer abroad. You wanted me to get an internship instead, so I'd have a job when I graduated. After college, when the company I worked for wanted to send me to Australia, you told me not to do it. I'd be far away from the action, and I'd never get promoted.

"It's time to start doing the things I want to." Daphne ate a bite of scallop. "I don't want to die without having lived."

Caroline was silent. Luke was about to say something, but Daphne jumped up.

"Excuse me, I'm going to the restroom."

Caroline waited until Daphne left. She turned to Luke.

"I'm sorry, I didn't mean to interfere."

Luke offered a small smile. "She's your sister, you want her to be happy."

Caroline debated whether she should be honest with Luke about her fears. Daphne would be furious, but Caroline might not get another chance to talk to him.

"Daphne can sound like a dreamer, but she's really smart and grounded," Caroline began. "The engagement is so sudden. I wonder if . . ."

"She's reacting to your mother's death." Luke finished the sentence for her.

Caroline flushed. "You're a great guy, it's just all happening so fast."

Caroline wondered if Luke was going to agree with her. He'd tell Daphne they should postpone the wedding until spring. Daphne could settle into her job in Boston, and Luke would have more time to devote to the restaurant.

He took a sip of his cocktail.

"Before I met Daphne, I never thought about marriage," he said slowly. "But the first hour of talking to Daphne on the beach, that changed. If we don't get married in Aspen now, I'll be waiting until the day we do. I love Daphne and I want to be with her."

Caroline finished her Silver Queen.

Luke really was a good guy.

"I believe you." She stood up. "I better go talk to her."

Daphne was sitting on a velvet stool in the powder room. A box of tissues lay on the dressing table.

"I'm sorry if I made you upset," Caroline apologized.

"You could have waited until after dinner." Daphne balled up a tissue. "I'm so embarrassed, Luke will think all we do is fight."

"That's not true," Caroline said. "He knows how much we care about each other."

Daphne turned from the mirror. Her blue eyes were bright.

"I always thought you and Mom knew more than me. I remember when we were teenagers and Walter's mother gave us Christmas money. We were each going to buy a pair of shoes. I wanted yellow ones with bows. You told me not to get them, they wouldn't go with anything. So, I bought a pair of boring white ones instead. They sat in my closet for a year, I never put them on."

"Getting married isn't like buying shoes, it's forever."

"And I always listened to Mom." Daphne ignored her. "Mom said that nothing was more important than being independent and having careers. It was easy for you, you loved books. I don't feel the same about public relations. It's fun and I like to travel, but it isn't my whole life."

Daphne was right. Caroline had never considered doing anything else. But Daphne fell into public relations. A friend knew someone at a PR company and recommended Daphne for the job.

"I'm worried that you're acting hastily because Mom died." Caroline tried to steer the conversation.

"I would want to marry Luke no matter what," Daphne snapped. "You'll never know what I'm talking about because you keep yourself all closed up." She narrowed her eyes. "I dare you to break your one-month rule."

Caroline's mouth dropped open. That was impossible. She'd lived by those rules for years. And now that she was in danger of losing her job, she had to focus on her career.

"I can't." She shook her head. "I'm going through a rough patch at work."

"You'd be surprised how energized you feel when you're in love," Daphne challenged. "Mom was brave, for the way she fought cancer. It's time you were brave too."

The spring after Anne had been diagnosed, she almost never stopped working. She took on three new authors, and spent endless hours editing their books. Caroline thought she rested on the weekends, but when she drove up to the cabin one Saturday, Anne was planting flowers in the garden. It was only later that Caroline realized what she was doing. It was Anne's way of believing she'd be around the following year. She had to stay alive to see the books get published, and to see the flowers bloom.

Caroline was brave, that's why she was determined to take care of herself.

Daphne took her lipstick out of her purse. "Have a real relationship with the next man you're interested in, and I'll never say anything again."

Caroline thought about Max. The attraction was there, but she'd been checking her phone all day, and he hadn't called or texted. Besides, he lived in Aspen and she was in New York.

But Caroline had never backed down from a challenge. And if she agreed to Daphne's challenge, it would end their recent bickering.

"There's Max, but he lives in Aspen. I'm going back to New York."

"Max is definitely cute, and lots of relationships start long distance," Daphne said.

"All right, I accept your dare. As long as you don't take offense if I question your relationship with Luke."

A smile played across Daphne's face. She was her light, bubbly self.

"You can have all the doubts you want, it's not going to change the way I feel."

Even if Caroline couldn't stop Daphne and Luke from getting married, she could at least convince Daphne not to quit her job.

Daphne smiled mischievously.

"You have to get rid of your other rules." Daphne counted on her fingers. "Not letting him see your place, and not staying at his for your morning coffee. Oh, and you have to let him leave a toothbrush in your bathroom. You're going to be a normal woman who's open to love and finding the right man."

It was Christmas, and she was stuck in Aspen until she met Anne's lover at Santa's Little Red Mailbox on New Year's Eve.

Caroline held out her hand. "All right, you have a deal."

They went back to their table and joined Luke. The entrees were venison and homemade pasta and grilled trout. For side dishes, there were pureed vegetables and baked potatoes. The desserts were delicious—roasted hazelnuts with whipped cream, pecan pie, a custard fruit tart. Caroline couldn't resist trying each one.

After dinner, they returned to the inn and exchanged presents. Luke gave Daphne a charm bracelet with charms of the places he wanted to go together. Daphne gave him a pair of suede boots and a book of the best restaurants in New England.

Daphne presented Caroline with a small box wrapped in silver paper. Inside was a miniature grandfather clock. It was painted white with yellow and red flowers.

Caroline gasped. It was almost the same as the clock Caroline had received as a child.

"I know it's silly, people don't use clocks anymore," Daphne said, pleased at Caroline's reaction. "I found it in the gift shop next to Santa's Little Red Mailbox. They have all sorts of things. I wonder if Mom shopped there when she was here."

Anne had loved to explore local shops when she traveled. She always brought something back for Caroline and Daphne. Hand-carved nutcrackers when she attended the Frankfurt Book Fair, flamenco skirts from a book tour of Spain.

Caroline gave Daphne and Luke the presents she had bought the first morning she was in Aspen. A snowflake sweater for Daphne, and a pair of wool gloves for Luke.

"We're going to play board games in the lobby," Daphne said when the wrapping paper had been put away.

Caroline was feeling too emotional. She needed to get some air.

"I'm going for a walk. Plus, you always beat me at Monopoly." Caroline turned to Luke. "Daphne is a real estate magnate. She bankrupts me with her rents every time."

Main Street was more beautiful than Caroline had seen it. Christmas lights twinkled everywhere. On the silver bells tied to lampposts, and on the banner strung across the street.

A horse and carriage stood next to the sidewalk. A little girl was feeding sugar cubes to the horse, while a man talked to the driver.

The man looked up. It was Max.

"Caroline!" Max exclaimed. "This is my niece, Lily."

Lily had dark hair cut in a cute pageboy style, and large brown eyes. She wore a red dress and long wool socks.

"Did you get any goldfish for Christmas?" Caroline asked Lily.

"I didn't ask for goldfish this year. I'm getting a guinea pig instead. Max and I are going to pick it out at the pet shop."

"My sister had to go to Denver Airport to pick up her husband," Max said. "I've been hanging out with Lily while she's gone."

"I made Max turn off his phone. Grown-ups spend too much time on their phones," Lily said. "My mom got a time-out because she was texting when she was supposed to be reading me a Christmas story."

Caroline felt lighter. That was why Max hadn't answered her text.

Caroline took her phone from her purse. "I'll turn mine off too."

"Max was mad at first, but we had fun," Lily went on. "After we opened presents, we made Christmas cookies. Max took me tobogganing and we saw the puppet show. Now we're going on a horse and carriage ride." Lily patted the horse's nose. "You should come with us."

Caroline still didn't know if Max was still interested in her. Christmas Eve had ended so awkwardly.

"I don't want to intrude," Caroline said hastily.

"I bet Max would like you to come," Lily persisted. "You smell good, guys like girls who wear perfume. My best friend, Emily, told me that. She has an older sister so she knows."

Max smiled at Caroline. He looked handsome in a down parka and boots.

"Lily is right, you should come. Lily wants to sit up front with the driver, now I won't be alone."

Caroline climbed into the carriage next to Max. She was afraid they wouldn't have anything to say. But Lily kept up a steady conversation about which house had the prettiest Christmas lights.

The carriage stopped in front of a Victorian mansion. A group of carolers stood on the doorstep and listeners were scattered over the lawn.

"These are the Aspen Carolers, they're members of the Aspen opera company." Max pointed at them. "Every summer, the opera performs at Maroon Bells Amphitheater. People come from all over the world."

Caroline pictured her mother watching the opera in a floppy sun hat and a pair of Italian sandals. Besides books, opera and ballet had been Anne's favorite things.

"You look far away, I must be boring you." Max cut into her thoughts.

"I was wondering if my mother attended an opera while she was here."

"Aspen is beautiful in the summer. And there's so much to do. Horseback riding and hot-air ballooning." Max grinned. "I'd invite you to come, but I don't want to break your rules."

Caroline almost blurted out that she had decided to bend her rules. But she would have to explain that it was for a dare with Daphne, and Max wouldn't understand.

Max kept talking. "I'd like to believe that last night, you got chilly and wanted to go back to your hotel. But I think you got cold feet."

"I didn't mean to." She looked at Max. "I'm over them now, I'd like to try again."

Lily had gotten out of the carriage. Now, she ran up to it. She was holding a giant candy cane.

"Can you believe how big this is?" She waved it proudly. "And each child got a coloring book."

Max pulled away from Caroline. "You can keep the coloring book but you better give me the candy cane. If your mother finds out I've fed you more sugar, she'll be furious."

An hour later, Caroline sat on the armchair in her room. Her new clock was on the bedside table, and a plate of peppermint chocolate truffles sat on the sideboard.

Max had asked Caroline to join them for the fireworks but she decided to go back to the inn instead. Caroline had enjoyed Max's company and Lily was sweet and fun, but she wanted to be alone.

She couldn't stop thinking about what Max said about Aspen in the summer. Caroline hadn't come with her mother in June because she was too busy working. It would have been lovely to take in an outdoor concert together. They could have ridden the gondola and eaten at one of the restaurants at the top of the mountain.

Perhaps Caroline would have met her mother's lover. She wouldn't be sitting here, wondering if he was going to show up on New Year's Eve.

Now her mother was gone, and she'd never get another chance.

Chapter Twelve

The next morning, Caroline woke early and checked the texts on her phone. The first one was from Max.

"I had fun last night. Lily can sound like a walking ethics textbook, but she's a sweet kid when you get to know her. Now that you and I have the dating rule book squared away, how about lunch? There's somewhere I want to take you. Wear warm boots. I don't want you to get cold feet."

Caroline laughed to herself. She tapped on the screen.

"Lily is delightful. She should write a book on advice to grownups from an eight-year-old. I always turn everything into a book idea. Hazard of the job. As for lunch, I'd love to. I promise not to get cold feet this time. If I do, you can warm them up."

Caroline reread it before she pressed Send. She wasn't usually so flirty by text. But if she was going to show Daphne that she was serious about winning the dare, she had to move the relationship along.

The second text was from Daphne.

"Luke and I are going skiing. Then we're going to have après-ski cocktails at the bar. I'm going to need one. I hope I can keep up, Luke was on his high school ski team."

Caroline sent a quick reply with an emoji smiley face. She was glad she and Daphne weren't fighting anymore. Then she jumped in the shower and got dressed. She was meeting Nick for their first meeting to discuss her editorial ideas for his book, and she couldn't wait to dive in.

Nick was waiting for her when she arrived at Paradise Bakery. It was cozy inside, and smelled of fresh-baked pastries. Skiers trudged around in ski boots, and couples drank cappuccinos and hot chocolates.

"This café is the best," Nick said when Caroline sat down. "The owner lets me sit here all morning, even though I can only afford one cup of coffee."

Caroline ordered a flat white and a pumpkin-nut muffin.

Nick spread the manuscript on the table. "I read your edit notes about the revisions I made for your mother," he began. "She had the same concerns about the section where Josh and Maggie meet for the first time. Josh doesn't show enough emotion. I tried to revise it in the current draft but judging from your notes, I didn't succeed. How do I show his emotions when he doesn't even reveal them to himself?"

Caroline thought about it. "How did you feel when you met Savannah?"

"Maggie and Savannah aren't alike. Savannah is from a wealthy family in Atlanta. In the book, Josh is a schoolteacher and Maggie has a boring job at a pharmacy."

"The characters might be different but the emotions are the same," Caroline urged. "That's the wonderful thing about books. The themes are universal."

Nick sipped his coffee. He leaned back in his chair.

"I was surprised when my parents hired Savannah. Savannah attended some fancy private college in Atlanta. She wore nail polish, and she had never done physical labor. Being a ranch hand is hard work. Getting up at sunrise to feed the animals, helping with the cooking. I figured she'd last two weeks. She'd go back to Atlanta and spend the rest of the summer sitting beside her parents' pool.

"I tried to be friendly, but she kept to herself. The second week, I understood why. Even though I didn't enjoy horseback riding, I'd always been around horses. I knew how to handle them. I saddled up Savannah's horse and watched her try to get on."

She tried to get on the horse, but slipped off.

"I explained that she was doing it wrong," Nick said to Caroline. "First she had to grab the reins, then place her foot in the stirrup.

"She did what I suggested, but she lost her footing and slipped off again. She must have gotten on a horse before. My parents wouldn't have hired her otherwise.

"She looked at me guiltily. She really was beautiful. Huge green eyes, and a heart-shaped mouth. She admitted that she may have fudged that part of the application. I was furious. It was a dude ranch! All the guests took horseback riding lessons.

"She argued that there were other activities like fly fishing. She was good at fishing. Her parents had a house on the Gulf Coast. I asked her why she was there if she didn't know anything about horses, and she said she was an archaeology major. She liked going to different places. And she was a fast learner. If I showed her how to get on the horse, she'd be fine.

"I led her through the steps. She did it right the first two times to practice, but the third time the horse started bucking. She rubbed his neck the way I showed her, but that made it worse. The horse reared and Savannah fell on the ground.

"I ran over and helped her up. It was the first time I noticed how good she smelled. Like wildflowers in the spring.

"I inspected the horse's neck and explained the horse bucked because it got stung by a bee. She didn't say anything, instead she walked to the house. I figured she'd had enough and wasn't going to try again. A few minutes later she returned. She was holding a teacup.

"She placed the cup under the horse's nose. He sniffed, then he lapped it up. Then she put the cup down and climbed on the horse. She grabbed the reins and the horse did a slow trot around the ring before she hopped off. She smiled smugly and said she'd given the horse Southern sweet tea. Tea steeped in sugar water. Her dog Moonie used to get stung by a bee and it worked every time."

Nick stopped talking. He took a sip of his coffee.

"I learned her parents were doctors, they didn't approve of her major. She called her dog Moonie because *Legally Blonde* was her favorite movie. She was tired of people judging her for her Southern accent and strawberry-blond hair. And just because she was studying archaeology, that didn't mean she wanted to get a suntan in exotic locations. She was serious about it. She asked what kind of future we could have if we don't learn by our past mistakes.

"That summer, I fell in love with Savannah and writing, and even with working on the ranch. My favorite time of day was evening, when Savannah and I strolled around the ranch. The sky was full of stars and it was so romantic."

Caroline tried to think whether she had ever felt that way about a guy. Often there was an electric spark when she met someone new, but after a few dates it faded. If her dating rules weren't so strict, would the spark grow instead? Then she remembered how things ended with Jack. Her rules made sense; she had no plans to change them after she won Daphne's dare.

Caroline pulled her mind back to Nick's book. "Josh might not be clear about his feelings for Maggie, but he knows how she makes him feel about other things."

Nick scribbled some notes. "Your mother said the same thing. That falling in love was like Aspen after a summer thunderstorm. The clouds cleared, and the colors were so vibrant."

Caroline wondered if her mother had been talking about herself. Nick had seen Anne at the conference. Maybe he met her lover.

Caroline told him about the letter from Santa's Little Red Mailbox. "Was there a man with my mother at the conference?"

"She attended the events by herself, but she did seem happier the last time I saw her," Nick mused. "It was the last day of the conference. She was wearing yellow sandals." Nick smiled. "That's the thing about being a writer, I remember every detail. I mentioned how I liked her sandals. She smiled and said they were a gift."

"Thank you for telling me." Caroline gulped. "It sounds like she was happy."

They talked more about the book and then Nick had to go to work. Caroline went back to the inn and got ready to meet Max for lunch.

An hour later, Caroline stood on the front steps of the inn. A red Jeep pulled up and Max jumped out.

"I brought a thermos of coffee." He handed it to her. His smile was bright as the snow. "I wasn't taking any chances that you'd get cold on the drive."

The scenery was breathtaking. The mountains formed a ring around them. There were forests, and a valley, covered in snow. Caroline saw elk, and a few moose.

They talked about Christmas and Lily.

"Lily likes you, and she's a harsh critic. She doesn't like the heroines in most Disney movies. They spend too much time worrying about finding a Prince Charming, when they should be concentrating on themselves."

Caroline laughed. "It's hard to be a male character in a Disney movie these days. In real life, most Prince Charmings would be out of the job."

Max turned onto a side road. He glanced at Caroline.

"I don't know if this is okay to say with the rules, but I like you a lot too."

They were somewhere up in the mountains. A few wooden buildings lined a pathway. One had a sign that read POST OFFICE, another was a bank. There was a building with a sloped roof.

"Ashcroft is one of Colorado's ghost towns," Max said. "During the summer there are a lot of tourists, but it's quiet at Christmas." He pointed to a building with a blue roof. "That was the Blue Mirror Saloon. The owner painted the roof blue, so newcomers couldn't miss it. At the height of the silver rush, Ashcroft had twenty saloons and two thousand residents."

Ashcroft was settled before Aspen, by a guy called "Crazy Culver" because he left the boomtown of Leadville to look for new silver deposits. He discovered silver in Ashcroft, and other prospectors joined him. Miners were given building lots, and erected houses and a school. Then the silver mine dried up and a new silver rush started in Aspen.

"That's where my ancestor Finn came in. Finn saw how much silver there was in Aspen, so he returned to Ashcroft and convinced other miners to come to Aspen. He even created a contest—the first miner who reached Aspen won a ham sandwich."

"That doesn't sound like a good prize," Caroline laughed.

"The men were always hungry, it was hard to find food during winter," Max replied. "The point is Finn didn't give up. When something didn't work out, he figured out how to do better." Max fiddled with his jacket. "There's something I want to tell you. I . . ."

His phone rang, and he took it out of his pocket.

"It's Lily," he said, frowning. "I told her not to call unless it's important."

Caroline waited until he hung up. "Is everything all right?"

Max looked sheepish. "She wanted to tell you that she packed nutmeg brownies for our picnic. She read that nutmeg can cause a bad reaction and she wanted to make sure you weren't allergic."

Caroline waited for Max to finish what he was saying. Instead, he concentrated on zipping up his jacket.

"You were saying something when Lily called," she prompted.

Max opened his mouth. Then he closed it again, as if he decided to say something different.

"It's about the picnic. I made the stuffing. Lily said I used too much mayonnaise the first time, but I think I got it right."

After they toured the buildings, they climbed back into the Jeep.

Max had packed roasted turkey on baguettes. There was

stuffing, and macaroni and cheese, and a plate of Lily's brownies. They talked about Daphne and her love of cooking.

"I want to learn more about you," Max said.

"There isn't much to tell." Caroline shrugged. "I love books and New York. And my sister and I have always been close."

"There must be something," Max prodded. "Most people have secrets they keep from everyone but themselves."

"There is one thing." Caroline toyed with her brownie. "I learned the truth about Santa Claus when I was in third grade, but it didn't stop me from believing in him. I still do. Christmas is the only time of year that everyone stops what they're doing and concentrates on other people. What can be more magical than that?"

After they finished the picnic, Max drove back to the inn.

Caroline turned to him. "Would you like to have dinner tonight? We could go to the Silver Nickel and order more of your rye whiskey."

"I'd love to, but I'm taking Lily to see *The Nutcracker*. I'd invite you, but it's sold out."

Caroline was about to get out of the Jeep but Max stopped her.

"Why don't we spend the day together tomorrow?" he suggested. "We can go snowtubing, and do some night skiing."

"Daphne and I are going shopping for her wedding dress in the morning, but I'm free after that."

Max leaned forward and kissed her. It was only a short kiss, but it was warm and sweet.

He pulled back and smiled. "I'll tell Lily our date was a success. She was afraid I'd mess it up."

After Max left, Caroline sat by the fireplace in the lobby. The lights on the Christmas tree twinkled and Christmas music played over the loudspeakers. Outside the window, the sun was setting and the mountain was bathed in a purple glow.

She was almost glad that Max wasn't free for dinner. Being with him had been like celebrating Christmas Eve. It was still her favorite day of the year. When the excitement of Christmas was before her, and there was so much to look forward to.

Chapter Thirteen

It snowed overnight. In the morning, the view from Caroline's window was like a postcard. The mountain was a bright white, and the branches of the aspen trees were heavy with snow. Caroline spent a lazy hour drinking coffee and watching a squirrel make footprints in the forest.

Daphne sent a text saying she and Luke were going to take a morning Jacuzzi and she'd meet Caroline at the dress shop at 11:00 a.m. Caroline was too relaxed to leave her room.

She picked up Nina's next letter and started reading.

Dear Anne,

It was lovely to meet you for lunch, you could have at least let me pay. You've done so much for me already, who knows when you'll see a return. That must be the funny thing about being an agent. You invest so much time in an author, and sometimes the book never sells. I was thrilled with your critique of the first ten pages of my novel. I don't usually drink at lunch but I was so nervous, I needed that vodka martini. When you said you loved it, I felt like a puppy having his fur stroked. Most authors are the same, without a shred of self-confidence about our work.

I understand why you need to tell editors why I haven't written for forty years. When I sat down to write these letters, it was because it was too complicated to explain over dinner. But the letters have come to mean so much more. I've always been a visual writer. When I take out my writing paper, I see myself as a young woman, and Teddy . . . well, Teddy being as handsome and irritating as ever.

So, if you'll indulge me by reading the letters, I promise you'll hear the whole story.

Teddy was never more infuriating as when we went to Vermont. Or maybe that's because I was feeling guilty. I was still furious at him for what happened with Gwendolyn. And for letting his mother come between us. But a week at a farmhouse in Vermont when he could be enjoying Christmas in New York was a harsh punishment, on top of the fact that we were no longer engaged.

Then I pictured Gwendolyn's parents' villa on Saint Kitts and I was happy to banish Teddy to Vermont. I only wished I didn't have to go with him.

Teddy drove. I was a New Yorker, I didn't have a license or a car. Teddy wasn't rich, remember, so his car wasn't anything special. And it wasn't made for the snow. The tires skidded, the heater blinked on and off.

We arrived in the late afternoon. From the outside, the farm was as I imagined it. A low-slung wooden farmhouse with a white picket fence, and a red barn. Inside, I was pleasantly surprised. There was central heating as well as a fireplace, and the kitchen had every utensil.

"Where did Margaret find this place?" Teddy asked, inspecting a rocking chair. "It's right out of an L.L.Bean catalog. I bet the closets will be full of herringbone sweaters."

"I like it." I opened the bedroom door. "As long as the bedrooms are heated, we'll be fine."

Teddy walked through the rest of the house. The master bedroom was off the living room, and there was another bedroom behind the kitchen.

"The bedrooms might be a problem," he said. "There are only two of them."

"Well, there are only two of us . . ." I said, and stopped. Teddy must have realized what I was thinking because he started laughing.

"I was thinking the same thing," he admitted. "When your contest winner arrives, we're going to have to share a bedroom."

"We'll do no such thing!" I exclaimed. "I'd rather sleep in the bathtub."

"You'd be welcome to, but I saw the bathroom. There's only a shower."

I had expected to pretend that Teddy and I shared a bedroom. We were supposed to be engaged, and it was the 1970s. Even a matron from the Midwest would assume that we'd sleep together. But after everyone went to bed, Teddy would move to the study. Except there was no study.

"I can't bunk down in the living room," Teddy said as if

he could read my thoughts. "That would hardly show how much we're in love. Besides, the sofa is lumpy and I have a bad back."

"Sharing a bed with you is out of the question," I said, stepping outside.

There was a covered porch but that would be impossible. Teddy would die of frostbite.

I kept walking to the barn. It was one large space with a loft.

"I solved our problem," I announced, walking back into the house.

Teddy had already found the alcohol. Two bottles of scotch and an ice bucket on the sideboard in the living room.

"I said I'd watch out for bears, but if you think I'm going to sleep on the porch . . ."

"It wouldn't do Laura Carter's column any good if her fiancé got eaten by a bear," I agreed. "You can sleep in the loft above the barn. We'll take up a space heater, and there are plenty of blankets."

"I will not! I'm allergic to horses," he protested.

I narrowed my eyes. "You never mention that when you go to the racetrack with a client, and they want you to meet the jockey."

"My allergies are changeable. Like your affections." He walked to the door. "All right, I'll sleep in the barn. I'll see you later."

I asked where he was going.

He turned and looked at me. It was times like that when

I wished he weren't so handsome. Just looking into those blue eyes made me melt.

"To the general store to buy more scotch. I can already tell that two bottles isn't going to last the week."

While Teddy was gone, I inspected the kitchen pantry. Margaret hadn't told me the name of the contest winner but I assumed she would reflect the magazine's core demographics. A married mother in her forties who used artificial sweetener in her coffee because she watched her weight, but still ate a few of the chocolate cookies she put in her child's lunch box.

A car appeared in the driveway. It was big and luxurious, not the type you saw in Vermont. A man got out. I ran into the living room and hid behind the curtains. He might be the photographer who had taken photos of the farm. If he took photos of me, I'd have to pretend to be Laura Carter forever.

There was a knock. I ran to the hall closet and found an old fishing hat. I put it on and opened the front door.

"Good afternoon," I said. "Can I help you?"

The man was in his mid-thirties. He was slender and attractive. Wide shoulders, amber-colored eyes.

"I'm looking for Laura Carter."

"And you are?" I prompted.

He took off the hat he was wearing.

"I'm not being polite, my grandmother would be furious." He held out his hand. "James Stanley."

I still didn't want to ask him inside. But I couldn't stand at the door forever. I wasn't wearing a coat and it was freezing.

I motioned for him to follow me. When I turned around, he was looking at me strangely.

"Is something wrong?" I questioned.

"I've never seen anyone wear a fishing hat in Vermont in December. The lakes are frozen."

"I'm writing a column about including fish in your Christmas menu. The hat gives me inspiration." I flashed him my widest smile. "It reminds me of the trout I caught last summer."

James kept looking at me oddly. I was getting impatient.

"Look, if you need more photos of the farm, go ahead. But I'm writing, so you'll have to show yourself around."

"I'm not here to take photos. Though I probably should, my grandmother would love them."

"Why are you here, Mr. Stanley?"

He twirled his hat in his hand. "Didn't your publisher tell you? I'm the contest winner."

My mouth couldn't have opened wider if a black bear had been standing in the living room.

"Do you always enter women's-magazine contests?" I asked when I regained my composure.

"To be honest, I don't read *Women's World Monthly*. My grandmother loves your column. She's too old to travel, and she wants to know everything about your life on the farm. I couldn't say no to her. It's Christmas and she's always been good to me."

I took off the fishing hat and sank onto a chair. The scotch on the sideboard looked incredibly tempting. But I doubted Laura Carter downed a scotch on the rocks at five o'clock in the afternoon.

"So, we're going to spend Christmas week together?" I gulped.

His face broke into a smile. When he smiled, he had an adorable dimple on his cheek.

"Don't worry, I won't get in your way. And I'm pretty handy. My family has a ski cabin in the Adirondacks."

I was about to ask what he did for a living when there was the sound of tires crunching. I'd forgotten about Teddy!

Then I really panicked. What would Teddy say when the middle-aged matron from the Midwest turned out to be a handsome man who drove a fancy car and whose family owned a ski cabin?

Teddy entered carrying a brown paper bag. There was mud on his trousers.

"I parked in front of a mud puddle at the general store." He walked straight to the closet and hung up his jacket. "And I forgot to stop at the bank, so I could only afford one bottle of scotch."

He turned around and noticed James.

James reached into his pocket and took out a wallet. "Since I'll be here all week, I'd be happy to contribute to the groceries. I only have a hundred dollars on me, I can get more when the bank opens tomorrow."

"Who are you?" Teddy asked.

"James, this is my fiancé, Teddy Chandler," I introduced them. "Teddy, this is James Stanley, the contest winner."

I could see Teddy sizing him up. James was wearing an expensive-looking wool jacket and leather boots.

"You entered a women's competition?" Teddy said, puzzled.

"My grandmother assured me anyone could enter." James turned to me with a worried expression. "I didn't want to do anything wrong."

"Of course you could enter," I said hastily. "Teddy and I are thrilled you're the winner." I shot Teddy a look. It wouldn't be good for the magazine if James wrote a letter to the editor saying he had been treated badly.

I opened a bottle of scotch. It was close enough to cocktail hour and we all needed a drink.

"Teddy will have someone to talk to while I prepare Christmas dinner." I filled the glasses with ice cubes. "Here on the farm, I can't rely on ready-made stuffing or pre-roasted turkey. I make everything myself."

Teddy noticed my look and put on his sweetest expression.

"Laura is practically Julia Child in the kitchen," he gushed. "You can help me milk the cows. I can lend you some clothes, if you didn't bring any."

"I have a couple of suitcases in the car," James said. "I'm used to working on a farm. My family owns a horse farm. I don't spend much time there, but I enjoy it."

"A horse farm?" Teddy repeated.

"I grew up in Washington, D.C., but my parents love the countryside. There's the horse farm, and the ski cabin. Now that my father is retired, they're buying a villa in the South of France."

"What did your father do?" Teddy asked.

Teddy didn't have any respect for men who lived off their trust funds. He believed everyone should have a career.

"He was in the diplomatic service. My mother ran the company that my grandmother started. Barbara's Pies."

At the time, Barbara's Pies was one of the most successful frozen-cake brands. It started with frozen apple pies in the 1940s, and quickly added more flavors. Cherry pies, peach pies, and pecan pies at Christmas and Thanksgiving. You couldn't open a freezer without finding a Barbara pie box, with a picture of Barbara in her signature red apron.

"My grandmother Barbara grew up on an apple farm in upstate New York. She moved to Washington, D.C., when she got married. She didn't fit into Washington social life, so she filled her hours by baking pies. The pies were so good, a friend urged her to get them in a supermarket and it grew from there. A few years ago, she had a stroke and stopped working."

I glanced uneasily at Teddy. He had already finished his scotch, and was pouring another.

"Do you work there too or live off the proceeds?" he asked.

"Neither, I've never been good at business." James shook his head. "I do love to bake, it's a great stress reliever. I'm a pediatric oncologist. Someday, I'd like to teach medicine at my alma mater."

Teddy never finished college. It was one of the things he was sensitive about. He was offered the job at Colgate-Palmolive during his senior year at Cornell and dropped out.

"Let me guess, you're a Harvard man," Teddy said dryly.

James let out a small laugh. "Hardly, I'm not that smart." He finished his scotch. "Georgetown for undergraduate and Johns Hopkins for medical school. Johns Hopkins was expensive but I was lucky. I got a full academic scholarship."

Anne, I must stop there, I promised my neighbor I'd walk her dog. That's one thing I miss about the farm. I love animals. They're so uncomplicated compared to men. At my age it's too hard to have a dog in New York so I walk the neighbor's dog instead.

I can see the three of us in that living room in Vermont so clearly, as if we were all still young. These letters bring me more joy than I've had in years.

Warm regards,
Nina

Caroline placed the letter back on the stack. Nina was the best kind of writer. When Caroline was reading the letters, she lost track of time. But Daphne would be waiting for her at the dress shop. She grabbed her jacket and went to join her.

Aspen Clothiers was on Cooper Avenue in a quaint Victorian building. Inside, there were racks of vintage dresses. Styles from the 1950s with calf-length pleated skirts and tucked waists. A multicolored dress from the 1970s made in Morocco, and a yellow ski suit that was the kind seen at European ski resorts.

For a moment, Caroline wished she were more adventurous with her wardrobe. But publishing in New York had its own dress code. Pants and turtlenecks, and one good winter coat that could be worn at author events.

Daphne already had a dressing room filled with dresses.

"There you are," she said to Caroline. "I've been here awhile. Ask the saleswoman, Marissa. I've already tried on a dozen dresses."

Marissa smiled at Caroline. "Matching up a bride with her dress is my favorite part of the job."

"Don't you want to wear white?" Caroline frowned.

Daphne zipped up a pale pink crepe dress. "A bride doesn't have to wear white. The wedding dress is like anything else. You have to fall in love with it."

Daphne tried on more dresses, and put the pink one on again. The skirt fell below her knees and it had a lace bodice and pearls sewn into the hem.

"This is the dress. I'll wear the turquoise earrings Mom gave me last Christmas for something blue."

"I agree, the dress is perfect." Marissa nodded. "You remind me of a customer I had last summer. She had the same-shaped face and blue eyes."

Caroline and Daphne exchanged a glance. Daphne showed Marissa a photo on her phone.

"Is this the woman?"

"Yes!" Marissa said in surprise. "She came in a few times. She bought one of our prettiest dresses, an orange sundress with a huge belt. She said she was going to wear it if either of her daughters ever got married." Marissa paused. "She sounded sad, as if she thought that would never happen."

Caroline's stomach made a small lurch. In June, Anne had been in remission. Had she lied to them about her health, or did she somehow have a premonition that the cancer would return?

"I'll take it," Daphne said firmly.

Caroline could see the tears in Daphne's eyes. She wondered if she was thinking the same thing.

Daphne put on a brave smile. "Now we have to shop for Caroline. The maid of honor's dress is as important as the bride's."

They chose a navy wool dress and a cashmere wrap. Caroline insisted on paying for both dresses. It was her wedding present to Daphne.

When they left the shop, they were both lost in their thoughts. Daphne spoke first.

"We should have come to Aspen with her. It would have been the last time we were all together."

"The doctor wouldn't have let her go if she wasn't in remission," Caroline reasoned. But what if her mother had lied to the doctor about how she was feeling?

"We should have known, we were her daughters," Daphne persisted.

"No one knows someone else completely," Caroline said. "Max was talking about that yesterday. Everyone keeps secrets. Have you asked Luke why he didn't tell you that his parents are spending Christmas in Paris?"

Daphne shrugged. "There hasn't been time to bring it up. We're meeting a Realtor this afternoon to see spaces for a restaurant."

Caroline stopped walking. "You can't be serious! You promised you'd listen to me. At least wait until after you've been married for a while."

"Luke and I get along so well, it would be fun to work together," Daphne returned. "Anyway, you're not going to win the dare. You're not even trying."

"What do you mean?" Caroline demanded.

"You're spending time with Max but you haven't done more

than kiss him," Daphne replied. "That's fine for most couples. Luke and I didn't sleep together for two weeks. But that's not your style. You haven't slept with Max because you're afraid of what will happen next if you do. It's easier not to keep a relationship going if it never starts in the first place."

Caroline shielded her eyes from the Aspen sunshine. She wondered if Daphne was right. She did like Max, but something was stopping her from being as flirty and casual as usual.

"I invited Max to dinner last night, but he had plans with Lily."

"You could have asked him to come over for a drink afterward." Daphne twirled her shopping bag. "If you move beyond a few kisses, I promise we won't sign any real estate papers for three months."

"You'd do that?" Caroline asked in surprise.

Daphne gave one of her best smiles. "Someone has to crack that ice castle you live inside. Besides, it's Christmas. A miracle might happen and you could fall in love."

Chapter Fourteen

Max picked Caroline up after lunch.

He gave her the afternoon's itinerary. They were going to drive to a place called the Lost Forest. There was snowshoeing, and cross-country skiing, and a restaurant at the top of the mountain. The best part was the alpine coaster. It was a roller coaster that wound through the forest and ended with a thrilling drop.

"This is from Lily." He handed her a package. "She apologized for taking up my time last night."

Caroline unwrapped it. Inside was a *Nutcracker* toy soldier Christmas tree ornament.

"It's lovely, but please tell her she didn't need to give me anything."

"Lily believes female friendships are important." Max kept a serious expression. "Especially where men are involved. She didn't want to come between you and me."

Caroline glanced at Max curiously. She put on a flirty smile. "Am I important to you?"

Max smiled back. "Lily seems to thinks so. She said I showed all the signs of having feelings for someone. Last night, I checked my phone for messages from you, even when I forgot I had turned it off. And today, I brushed my teeth twice before I picked you up."

Caroline felt a small jolt, like an extra-strong cup of coffee. It was fun to flirt with Max. Maybe Daphne was right, she just had to try harder.

"I'll hang the ornament on the Christmas tree in my hotel room," Caroline said. Aspen trees sped by and she pushed herself to keep talking. "Maybe we can order room service tonight, and you can see the Christmas tree."

Max pulled his eyes from the road and glanced at her.

"I thought inviting me to your place was against the rules."

She couldn't show Max that she was changing her rules all at once. He'd ask why and she'd have to tell him about her dare with Daphne. It was better to bend the rules gradually.

"A hotel room isn't the same as my apartment," Caroline reasoned.

"Then I accept." Max's tone was light. "Now, let's say that at dinner we drink a few glasses of eggnog and I'm too tipsy to drive home."

"That could be a problem," Caroline agreed. "Especially if all the Ubers in town are taken."

"It's a real problem over Christmas week. There are always more tourists than Ubers."

"You could walk, Aspen isn't very big."

Max shook his head. "It's supposed to snow tonight. The sidewalks will be slippery."

"Wear boots?" Caroline said with a laugh.

They reached the Lost Forest and Max stopped the car.

"My boots will get wet when we ride the alpine coaster. They won't have time to dry out."

Before she could say anything else, Max leaned over and kissed her. It was longer than their last kiss, and his lips were sweet and warm.

"We're two intelligent adults," she said when they parted. "I'm sure we can work it out."

The next hour was spent snowshoeing through the forest. There was a lookout where they stopped and took in the entire Elk Valley. Aspen and Snowmass snuggled next to each other like two clusters of Monopoly houses.

It didn't snow every year in Hudson. But when it did, Caroline and Daphne loved to snowshoe near the cabin. Anne would pack sandwiches, and nuts for the squirrels. For a moment, Caroline wished it were the previous Christmas, with Daphne snowshoeing beside her, and their mother pottering in the cabin's kitchen.

Daphne was right. Life was precious, it had to be lived now. But that didn't mean falling recklessly in love, even if Max was handsome and fun. It would be too easy to get her heart broken. Besides, for the first time in months, Caroline was excited about a new author. And she was enjoying reading Nina's letters.

After they finished snowshoeing, they sat at a table on the restaurant's terrace. Skiers piled out of the gondola and started eagerly down the mountain. Caroline watched them in their bright ski parkas and felt happy. It was wonderful to sit outside, drinking a cold beer and tipping her face up to the sun.

They ordered bowls of beef chili and fresh-baked corn bread.

"I love this restaurant, everything is locally grown," Max said. "The chili is made from grass-fed cows, and the corn is organic. Even the beer comes from a local brewery."

"That's important to you, isn't it?" Caroline said.

Max nodded. "If we don't take care of the environment, we

won't have anything to leave to the next generation. That's why I started the distillery. It doesn't take anything from the planet that it doesn't give back."

Caroline thought again how much she liked Max when he talked about the distillery. The beer combined with the high altitude was making her flirty.

"So, tell me more about you. You're charming and successful. There had to have been a great love somewhere."

Max glanced at her in surprise. "You're interested in my dating history? Doesn't that go against the rules?"

"I just want to know if there was anyone serious," she said playfully. "I can see you dating an indie musician whose latest song had five hundred thousand downloads."

"There was a woman a few years ago," Max offered. "Her name was Jessica, I thought we were in love." He sipped his beer. "My parents own a winery near Santa Barbara. I was helping my father run it, and Jessica worked in Santa Barbara.

"After we'd been dating a few months, I invited her to the winery for dinner. I selected a bottle of my father's reserve wine for our meal. I told Jessica that I wanted to get serious and she agreed. A few weeks later she convinced my mother to let her throw a surprise party for me at the winery. She invited all her friends, and opened half a dozen bottles of his best reserve wine. The next day it was all over her Instagram. It turned out that she wanted to be an influencer and thought dating the owner of a winery would be cool. My father was furious with me, and I couldn't blame him. I shouldn't have let it happen."

"Is that why you came to Colorado?" Caroline asked.

Max shrugged. "I've always loved the mountains. And I like being my own boss. I get to make all my own mistakes."

Caroline's heart went out to him. Everything in Max's life seemed so perfect—the Queen Anne mansion on Walnut Street, the sleek, modern distillery.

He took out his phone and started typing.

"Enough about me," he said. "Now, let's say I spend the night, do I stay for morning coffee?"

Caroline peered at his phone.

"You wrote that down?" she asked.

Max stopped typing. He gave his most electric smile. "I guess Lily's right, you are important to me. I don't want to get anything wrong."

After they finished their chili, they climbed into the alpine coaster. Caroline sat in front and Max wrapped his arms around her waist. The coaster started slowly, then gradually picked up speed. It ended at the foot of the mountain with an almost vertical drop. Caroline loved the wind in her hair, and the feeling of weightlessness.

They drove back to Aspen, and Max went to run errands. There were a few hours until dinner. Caroline decided to go and see Nick.

Nick was in a supply room at the Limelight Hotel. He was sitting on a folding chair at a folding tray table, tapping on his computer.

"My boss lets me write here before my shift," Nick said when she entered. "It's not very big, but I do my best writing here."

Caroline gave a small smile. "Lots of writers work in odd spaces. I know an author who writes on the floor of her closet. She doesn't do her revisions there, those are done on the window seat in her bedroom."

"Writing and revising use different parts of the brain." Nick nodded. "I've been working on your revision notes. I'm having trouble with chapter four."

"That's where Josh realizes how much he cares for Maggie," Caroline recalled. "Most love stories are the same. Boy meets girl, they fall in love, then something pulls them apart. What I adore about your book is that we don't know until the end whether they're going to make it. But we need some foreshadowing. How far will Josh go to hang on to Maggie?"

"I don't know," Nick said truthfully. "Sometimes it's hard to get inside his head."

"At the beginning, Josh is unknowable," Caroline agreed.

She remembered how much she loved discussing books with their authors.

"We need a hint, one extra scene," she said thoughtfully. "Draw from your own experience. The first time you thought you might lose Savannah."

Nick's cheeks flushed. He looked even more boyish than usual.

"It was a few weeks into the summer. We were having a wonderful time. We went on long rides together. We even went camping." He smiled ruefully. "Savannah wasn't a good camper. She had never slept without thousand-thread-count sheets in her life. Then Elliot arrived. It was a surprise to Savannah, she didn't know that he was coming."

"Who was Elliot?" Caroline wondered.

"I thought he was just another guest." Nick's calm expression changed. "It turned out he was the guy she was supposed to marry."

Nick closed his laptop and told her the story.

"Elliot was in his mid-twenties. He had New England prep school good looks. Crew-cut hair, firm jaw, wide shoulders from playing lacrosse," Nick began. "But he was friendly and he was good with horses. The second night he was there, I heard him and Savannah talking. I didn't mean to eavesdrop. They were sitting on the porch. I was doing the dishes, the kitchen window was open. They were arguing that Savannah should have accepted his mother's invitation to spend the summer in Cape Cod. Savannah was going to be there for two weeks. She didn't want to spend more time there. She didn't like sailing and she wanted to be on her own.

"That's when Elliot said he was in love with her. I turned off the faucet in the kitchen. I had to hear her reply. Savannah took a few moments to answer. The time seemed to last forever.

"She suggested they do something special the next day, which was her day off. I was tempted to run out to the porch and confront Elliot. What would I say? Savannah and I had only kissed a couple of times. I hadn't told her my feelings.

"I waited until Elliot went to bed, then I tapped on Savannah's door.

"Savannah looked so pretty. Her hair was even blonder from spending so much time in the sun. She told me that she and Elliot had been together since freshman year. He was going to law school. Both sets of parents thought they were a perfect couple.

"When I asked if she was in love with him, she shrugged and said she wasn't sure. She had to get married someday, that's how things were done in her circle. Elliot was better than most of the guys in Atlanta.

"I should have said that I was in love with her then, but I was scared. Elliot had a combination of smoothness and good looks that I couldn't compete with.

"The next morning Elliot asked me to pack a picnic. He was taking Savannah to the top of Smuggler Mountain. Then he pulled a velvet box out of his pocket. Inside was a square-cut diamond ring. He wanted to hide the ring in the dessert.

"I packed ham and turkey sandwiches, strawberries, a couple of sodas. I rummaged through the fridge and found two slices of sponge cake. Elliot could hide the ring in the whipped-cream topping.

"When I finished, Elliot was looking at his phone. There was supposed to be a thunderstorm. That was my chance. If the picnic got washed out before Elliot proposed, I'd have time to tell Savannah that I was in love with her. I told him the weather app was often wrong. Thunderstorms usually passed by our part of the valley.

"That wasn't exactly true. We occasionally got summer thundershowers. But they weren't dangerous and they didn't last long. It wouldn't hurt Elliot and Savannah to get wet.

"The moment they set off, I felt guilty. Elliot wasn't a bad guy. But they had already left, and my feelings for Savannah were too strong to ignore.

"Several hours later they returned. It had started raining as they reached the peak of Smuggler Mountain, before Elliot had a chance to pull out the ring.

"That night, I confessed to Savannah my feelings, and she acknowledged she felt something for me too. Elliot left the next day. He made up some excuse that his father bought a new sailboat, but I knew the truth."

Nick stopped talking. He brushed hair out of his eyes.

"I'd never done anything like that before. I couldn't help myself. Savannah was like a drug."

"You have to give some of that emotion to Josh. Write a scene where Josh behaves out of character to keep Maggie in his life."

The tension in Nick's shoulders eased. He opened his computer and started typing.

After Caroline left the Limelight Hotel, she strolled down Main Street. It was late afternoon and the sun was setting over the mountain. The sidewalk was filled with couples looking for a place to have après-ski cocktails.

Her phone rang, Max's number flashing on the screen.

"This is a surprise," Caroline answered. "Dinner isn't for a couple of hours."

"I can't make dinner," Max groaned. "I was helping Lily hang a *Nutcracker* ornament on the Christmas tree. I fell off the ladder. I'm lying on the sofa with a twisted ankle."

"Would you like me to bring you something? Frozen peas are good for sore ankles."

"I'm stocked up on frozen vegetables, but a bottle of wine and two glasses would be nice."

"You want me to come and see you?" Caroline gulped. Somehow the request was more intimate than Max asking her to dinner.

"As long as it's not breaking any rules." His tone grew softer.

A small thrill shot through Caroline's body. "I can't think of a single rule. I'll see you in an hour."

Chapter Fifteen

Caroline went back to the inn and changed into a cashmere sweater and beige slacks. She bought a bottle of chardonnay at the Aspen Grog Shop, and a slab of Gruyère cheese at the Meat & Cheese Restaurant and Farm Shop. Anne would have adored the farm store. The shelves were stocked with wooden pâté boards and marble rolling pins. There were jars of bourbon maple syrup and goat's milk caramels and moonshine cookies.

A pang formed in Caroline's throat and she wished again that she and Daphne had accompanied their mother to Aspen last summer. They could have taken home chili sauce and raspberry jalapeño jam.

When she arrived at the Queen Anne mansion on Walnut Street, Max was lying on the sofa in the sunroom. A few books sat on the side table, next to a pile of towels and an ice pack.

"My mother and Helen are out. Lily is taking care of me," Max said, trying to put on a smile. "She's in the kitchen making a salad. She read that leafy vegetables have nutrients to help my ankle heal faster."

"Does it hurt?" Caroline asked.

"Only when I move it." Max winced. "I wish it made for a better story. You know, I was skiing Aspen/Snowmass's hardest run, Hanging Valley Headwall, and someone ran into me. Instead, I was standing on a ladder trying to put back an ornament that had fallen off a Christmas tree."

"You were doing it for Lily," Caroline reminded him.

Max beamed. "I assured her it wasn't her fault and she's taking wonderful care of me. We're reading her favorite books. We read *The Polar Express* and we just started *Anne of Green Gables.*"

Caroline went into the kitchen to get wineglasses. Lily was standing on a chair at the counter. She was washing a bunch of kale.

"Would you like help?" Caroline asked.

Lily shook her head. "I'm used to not being very tall. You didn't meet my father. He was only here for a day, he had to go back to Los Angeles. He's a surgeon at UCLA and he's not tall either. But he never let it hold him back."

"I'm sure you'll accomplish anything you set your mind on." Caroline nodded.

"I'm glad you're here. Max is a grumpy patient," Lily continued. "The kale will make the swelling go down faster, and I found some chia seeds. They help build strong muscles."

Caroline took two wineglasses from the cabinet. She noticed a red envelope on the table. It was like the envelope Anne had received from Santa's Little Red Mailbox.

"I'm writing letters from Santa to my mom and dad, and Grandma and Max." Lily followed Caroline's gaze.

"But it's only two days after Christmas," Caroline replied, puzzled. "The letters won't be delivered until next Christmas."

Lily jumped down from the chair.

"I have to mail them now, I'm not coming back to Aspen until summer." Her small forehead puckered. "Last summer when I was here, Santa's Little Red Mailbox was stuffed with letters. I don't want to miss out."

"You were here last summer?"

Lily nodded. "I love summer in Aspen. Max took me swimming, and Grandma and I saw children's plays at the outdoor theater."

"My mother was here for the writers' conference."

"Do you have a picture of her?" Lily asked. "Aspen is so small, maybe I saw her."

Caroline searched through her phone and handed it to Lily.

"I did see her!" Lily exclaimed. "She used to come into the used bookstore on Cooper Avenue. I went there all the time with my grandma. I remember your mother because she and the girl behind the counter talked for ages. And your mother wore the prettiest sandals."

Anne loved buying beautiful shoes. It was one of her indulgences.

A thrill surged through Caroline. Perhaps Anne and her lover had visited the bookstore together. She'd have to go and ask the salesgirl.

"Is the bookstore open over Christmas week?" Caroline asked.

"It's open three hundred and sixty-four days a year," Lily said knowledgeably. "The owner believes that books are more important than anything."

Caroline and Max and Lily read *Anne of Green Gables*. Lily had hot apple cider and Caroline and Max drank glasses of wine. They toasted marshmallows in front of the fireplace, and Lily announced she had a name for her new guinea pig. She was going to call him Rudolph, because he was the best Christmas present she ever had.

"Better than a goldfish?" Caroline asked, as she was leaving.

"Much better," Lily declared. "Rudolph lets me pet him. The goldfish slipped away when I put my hand in the fishbowl."

After Caroline left, she walked down Cooper Avenue to Aspen Used Books. It was empty inside but the lights were on.

"Are you open?" Caroline asked, peeking in the door.

The girl glanced up from the cash register. She was in her early twenties with thick, dark hair.

"Until nine p.m." The girl nodded. "Can I help you find something?"

Caroline shook her head. She didn't want to start by asking questions. First, she'd buy some books.

A display table held paperbacks with worn covers. There was a bookcase where the books were shelved by genre, and a counter stacked with old comic books.

Caroline could see why her mother had come here often. She loved used books, they had a history. Once she bought a book from a used bookstore in New York and discovered a familiar-sounding name scrawled on a hotel napkin. She traced the napkin back to the previous owner of the book. It turned out she was a Broadway actress. The actress wanted to write her autobiography and Anne ended up becoming her agent.

Caroline selected a Judy Blume book for Lily, and a book of Maya Angelou poems for herself.

"I have a question," Caroline said after she had paid for the books. "My mother was here in June. I wonder if you worked here."

"I've worked here every summer since I was sixteen." The girl smiled. "My mother is the owner."

Caroline took out her phone and showed her a photo of Anne.

"I do remember her," the girl said. "We had a long conversation about Toni Morrison. I hadn't read any of her books and your mother said I was missing out."

"Did she ever come in with a man?" Caroline asked.

The girl shook her head. "She did say she was buying some books as gifts."

Caroline's pulse beat faster. "Do you remember what they were?"

"We keep records of the books we sell." The girl clicked on her computer. "If you give me the dates she was here, I can look it up."

Caroline gave her the dates of the writers' conference in June.

"On June eighth, she bought *French Lessons: Adventures with Knife, Fork, and Corkscrew* by Peter Mayle, and *White Teeth* by Zadie Smith."

French Lessons must have been for Daphne. *White Teeth* had been for Caroline.

"Is that all?" she asked, trying not to show her disappointment.

"On June tenth she bought a biography of Abraham Lincoln and a book on the Civil War."

Anne wasn't interested in war. The book on the Civil War must have been for Anne's lover.

A lightness filled Caroline's chest. She pictured her mother debating which book to buy. Then she would have laughed and handed both copies to the salesgirl. One could never have too many books.

Caroline thanked her and walked back to the hotel. The ornaments in the shop windows seemed brighter, and even the stars on the lampposts had an extra shine. She couldn't wait until New Year's Eve. To talk to a man who had been in love with Anne. Someone who had been with her during the last summer when she was happy and alive.

Caroline imagined them sitting in a coffee shop together, drinking lemonades and reading their books. Afterward, they would have taken a stroll through Aspen Meadows, or sat in the inn's outdoor Jacuzzi.

When she reached her hotel room, she texted Daphne. It would be nice to see Daphne and tell her what she discovered. But Daphne texted back that she and Luke were at Ullr Nights at Elk Camp. They wouldn't return until midnight.

Caroline let out a deep sigh. She was too wound up to go to sleep, but she didn't feel like going out. She changed into a robe and curled up on the bed. Then she picked up Nina's next letter and started reading.

Dear Anne,

I spoiled myself today, I went to SoHo and bought a Christmas tree! It's not very tall, my apartment is tiny and I've no one besides your girls to buy presents for. But I love seeing it in the living room. I even went to the local Duane Reade pharmacy and bought ornaments and a star for the top of the tree.

One of the wonderful things about Vermont had been the Christmas trees. The tree lots were full of them, or you could go into the woods and chop down a tree yourself. Everything about Christmas in Vermont was like a postcard. Towns with quaint main streets. Horse-drawn carriages and sleds pulled by real reindeer.

The first day that James arrived at the farm, I thought everything would be all right.

Teddy and James were both New York Giants fans and they watched the football game on television. James produced a delicious wine from the trunk of his car to accompany the premade chicken that I discovered in the fridge. After dinner, we all piled into James's car and drove the short distance to town to see the Christmas lights.

James really was sweet, I could tell that Teddy liked him. They even planned to go snowshoeing. The next morning, James made maple syrup pancakes for everyone and then Teddy went to run some errands.

"You don't have a Christmas tree," James said to me.

We had just finished doing the dishes and were standing in the living room.

I gulped. How could Margaret have forgotten to get a Christmas tree? Teddy's car was so small, we couldn't use it to pick up a tree.

"My editor thought it would be fun for the contest winner to pick out the Christmas tree," I said hastily. "But you're driving that beautiful car. I can call a Christmas tree lot and have it delivered."

"It will be more fun to choose it ourselves." James shook his head. "I'll put it on top of the car, I have some rope in the trunk. I'm good at knots, I was a Boy Scout."

Of course James had been a Boy Scout! I was glad that

Teddy wasn't there. He didn't need to hear another thing to add to James's list of accomplishments.

"I have an even better idea." James kept talking. "Why don't we chop a tree down ourselves. I'm sure there's a saw in the barn."

"You want to get a tree from the forest?"

It was one thing to go with James to a crowded Christmas tree lot, but I didn't think Teddy would approve of us going into the woods together. Not that Teddy had any say in the matter. I heard him talking to his mother on the phone about Saint Kitts. Dolly had been invited and she insisted that Teddy go too. If Teddy had put up some resistance, I might have forgiven him. I was tired of him putting his mother first. But at the same time, I couldn't blame him. Even if he was telling the truth about what happened with Gwendolyn, an invitation to a Caribbean island did sound enticing. Especially when we were in Vermont, where it was so cold your cheeks felt frozen.

And Teddy and James and I had to spend the week together. I wanted everyone to get along.

"I used to chop down the tree every Christmas that we were at the cabin in the Adirondacks," James said.

We drove into the woods and picked out a large white spruce tree. It was one of the most beautiful trees I had ever seen. After that, we stopped at the general store and bought all the Christmas ornaments left on the shelves. I made a quick stop at the candy store and bought a packet of Teddy's favorite nougats. He wouldn't be happy when he saw the tree, and he had a serious sweet tooth.

Teddy still wasn't back when we arrived at the farm,

so we decorated the tree ourselves. It really was stunning. Blue and silver ornaments, glass balls, and a glittering gold star.

James was stringing the branches with tinsel when I heard a car drive up. I ran outside. I wanted to tell Teddy about the tree before he saw it.

"There you are." Teddy walked toward me. "I have a surprise for you."

"What kind of surprise?" I asked anxiously.

"I felt bad for complaining about coming to the farm. James is a decent guy, and it's nice to be out of New York. The fresh air alone is worth it. I know how much you wanted a Christmas tree this year, so I thought I'd make it up to you."

My landlady in New York wouldn't let me have a Christmas tree, and Teddy refused to get one for his apartment. He didn't like pine needles on his carpet.

"You didn't have to do anything," I replied. "In fact, I have a surprise for you."

"Let me tell you mine first." His eyes danced. "Look inside the car."

I peered in the window. A small Christmas tree was jammed into the back seat.

"There weren't many trees left at the lot, so I got a good price," Teddy said proudly. "Then I went to the general store but some young couple had bought all the ornaments. I had to drive to Burlington."

My stomach dropped and the muscles in my neck tightened.

"It's beautiful, but there's something . . ."

"Let's not talk about anything now," Teddy interrupted. "You and I can decorate it together."

Before I could warn him, Teddy pulled the tree out of the car. I gathered the pine needles that had fallen on the back seat and followed him into the house.

"What's that?" He pointed to the huge tree next to the fireplace.

James climbed down from the ladder and joined Teddy.

"Isn't she a beauty? It's a Vermont white spruce tree, we chopped it down in the forest."

"You cut down the tree yourself? Teddy gaped.

"It's easy if you have the right saw." James shrugged. "Laura helped me carry it, she's quite strong."

Teddy glanced from the tree to me. His temple was pulsating and his cheeks were pale.

"Laura has all kinds of hidden strengths," he grunted. He turned to the door. "I'll return this one."

"You can't return a Christmas tree." I stopped him. "We'll put it in the dining alcove. I was going to write a magazine column about having more than one Christmas tree. It makes a house more festive."

"We have plenty of ornaments," James said. "Laura and I bought all the ornaments at the general store."

Teddy's cheeks turned from pale to bright red. He set the tree down so hard, pine needles fell on the rug.

"I'll let you two decorate it," he said. "I'm going to go lie down."

"It's daytime!" I exclaimed. It was late afternoon, and we hadn't even had dinner.

"My back is acting up from carrying the tree." Teddy

clenched his teeth. "And I caught a cold last night. It's my fault, I spent some time in the barn."

He marched into the bedroom and slammed the door.

James and I decorated the small tree. It looked quite pretty in the dining alcove. And it was thoughtful of Teddy to pick it up. I owed him an apology.

I heated a bowl of chicken soup, and cut up some bread and cheese.

When I entered the bedroom, Teddy was sitting up in bed, reading a travel brochure about Saint Kitts.

"The temperature in January in Saint Kitts is eighty degrees. And, it's carnival season. There's calypso dancing in the streets, and everyone drinks rum and pineapple juice."

I didn't feel like making some snide remark. Instead, I set the tray on the bedside table.

"I'm sorry we picked out the Christmas tree without you."

"I don't know if I can keep up the charade," he said.

"What do you mean?" I asked. "I promised Margaret. And I apologized about the tree . . ."

"It's not the tree, though I did hurt my back." He winced. "It's about us."

"What about us?"

"We shouldn't be pretending to be engaged, we should really be engaged. I thought about it the whole time I was driving to Burlington. You and I belong together."

"You should have thought of that before you made your travel arrangements." I waved at the brochure.

"Those can be canceled." He shrugged. "Nothing happened between me and Gwendolyn. It was my mother's doing. If you want me to, I'll call her and she can tell you herself."

I almost gave in. All I wanted was for Teddy to take my side when it came to matters between Dolly and me. But he wasn't saying that his mother would apologize, only that she would talk to me. I imagined how the conversation would go. Dolly would accuse me of not trusting her son, and I'd end up feeling bad. Still, at least Teddy was trying to make it right. And he looked so handsome. I was tempted to kiss him.

"I'll call her right now," he said, sensing my indecision. "Then we'll tell her that we're getting married."

I almost agreed, when I saw a pink envelope peeking out of his jacket pocket.

I snatched it up and opened it.

> Dear Teddy,
> I can't wait until you arrive. I told Mommy to put you in the pool house. She said that you'd be more comfortable in a guest room in the main house, but we'll want privacy. I didn't say anything to my mother but I'll arrange it.
> Love,
> Gwendolyn

I threw the letter on the bed. Then I grabbed a pillow and some blankets.

"You can have the bedroom, I'll sleep on the sofa tonight. I'll tell James that you have a bad cold and I don't want to catch it."

Anne, I'll stop there. Perhaps I shouldn't have written about the Christmas tree in the first place. I can feel my blood boiling and I don't want to spoil the joy of having my Christmas tree now. It looks so pretty in my living room.

That's one of the problems of being a writer. Writing about unpleasant things isn't easy. But without them, there wouldn't be a story.

Regards,
Nina

Chapter Sixteen

The next morning, Caroline went for a run on the Rio Grande Trail. The air was chilly, but the views—the craggy, snow-crested peaks of Snowmass and Aspen Highlands towering above her, and the frozen Roaring Fork River below—were breathtaking.

Afterward she took a hot bath and treated herself to a room-service breakfast of oat milk pancakes, coffee, and eggs the way her mother used to make them: sunny-side up with sliced avocado and salsa.

She was feeling happier than she had in months. Reading Nina's letters always made her feel better. Nina was a wonderful writer; her words transported Caroline to another time and place. She wondered again if Nina ever finished her manuscript. But Anne would have had every publisher in New York excited about it. Something must have happened to stop her from completing it.

And it had been thrilling to learn something new about Anne's lover. He lived in Philadelphia and he was interested in the Civil War. Caroline tried to picture him. Was he very tall? What color was his hair and did he have kind eyes and a warm smile?

Then there was Max. It had been so pleasant spending the

evening together without wondering how far things would progress, or whether this was the night that she'd sleep with him. And
she loved being around Lily. Lily made her laugh; she was sweet
and mature at the same time. Caroline wondered if she and Max
could have a future if they lived in the same place. But she quickly
put the thought out of her mind. They hadn't done anything more
than kiss, and she didn't know if the attraction would last. Even if
it did, this was no time to rethink her rules. She had to edit Nick's
manuscript and focus on her career.

Caroline's phone rang as she was finishing her second cup of
coffee. Daphne's number flashed on the screen.

"Where are you? I've been calling for ages," Daphne demanded.

"I had my phone on silent. I went for a run and took a bath,"
Caroline said happily. "I'm eating sunny-side-up eggs, the way Mom
made them. You should join me."

"I'm not hungry, but I need to talk to you."

"Why didn't you text?" Caroline asked.

"I didn't want Luke to see." Daphne's voice wobbled. "I can't
tell you over the phone. I'll be there in fifteen minutes."

When Caroline opened the door, she was shocked at Daphne's
appearance. Daphne's hair had escaped its ponytail and there were
circles under her eyes. She wasn't wearing makeup and her cheeks
were pale.

Caroline offered Daphne a sunny-side-up egg but Daphne
shook her head.

"I couldn't even manage a slice of toast at breakfast. I had to
pretend to Luke that I already ate."

"Are you pregnant?" Caroline asked in alarm.

Daphne's large blue eyes filled with tears.

"Of course I'm not pregnant. I don't know if there's going to be a wedding. I found out something about Luke and I don't know what to do."

A feeling of dread formed in Caroline's stomach. She didn't want Daphne to get hurt.

"Found out what?" she asked.

Daphne pulled out her phone. She thrust it at Caroline. "Read this."

It was a column in the *New York Times* food section.

Caroline read out loud:

"'With signed paintings by Picasso on its hotel's walls, and the grave of Marc Chagall in its graveyard, the picturesque French village of Saint-Paul-de-Vence had everything except a Michelin star restaurant. Until now. The husband-and-wife restaurant duo Allan and Evelyn Bernard have a new Michelin star to accompany the one they received for Bernard's in Paris. Le Miel received its star only six months after opening, and promises to be a great addition to the food scene in the hill towns of the French Riviera.'"

Caroline stopped reading. "What does this have to do with Luke?"

Daphne looked even more wretched. She let out a sigh.

"I read about Bernard's a few years ago, it's one of the hottest *petits plats* restaurants in Paris." She took a deep breath. "Allan and Evelyn Bernard are Luke's parents."

Caroline scanned the article again. There was a photo of a couple in their late fifties. The woman was attractive; the man had silvery hair and sharp cheekbones.

"I don't understand, why didn't he tell you?"

"I don't know, and I can't ask him. He'll think I was snooping," Daphne said.

Daphne had been doing a Google search for an image of Luke's restaurant in Hudson to show the Realtor. Instead, she found the article.

"Luke said he grew up on a farm in Wisconsin, I assumed his parents were farmers," Daphne said. "When his mother called from Paris, I didn't mention it to him. I wanted him to tell me they were in Paris himself."

Suddenly, Daphne's expression changed. Her eyes brightened.

"If you ask about his parents, he'll know we discussed it. If Max brought it up, he'd have to answer Max's questions."

"Max!" Caroline exclaimed.

Daphne grew excited. "He can say he's planning a trip to France, and he's going to try some Michelin-star restaurants."

"I've only known Max for a few days," Caroline replied doubtfully. "I don't want to ask him to do something underhanded."

"We'll all go to lunch." Daphne ignored her. "Luke wants to thank Max for sending his doctor when he got the concussion."

Daphne's eyes dimmed again, and she glanced down at her engagement ring.

"You have to help. Whatever Luke's reasons, he's keeping something from me. I can't marry someone with secrets. But I'm in love with him and I don't know what to do."

An hour later, Caroline stood at the door of the Queen Anne mansion on Walnut Street. Max answered the door. His hair was damp, and he was freshly shaven.

"When you called, I decided it was time to get off the sofa and take a shower." He grinned, leading her inside.

Caroline handed him a box of cinnamon apple muffins.

"I picked these up for you and Lily from Paradise Bakery." She smiled back.

"Lily is upstairs feeding the guinea pig. Apparently, Rudolph doesn't understand he's not really a reindeer. She's been giving him carrots and he likes them."

They sat in the living room. A Christmas tree strung with red and green lights stood near the window. A bowl of chestnuts sat on the coffee table, next to a silver nutcracker.

"You said you had something important to talk about," Max said.

"It is important," Caroline said. "It's about Daphne."

Max made a fake grimace.

"I thought you came over to say how disappointed you were that we couldn't have dinner last night."

"I am disappointed," Caroline returned teasingly. "I'm enjoying our time together."

"So am I." Max nodded. "Lily commented that I was a much better patient after you left."

Caroline told him about Luke's parents.

"I hate to ask you to make up something," Caroline said. "But Daphne is so upset. She hates that Luke didn't tell her the truth."

"You care a lot about your sister."

Caroline nodded. "I've never seen her like this. She looks worse than after our mother died."

"Of course I'll do it," Max agreed. "We'll go to White House Tavern, they serve the best burgers in Aspen. I do have one condition."

"What kind of condition?"

He leaned forward and kissed her.

"That we have a make-up date for last night. Indoor Jacuzzi at the inn, followed by cocktails at the Silver Nickel, and then room-service dinner of oysters on the half shell and sirloin tips in your room."

Caroline pretended to think about it.

"Those are pretty strict terms. Perhaps I need some incentive."

"Incentive?" Max repeated.

She leaned forward and kissed him. "Something like this."

Max placed his arms around her and she let herself fall into his embrace.

"So, what do you think of my terms now?" Max asked when they parted.

"I can work with them." Caroline tried to keep her tone serious. "In fact, I could have made them myself."

The White House Tavern was in a white cottage on East Hopkins Avenue. Inside, there were high ceilings and timbered walls. The bar was lined with bottles, and logs crackled in the brick fireplace.

"This is the A. G. Sheppard House," Max said when the waiter had taken their order. "Sheppard bought the lot in 1883 for three hundred dollars. The house was used as a miner's cottage at the turn of the century. My ancestor Finn Steele owned a similar house a few doors down."

"Max's family has lived in Aspen for generations," Caroline said to Daphne and Luke. "His ancestor was part of the silver rush."

"I love Aspen's history, it's so different from New England," Daphne gushed.

Daphne wore a pink cashmere turtleneck and faded jeans. Her cheeks were brushed with powder and she wore pink lipstick. But Caroline could tell that she wasn't herself. The wonderful smile that usually lit up her whole face stopped before it reached her eyes.

Max and Luke ordered the white cheddar cheeseburgers with spicy slaw. Caroline and Daphne split a kale salad with rotisserie chicken.

"I'm sticking with the burger," Max said when Caroline offered him some salad. "Lily fed me kale all day yesterday. I feel like her guinea pig."

They talked about the distillery and Luke's restaurant in Hudson.

"Owning a distillery is hard, but a restaurant must be worse," Max said to Luke. "I spent a summer in Paris during college. I ate at the same café every day, some of the customers were so rude. They blamed the waiter that the soup was cold, or the mustard was spicy. They even complained to him about the weather."

Luke didn't say anything. Daphne's shoulders tensed and she set down her fork.

"I've been thinking we should go to Paris for our honeymoon," she announced.

Luke put down his burger. "But we're using that company that decides where we go."

Daphne told Max about Where Are the Bride and Groom. "I read some negative reviews online. One bride complained that their reservation was for a cruise down the Amazon River, even though her fiancé is allergic to mosquitoes."

Luke turned to Daphne. "You've been to Paris for work, shouldn't we go somewhere new?"

"That was ages ago." Daphne waved her hand. "It would be so romantic to go together. We could walk in the Tuileries Garden and take a dinner cruise on the Seine." She paused and looked at Luke. "Unless there's a reason you don't want to go to Paris."

Luke smiled and squeezed her hand. "You're the bride. We'll do whatever you want."

Luke and Max kept talking, but Daphne wasn't listening. She pushed the chicken around her plate and her eyes were dangerously bright. Her hand brushed her water glass and it tipped on the table.

"Sometimes I'm so clumsy," she sighed, inspecting her wet skirt. "Excuse me, I'll be right back."

Caroline waited a few minutes. Then she followed Daphne into the powder room.

Daphne was standing in front of the air dryer. There was no one else there.

"Don't tell me that you spilled the water on purpose," Caroline said.

"Of course not," Daphne said. "You know I get clumsy when I'm upset."

It was true. Daphne had excelled at sports in high school. She played soccer and was a starter on the volleyball team. But during her senior year, her team lost the championship volleyball game. Daphne's ex-boyfriend attended with another girl, and Daphne fumbled her serves.

"I shouldn't have said I wanted to go to Paris, it just popped out," Daphne groaned. "I was the one who convinced Luke to use Where Are the Bride and Groom."

"He must have a reason for not telling you about his parents. Maybe he isn't close to them, or they had a falling-out," Caroline suggested.

Daphne shook her head.

"His mother congratulated me about the wedding."

Caroline tried again. "You keep secrets from me."

"I tried to tell you about the engagement. Then I decided to make it a surprise."

"I'm not talking about that. It was a few weeks after Mom died. I was at a bar with Jack, I saw you leaving with a guy," Caroline recalled. "The next day you mentioned you spent the night at a friend's apartment. It wasn't my business, so I didn't say anything."

"I was embarrassed," Daphne admitted. "I'm not like you, I don't do one-night stands. But he was hot, and you know . . ." She gulped. ". . . I needed something to blot out the pain of Mom's death."

Caroline wanted to say there was nothing wrong with casual sex, as long as one took precautions. But this wasn't the time. The important thing was concentrating on Daphne and Luke.

"You have to ask Luke yourself."

"I'm not ready," Daphne sighed. "You and Max could spend the afternoon with us, I'll ask Luke this evening."

Caroline had planned on going to the used bookstore and finding out more about Anne's lover. But that would have to wait.

"I suppose I could," Caroline said.

Daphne perked up. Her tone became brighter.

"The four of us can watch the Fat Bike Race."

"As long as we don't go ice-skating. Max already twisted his ankle, I don't want it to happen again."

They left the tavern and went to watch the start of the fat-bicycle race. The race was part of the 12 Days of Aspen. It was held at the Aspen Golf Course. Spectators wearing ski parkas lined the route, and a man holding a flag ushered the competitors across the finish line.

After the race, there was a dog fashion show. People borrowed dogs from the Aspen Animal Shelter and dressed them in costumes. The proceeds went to charity, and often the dogs were adopted after the fashion show. Caroline loved a mixed Labrador wearing a Santa hat, and Daphne fell for a terrier mix in red booties.

Now Caroline sat at the bar of the Silver Nickel, waiting for Max to arrive. The dog fashion show had run late, so they decided to skip the Jacuzzi and meet for drinks instead.

Max stood at the bar's entrance. She was reminded of when she first saw him. She had been hesitant to talk to him because she wasn't interested in a fling. But he had been so handsome, with those warm hazel eyes and chiseled cheekbones.

Max kissed her and sat on a stool.

"I was thinking of when we met," Caroline said. "You offered to order the sausage fennel pizza and give me a slice. I said that was a terrible pickup line."

"You had me all wrong," Max returned. "I don't do pickup lines. Besides, the sausage fennel pizza is too good to share unless it's with someone special."

"You couldn't have thought I was special. You only saw me across the room."

"You had this glow. You don't give yourself enough credit, but you're beautiful, Caroline."

Caroline blushed. She shouldn't have started this conversation.

Max touched her hand. "I'm glad you ate the pizza, and I'm glad we're here now."

They ordered duck fritters to share and two Sazerac cocktails. The bartender poured a small amount of absinthe into the glasses and added rye whiskey and sugar cubes.

They talked about Daphne and Luke.

"I wasn't much help," Max apologized.

"Did you really spend a summer in Paris?"

"Of course, I would never lie."

"I've been to Madrid and London. But I never made it to Paris," Caroline said. "I've always wanted to go."

The minute Caroline said it, she regretted it. It was the kind of thing women said to move a relationship along. She blamed it on the cocktail; she should never drink anything with even a drop of absinthe—it was too strong.

"I'd say something about going together, but that would be against your rules," Max said.

"I don't have time to go to Paris anyway." Caroline kept her voice light. "I've got to get Nick's book into shape before I present it to my publisher."

"If you didn't have to work on the book, would you go to Paris with me?" Max asked.

If she was going to beat Daphne at her dare, she had to pretend she was softening her rules.

"Well, I do have to help Nick, and you're busy at the distillery." She gave him a flirtatious smile. "Though I don't know anyone who can resist Paris in the spring. I'd love to visit Shakespeare and Company. It's the most famous bookstore in the world."

Max leaned forward and kissed her. His breath was sweet from the sugar cube. "I'll take that as a definite maybe."

They finished the fritters and talked about a new blend of rye whiskey Max was releasing, and Nick's novel. Caroline was about to suggest they go upstairs and order room service when Daphne appeared.

"I found you." Daphne rushed over to them. "You weren't in your room, the front desk didn't know where you'd gone."

Daphne's hair lay in damp clumps at her shoulders. Her lips were raw as if she'd been biting them.

"You must be freezing. Your hair is wet, you're not wearing a jacket." Caroline frowned.

"It started snowing and I didn't want to go back to the room to get my jacket," Daphne said. "Luke and I got in a fight and I left."

"You left?" Caroline repeated.

"I didn't know what else to do," Daphne said. "I thought I could stay with you tonight."

Max's face fell. He pretended to be studying the menu.

"Unless I'm interrupting something," Daphne said. "I could try to get my own room."

The images that had been going through Caroline's mind—Max and her sharing oysters on the half shell in front of her fireplace, Max leading her to the bed, Caroline taking off his sweater, seeing his naked chest for the first time—dissolved.

Caroline finished her drink. "Of course you'll stay with me."

Chapter Seventeen

Max went back to his parents' house, and Caroline took Daphne up to her room. A tray of chocolate truffles sat on the coffee table, next to a silver coffeepot. There was a scented Christmas candle and a packet of mistletoe.

Outside the window, the mountain was alive with night skiers. Colored strobe lights danced on the slopes, and the gondola was strung with twinkling silver lights. It was one of the prettiest sights Caroline had ever seen.

A bottle of brandy sat on the sideboard, with two glasses.

"You were going to invite Max to your room! Isn't that against your rules?" Daphne exclaimed, eyeing the two brandy glasses.

"I had to, I accepted your dare," Caroline reminded her.

Daphne sank on the sofa. "I'm sorry for ruining your evening, I didn't know what else to do."

Caroline poured a glass of brandy. She handed it to Daphne.

"Your teeth are chattering. Drink this, then tell me what happened."

Daphne had shown Luke the article about his parents in *The New York Times*. When Luke was eight, his parents went to Paris for the summer. A friend was opening a restaurant and Luke's father was going to be an investor. Then the chef quit, and Allan decided to become the chef himself. The restaurant was so successful, he and Luke's mother stayed in France. Luke was raised by his grandmother in Wisconsin, and he visited his parents every summer.

"His parents are well known in the food world, and Luke wanted to make it on his own. He took his mother's last name and opened the restaurant in Hudson," Daphne said. "He didn't tell me when we met, then we got serious so quickly. He was going to tell me before the wedding, but I suggested eloping."

"He was going to tell you eventually," Caroline said slowly.

"He left out a huge part of his childhood!" Daphne protested. "In a relationship, you can't decide when to reveal the truth, you should always be honest. What if he's keeping other things from me?"

Caroline thought about her own rules. She hardly ever told her dates anything about herself, and she didn't ask questions about them. Why was it different with Max? He was easy to talk to, and he seemed genuinely interested in her.

But it didn't mean anything. They were two people who met at a ski resort during Christmas week. Caroline would go back to her real life in New York, and never see Max again.

"I wish Mom was here," Daphne sighed. "We'd go into the kitchen and take out the Christmas leftovers. Then we'd cook something together. I think more clearly when I'm chopping vegetables or mixing cake batter."

Caroline had an idea. She sent a few texts on her phone. Then she grabbed Daphne's jacket and handed it to her.

"What are we doing?" Daphne asked.

Caroline put on her own jacket and opened the door.

"You'll see, follow me."

The first stop was the small supermarket called Aspen Groceries. Caroline filled a cart with butter and olive oil and double cream. There were cooked turkey and ham slices from the deli, and pie crust from the bakery. She added an assortment of vegetables, and spices.

Then the Uber drove them to Max's distillery. She found the key where Max had left it.

"Where are we?" Daphne glanced around the large space.

"Mad Finn Distillery." Caroline walked toward the back. "I texted Max and asked if we could use the kitchen. He left the key, he even turned on the oven."

Caroline took the groceries into the kitchen. An oak island took up the center of the room, and tall windows overlooked snow-covered fields. There was a six-burner stove, and two dishwashers.

"Max owns all this?" Daphne gasped. She took in the oversize pantry, the glass cabinets filled with plates.

"When the distillery opens, it's going to have a full-service restaurant." Caroline unloaded the shopping bag. "You're going to make Mom's turkey and ham Christmas pie. And we're going to figure out what to do about Luke."

For the next hour, Daphne didn't say anything. Caroline watched her heating the butter in the saucepan, splashing in vinegar, adding cream so that it simmered but didn't boil over. She longed for it to be last Christmas, with Daphne and Anne making the pie together, and Caroline reading in the living room. Eventually the wonderful smells—golden pastry crust, fragrant thyme—would reach her and she'd come and join them.

"This was a great idea," Daphne said when the pie was baking in the oven. She wiped her hands on a dish towel and sat on a stool.

"I told Max we'd save him a piece of pie." Caroline sat beside her. "He was happy to do it."

Daphne took a leftover slice of ham and popped it in her mouth.

"When I was a kid, I thought our parents had the best marriage. They didn't argue like other parents, and they were nice to each other," Daphne said. "Now, I'm not so sure."

"What do you mean?" Caroline asked.

"Luke and I aren't married yet, and I already feel so close to him. When we're fighting, I can't concentrate on anything else. Maybe that's part of love, and Mom and Dad never experienced it."

"Of course they loved each other," Caroline argued. "They were married for twenty years."

"Mom was busy with us and her career, and Dad was so easygoing. He just needed his weekend fishing trips to be happy. Maybe they liked each other a lot, but they weren't really in love."

"Even if that was true, what does that have to do with anything?"

Daphne drummed her fingers on the counter.

"Even if Mom was alive, she wouldn't be able to give me advice if she'd never been in love herself. I have to figure this out on my own."

The pie, when it came out of the oven, was delicious. The pastry melted in Caroline's mouth, the meat and vegetables were tender and buttery. They ate it with a bottle of wine that she found in the pantry. She wrapped the leftover pie in plastic wrap and left a note thanking Max for letting them use the kitchen.

An Uber drove them back to Aspen. The closer they came to the inn, the quieter Daphne became.

"I'm going for a walk," Daphne said when the driver pulled into the driveway.

"I can come with you," Caroline suggested.

Daphne shook her head. She pulled on her hood. "Don't worry about me. I'll be fine."

Caroline was about to walk up to her room, but the concierge stopped her.

"Miss Holt, you had a delivery."

"A delivery?" Caroline repeated.

"No one was there, so the delivery boy gave me the card."

Caroline read the card. She pulled out her phone and dialed Daphne's number.

"What's wrong?" Daphne answered.

"You have to come back, there's something you need to see."

Caroline waited for Daphne in the lobby. They went up to Caroline's room together. Caroline let Daphne walk in first.

Almost every surface held a bouquet of roses. Red roses sat on the coffee table, yellow roses adorned the side tables. A bouquet of white roses stood on the bathroom counter, and another on the bedside table.

"Are these from Max?" Daphne asked.

Caroline handed Daphne the card. "No, they're from Luke."

Daphne read the card. When she looked up at Caroline, her cheeks were wet with tears.

She gave Caroline a hug and turned to the door.

"I have to go see Luke. For the record, being in love sucks." Her eyes danced and her smile was white as snow. "But I wouldn't have it any other way."

After Daphne left, Caroline hung up her jacket and sat on the sofa. She was happy for Daphne. The concierge would move the roses to Daphne and Luke's room. Without Luke, Daphne had been like a fishing boat searching for the shore.

It was still early but she didn't want to call Max.

She picked up Nina's next letter and started reading.

Dear Anne,

I've been so naughty! Instead of working on the manuscript, I've been reading old love letters. It started innocently enough, I was going through a box of my press clippings. That's one of the funny things about being a writer. One can't help reading one's reviews. Not that mine were all bad. *The New York Times* and *The Washington Post* loved my work. But the reviewer in *The Boston Globe* said that my second novel didn't live up to my potential, and the *Los Angeles Times* wrote that I had traded my "bra-burning prose for a novel that would purely make money."

As if their reviews could change anything about the story. The story is the important thing. Why else do authors write in the first place?

At my age, it seems silly to reread love letters. But it's one of the surprises about growing older. One never gives up the dream of a great love. Love is still the best thing on earth. And sometimes the most painful.

I don't have to tell you, you're a beautiful woman in the prime of life. I was like you once, attractive and confident. I could have whatever I wanted. Only, I didn't always know what I wanted. Especially when it came to Teddy. Teddy was like the cotton candy you buy at the state fair. Light and sweet and irresistible. Until you finish it, and you're left with sticky fingers and a toothache.

I expected Teddy to be irritable the day after we put up the Christmas trees, but he was the reverse. That was the thing about Teddy, when something was bothering him, he became sweet as molasses.

I woke up to Bing Crosby's "White Christmas" playing on the phonograph. The smell of frying bacon came from the kitchen.

I wrapped my gold silk robe around me more tightly.

"You look wonderful in that robe. It brings out your eyes," Teddy greeted me.

"My eyes are brown," I said icily.

"Your eyes are the color of roasted almonds," Teddy corrected. He patted a dining chair. "Sit down, I made your favorite breakfast: eggs Benedict with bacon. And I went to the farm next door, and got a jug of whole cream. It's fresh, the farmer milked the cow this morning."

"We shouldn't eat without James," I said.

"He's still asleep, I made plenty," Teddy answered.

"Why are you doing this?" I asked when we sat down. Teddy made the best eggs Benedict. He wouldn't tell me his secret, but I think it had something to do with the amount of butter in the sauce.

"I've been acting like a jealous schoolboy. There's obviously nothing going on between you and James."

"What are you talking about?"

"I thought James had eyes for you, but I was wrong."

Teddy had gone to the public library and pulled up some

articles about James. He had a beautiful girlfriend named Rhonda. Rhonda came from an old Philadelphia family and graduated from Yale.

I don't know why it bothered me. I wasn't interested in James romantically, and I had never longed for a fancy education. I was happy with my life and my career.

"You're saying Rhonda is better than me because she has a social pedigree and a diploma from an Ivy League school?" I demanded.

"Of course she's not better than you," Teddy soothed me. "All I'm saying is I overreacted. Let's change the subject. I wrote down a list of things for the three of us to do together. We're going to give James a picture-perfect Vermont Christmas."

When James woke up, Teddy served him the same breakfast. Afterward we piled into Teddy's car. James offered to drive but Teddy insisted. James was our guest, he couldn't be expected to be our driver too.

We started by sampling Jersey cheeses at Billings Farm in Woodstock. They really were delicious. Apparently, Jersey cows produced milk with the greatest amount of butterfat.

After that, we visited an apple orchard, where we collected apples and ate freshly made hot apple cider doughnuts. We finished the tour by watching a Christmas parade in Woodstock. The mayor arrived on a Clydesdale horse and Santa and Mrs. Claus followed in a red sleigh.

Then we went back to the farm to dress for dinner. Teddy had invited a surprise guest. He wouldn't tell me who it was.

Teddy had prepared tenderloin beef in a red wine sauce, with sausage and sage stuffing. For dessert there would be a choice of mincemeat pie, and cinnamon crumble served with vanilla ice cream. I knew when I entered the kitchen that Teddy hadn't cooked any of it himself. Teddy's fridge never contained more than Chinese takeout and bottles of seltzer water. I found out later that he ordered the whole meal from the Woodstock Inn. It must have cost a fortune.

The meal made me suspicious. I couldn't figure out why Teddy was being so nice.

Teddy's guest was Father Joseph, the local pastor. I was shocked when Teddy introduced him. Teddy wasn't keen on religion.

"I met Father Joseph when I was looking for Christmas ornaments," Teddy said. "He heard me mention your name to the clerk and came up to say hello."

"My wife is your biggest fan," Father Joseph gushed.

"My biggest fan?" I repeated, questioningly.

"Of your column," he prompted. "Every other sentence in our house includes 'Laura Carter would paint the bedroom yellow' or 'Laura Carter buys her apples at the Happy Valley Orchard.' She doesn't do anything without checking to see if it's in your column first."

I'd almost forgotten I was Laura Carter. Thank God Father Joseph mentioned it before I introduced myself as Nina.

"I'll make sure to sign some columns before you leave." I shook his hand.

Teddy led Father Joseph into the living room. James stood at the bar, fixing predinner cocktails.

Teddy introduced them and we sat down on the sofa.

"Father Joseph is famous around here. He's performed almost all the weddings and funerals in town for the last forty years," Teddy said.

"It's been an honor." Father Joseph nodded. "The wedding day is often the happiest time in a man and woman's lives."

"Laura and I can't wait to tie the knot," Teddy said. "James is the only single man here. Unless he's hiding something."

James was wearing cashmere slacks, and brown Italian loafers. I could tell Teddy wasn't happy about that. Teddy prided himself on his fashion taste, but his clothing budget rarely included cashmere and Italian shoes.

"You're a successful doctor in your thirties," Teddy continued innocently. "There must be a pretty girl just waiting for you to propose."

"I'm afraid not." James shook his head.

"Not some Yale graduate whose family dates back to the 1800s?" Teddy questioned.

James blushed. "I have dated a girl on and off. Rhonda is in Geneva at the moment, her father is the U.S. ambassador. I haven't seen her in months."

Teddy looked at me triumphantly. I didn't know why. There was nothing going on between me and James.

"I urge you to put a ring on her finger when she returns." Teddy finished his Bloody Mary. He glanced at me mischievously. "Being engaged has changed my relationship with Laura in ways I never imagined."

During dessert, Father Joseph talked about the money being raised to build a new baptismal font at the church.

"I'll write you a check," Teddy said enthusiastically. He reached over and squeezed my hand. "Laura and I want lots of babies, I'm sure we'll take advantage of your services."

"You'll have to start soon if you want me to perform them." Father Joseph gave us a meaningful look. "I'm not as young as I used to be."

I excused myself and went to get more ice cream. I wasn't hungry but I refused to listen to Teddy talk about babies.

When I returned, everyone had moved into the living room. James offered to do the dishes, but Teddy said he'd take care of them later.

"You're right about not waiting to have babies." Teddy filled four glasses with sherry. "In fact, you've given me a marvelous idea. Laura and I were going to get married in the spring, but why shouldn't we get married now!"

I almost dropped my sherry.

"We'll get married right here in front of the fireplace on New Year's Eve. Father Joseph can perform the ceremony. James will be the witness and the best man. Laura knows everyone in town, she'll have her choice of matrons of honor. I'm sure someone in town can pull some strings and get a marriage license in time." He turned to me.

Teddy looked so innocent, like a child telling Santa Claus what he wanted for Christmas.

"We can't impose on Father Joseph during Christmas week," I said hastily.

"On the contrary, it would be my pleasure." Father Joseph beamed.

James set down his sherry glass. His brow furrowed.

"Is that really a good idea?" he asked. "You both must have family who want to be at the wedding."

"Let's face it, Laura and I are getting old to be newlyweds. Our families are anxious for us to finally tie the knot," Teddy sighed. "Perhaps we'll have a second wedding in New York."

"Then it's settled." Father Joseph stood up.

Father Joseph left and Teddy took the dishes into the kitchen. I waited until James had gone to his room, then I joined Teddy.

I turned the faucet on to hot and loaded dishes into the sink. I was so angry, I didn't notice it almost burning my skin.

"I wouldn't marry you on New Year's Eve if it stopped a flock of ravens from descending on us," I seethed.

"You're going to have to if you want Laura Carter to maintain her readership," Teddy announced. "And Father Joseph's wife is your biggest fan, you wouldn't want to let her down."

There was nothing more to say. I set the last dish in the sink and stormed out.

It was only when I entered the living room that I remembered Teddy was going to sleep in the bedroom. And I'd freeze to death in the barn.

I lay down on the sofa and closed my eyes. My last thought before I fell asleep was that Teddy should take up chess. He had me in check and there was nothing I could do about it. Checkmate.

Anne, I'll stop there. If I keep writing, I'll get angry with

Teddy all over again, and my heartburn will start acting up.
I suppose that's why it's rare for older people to fall in love.
Our bodies can't handle the pain.

It is Christmas so I'll end on a happy note. Which is that
I found you, and just knowing you makes me happy.

Warm regards,
Nina

Caroline imagined Nina celebrating Christmas alone in New
York in her seventies. Perhaps Daphne was right. If Caroline didn't
let love into her life now, she never would. When she was seventy,
she'd be alone too.

She replaced the letter and turned off the lights.

Chapter Eighteen

The used bookstore was already bustling when Caroline entered the next morning. A mother was trying to entertain her small son, while flipping through books at the same time. Two college students were picking through the classics table and an older man was browsing in the fishing section.

"I brought you a cappuccino." Caroline handed it to the salesgirl who had helped her two days ago.

"Thank you, but you didn't have to do that." The girl accepted the to-go cup. "My name is Allison."

Caroline introduced herself and told her why finding out more about her mother was so important to her.

"I'm sorry for your loss," Allison said. "I'm twenty and my mother is my best friend. She taught me to love books, now I'm getting a degree in library science. Girls in my sorority adore perfume, I love the smell of books."

"I'm the same, I can't imagine having a career that doesn't include books," Caroline acknowledged. "You were so helpful, I wondered if you remembered anything else about my mother."

Allison switched on her computer.

"She did come in another day. She bought a copy of *Under the Tuscan Sun,* by Frances Mayes."

Caroline had found a copy of the book on her mother's bedside table ages ago, and read it then. It was about a couple who bought a villa in Tuscany. They wanted to spend a romantic Christmas there, but when they arrived it was in shambles. It took them six months to fix up. There were so many obstacles along the way. Leaking faucets, workers who only showed up to eat the food in the pantry, a family of mice that wouldn't leave. It was finally ready the following summer and it was the best time of their lives.

Why would Anne have wanted to read it again after all these years?

Perhaps she had believed she was in remission and was planning her future. She was going to retire and buy a villa in Tuscany. She and her lover were going to renovate it together. Caroline imagined spending Christmases there with Anne and her lover and Daphne. Midnight services held in a six-hundred-year-old church. Going caroling with other villagers. Christmas dinners that included lasagna and panettone for dessert.

Allison scrolled further down the computer screen. "Oh, but she returned it a few days later."

"She returned the book. Did she say why?"

"I wasn't here." Allison shook her head. "I'm sorry, there's no note."

Caroline's hopeful feeling disappeared. She thanked Allison and walked back onto the street. A soft snow was falling, and a layer of fresh powder dusted the sidewalk.

She had been wrong. Anne bought the book because it brought back memories of when she was healthy and could plan a future. Or, even worse, being at the Aspen writers' conference—strolling along Main Street on warm summer evenings, browsing in the shops and having dinner at the outdoor cafés—made her believe she was going to be all right, but then something happened: the night chills caused by the cancer returned, and she knew that living in Tuscany would remain a dream.

Tears formed in Caroline's eyes. She wished she could talk to someone. But Daphne and Luke had gone cross-country skiing.

Her phone rang. It was Max.

"I was hoping I'd catch you," Max said when she answered. "How's Daphne?"

Caroline told him about the bouquets of roses.

"I'm glad they're working it out. Luke is a nice guy," Max said. He gave a low chuckle. "Lily is reading *Romeo and Juliet*. I'm beginning to feel like you and I are star-crossed lovers. First, I twist my ankle, then our romantic dinner gets interrupted by Daphne."

"Isn't Lily a little young to be reading *Romeo and Juliet?*"

"There's a 'Shakespeare for Kids' version," Max explained. He paused for a moment. "How about we go snowmobiling? Then there's a new exhibit at the art museum, and we could finish the day with room service in your room as planned. This time we'll turn off our phones, and keep the lights dimmed so no one can find us."

Caroline didn't say anything. She thought of Nina's letters, and Nina being alone in her seventies. Of Daphne's face when she saw Luke's grand gesture of all the roses. Of her mother's last brush with love the previous summer.

"Unless I'm being presumptuous and the offer is off . . ." Max said.

"Nothing has changed," Caroline replied. She took a deep breath. "I'd love to spend the day together."

Max met her in the lobby of the Aspen Inn two hours later. He looked handsome in a fleece-lined suede jacket over a green turtleneck.

"I brought you something." He handed Caroline a small package.

Caroline unwrapped the tissue paper. Inside was a silver coin.

"It's a copy of a coin that was made from the first silver rush," he explained. "Mad Finn kept one in his pocket, he swore it brought him good luck."

The coin was so different from the gifts her flings had given her to impress her: the Chanel perfume that Jack bought after they'd been sleeping together for a week (Caroline would never wear Chanel, other editors would assume she was being overpaid), the Gucci scarf Brad gave her on the last day of the London Book Fair (it was a sweet thought but she never wore it without feeling like a walking advertisement for Gucci).

Caroline slipped the coin into her pocket. "It's perfect, I love it."

"Not that you need luck, you're beautiful and capable," Max said hastily.

Caroline gave him a quick kiss. "Everyone needs luck now and then. I can't think of anything I'd like more."

Max had rented the snowmobile from the T-Lazy-7 Ranch. There was usually a tour guide, but Max knew the area so well, they crisscrossed the trails by themselves.

They drove through White River National Forest. Caroline was overwhelmed by the snow-covered mountains reaching up to the sky, the deep valleys below and frozen waterfalls. They stopped at a cabin owned by the T-Lazy-7 Ranch and took out Max's picnic. A thermos of hot chocolate, cheeseburgers from the Silver Nickel, a plate of Lily's brownies. After lunch, they drove to

Maroon Lake at the foot of Maroon Bells. Aspen groves opened up to wide meadows. The only sounds were of deer darting through the snow, and her own heart beating when she wrapped her arms around Max's waist.

They passed through the town of Independence on the snowmobile and Max told her the history of the town. At its peak in the 1880s, it contained a bank and three post offices and a stamp mill where they processed silver ore. Then, like in other mining towns, the silver began to dry up and the miners moved on. The blizzard of 1899 caused the remaining residents to leave. They skied down to Aspen on skis made from their dismantled houses. All that was left was a few stables and the old jail with a plaque of the town's history.

Max was a wonderful storyteller. She asked him to tell her more. He told her about Isabel, the girl in Aspen who stole Mad Finn's heart. Isabel's father worked in the post office, but he was often hungover from too many whiskeys at the saloon, and she took his place. About their four children, who wanted to get as far from Colorado as possible—to California, where there were so many opportunities, or to Philadelphia, where the railroads were creating new millionaires.

Max's stories made Caroline long for a father of her own in a new way. She wanted to know about her ancestors, to feel connected to places and times in history. If only her mother had told her something. Now she never would.

After they returned the snowmobile, they spent an hour at the Aspen Art Museum. It was housed in an old hydroelectric plant. There was an outdoor area with sculptures and a fountain. Caroline joked that it was no rival to the Guggenheim in New York. Max teased back: Where else could you find a steel statue made of reused horseshoes, or a papier-mâché landscape of the Aspen Highlands?

Max dropped her off near the inn and she spent an hour browsing in the boutiques on Main Street. She treated herself to a red wool dress to wear for dinner, and bought Max a small bottle of cologne. She put it back on the shelf twice before she decided to buy it. She rarely gave gifts to the guys she dated. The relationships were too brief, the smart tie would end up in a drawer and never be worn. But Max had given her the silver coin. And the cologne smelled good, like the aspen trees they had passed that afternoon.

For the first time, she envied the couples strolling arm in arm, the young families with a toddler perched on the father's shoulders. She was surprised at herself. She hadn't known she wanted those things. But she recalled how good it felt to wrap her arms around Max's waist when they were riding the snowmobile. It was more than the physical attraction; for the first time she felt part of something.

When Max arrived for dinner, he had changed into a white shirt under a snowflake sweater. His hair was smooth and worn to the side, and he wore navy slacks.

"I have something for you." Caroline ushered him inside.

The hotel room had never looked so lovely. A Christmas tree twinkled beside the window, and red candles flickered on the fireplace mantel. The dining table was covered with a silver tablecloth and set with white china and sterling silverware.

Max opened the package. He glanced at Caroline in surprise.

"I thought you didn't do that sort of thing—you know, give gifts."

She suddenly felt embarrassed. Had she told him that she didn't give presents? She couldn't remember.

"You gave me the silver coin, and it is Christmas," she reminded him.

Max unscrewed the lid and inhaled the cologne.

"Thank you. I'll wear it every day," he said, smiling. "Now, I think we should start the evening with cocktails."

Max found a bottle of gin and a Tom Collins mix in the minifridge. He stirred them in a cocktail shaker and poured two glasses.

"Lily said it's a good idea to drink on a first date." He handed her a glass. "Her best friend, Emily, said it makes everyone relaxed so there are no strained silences."

"Emily is Lily's age! How does she know?" Caroline asked with a laugh. The Tom Collins did make her feel relaxed. Suddenly she didn't know why the evening made her tense. She had done this kind of thing dozens of times before.

"Apparently Emily's mother watches a lot of reality shows." Max grinned.

They sat on the sofa and ate pumpkin balls as appetizers. Max told her a story about teaching Lily to play backgammon, and Lily beating him three times in a row.

"Lily is lucky to have you as an uncle," Caroline reflected.

"Now that I don't live in California, I don't see my sister and her family often." He shrugged. "Helen and her husband work hard, I'm happy to help out."

Caroline shared her fears about Daphne and Luke. Daphne didn't realize how difficult it would be to raise a child if they both worked in a restaurant.

After the appetizers, they moved to the dining table. The chef had prepared roast rack of lamb and shrimp risotto. There were soft rolls and a cranberry salad. Their conversation was light and easy. Caroline tasted the sweet Colorado butter and gazed at Max in the candlelight and a warmth spread through her.

"Now we move on to the best part of the evening," Max said after they had eaten dessert and were sitting on the sofa.

The dishes were stacked on the room-service cart and the lights were turned low.

"If this was a romantic movie, I'd put on slow music and ask you to dance." Max trailed his fingers across Caroline's thigh. "But we've had enough distractions."

Max's kiss was deeper and longer than his previous kisses. His hand slipped beneath her dress.

His palm felt good against her skin. But suddenly she had an image of other men she'd slept with. Lying alone in bed after they'd gone home, or waking to the empty coffeepot the following morning.

She pulled away, and straightened her dress.

"I think I need a walk. I ate too much lamb."

Max sat up straight on the sofa.

"I don't understand, I thought this was what you're all about. The sexy, successful New York editor having her little flings."

"I guess I'm not ready. With my mother dying and everything going on between Luke and Daphne . . ."

"People die, Caroline. Even parents," Max said crisply. "It's terrible and sad but it happens. At least Daphne is trying to build a life."

"You don't think it's a bad idea for Daphne and Luke to get married so soon?" Caroline repeated. The mood was broken and she felt confused and upset.

"It's not up to me to approve. All I see is a couple who are in love and trying to work it out. You're like a turtle retreating into its shell."

Caroline stood up. "I think you better leave."

Max opened his mouth to say something. Instead, he grabbed his jacket.

"You're special, Caroline. I could really fall for you," he said. "But you don't know how to give yourself a break. And no one can help you but yourself."

Chapter Nineteen

The weather the next morning matched Caroline's mood. The sky was gray, and the wind blew the snow sideways.

Caroline's voicemail was empty and Max hadn't sent any texts. She had been looking forward to the end of the evening and exploring Max's body. Something had stopped her, and she didn't know what.

Daphne knocked on the door. She was wearing a cable-knit sweater that had belonged to their mother, paired with jeans and short boots.

"Luke and I are going to meet the minister this morning, but I wanted to see you first." Daphne glanced around the room. "That is, if I'm not interrupting anything."

"Max didn't spend the night." Caroline turned off the coffee-pot. "He left right after dessert."

"You mean before . . ."

"We didn't sleep together, we didn't even get to second base," Caroline sighed.

She told Daphne what happened. Max had accused her of not living her life.

Daphne poured sugar and cream into a cup. "He's right. You promised you'd see how far this thing with Max would go, instead you've strangled it from the start."

"I don't know what you're talking about," Caroline huffed.

"You usually sleep with guys because there are no strings attached. This time, you were afraid that our dare would make you consider having a real relationship. So, you stopped it before it began."

"I did nothing of the sort!" Caroline drank her coffee. It tasted strangely bitter, even when she added sugar.

"Max wouldn't have left if you hadn't encouraged him to leave," Daphne said. "And he's right about other things. Mom is dead, nothing you do can bring her back."

"You miss her too. You're wearing her sweater."

"Because she had classic taste and we're the same size," Daphne replied. "I might make mistakes with Luke and even with my career. But at least I'm trying to move forward. I don't even know why you're trying to find out more about Mom's lover."

Caroline gasped. Anne's lover was the whole reason she was in Aspen.

"I hate the idea of him waiting at Santa's Little Red Mailbox and not knowing why Mom didn't show up," Daphne continued before Caroline could answer. "But it doesn't matter where he's from or what his taste is in books. Mom is dead, they'll never be together."

Caroline wanted to say that Daphne didn't know what it was like to be the older sister. To always worry about Daphne. When they were young, Caroline comforted Daphne when she had nightmares and couldn't fall back to sleep. She lent her money for her first apartment and answered her texts no matter what the time was, because she wanted Daphne to be able to count on her.

"Just because I like Max doesn't mean we have to move so fast."

"The dare is off. I have to go and meet Luke." Daphne walked to the door and turned around. Her blue eyes were fierce. "At least I can save money on a bridal bouquet. I don't have anyone to toss it to."

After Daphne left, Caroline finished her coffee and stared at the snow falling outside the window. She still didn't know what stopped her from going further with Max. Usually slipping into bed with a man was the most natural thing in the world. Even her mother would have approved. Caroline was a mature adult, and love affairs with sexy men were part of the tapestry of life.

She texted Nick and suggested they meet before his shift. Then she grabbed a jacket and walked to the Limelight Hotel. Right now, she might be a disaster at dating, and a lousy sister, but she was good at her job.

Nick was polishing silver in the banquet room.

"My shift doesn't start yet, but I think better when my hands are busy," Nick said when he saw her.

Caroline nodded knowingly. "One of my authors loves to vacuum, and another's favorite thing is ironing. Her husband loves it, he always goes to work with pressed shirts and slacks."

Caroline settled into the supply-room office and Nick brought in two cups of coffee.

"No, thank you." Caroline shook her head. "For me, coffee is usually a magic potion, but today it gave me a headache."

Nick studied her more closely. "Is something wrong?"

"Nothing that getting lost in your manuscript won't cure." Caroline tried to smile. "We need to work on Josh's feelings. For instance, when Maggie decides to stay in Colorado, Josh is the one who pulls back."

Nick opened his computer.

"I don't know where that came from. I was so sure that Josh would be ecstatic that Maggie decided to stay. Every time I tried to change the scene, it came out the same way."

"Characters often take over a story. Tell me more about you and Savannah. How did you feel after Elliot left?"

Nick ran his hands through his hair.

"I didn't see Savannah until two days later. She had the weekend off and went to Denver to go shopping. It was after dinner and I knocked on her door. She was arranging her purchases on the bed, work shirts and pairs of riding boots. She had decided to stay for the whole summer.

"I reminded her that she was spending two weeks at Elliot's parents' house in Cape Cod, but she told me the trip was off. Elliot had broken up with her. Oddly, instead of being thrilled, I had a choking feeling. I was in love with Savannah but I wasn't like Elliot. I wasn't ready to propose.

"I left so that Savannah could take a bath. We met again an hour later for a stroll around the ranch. It was a beautiful summer night. The moon was full and stars twinkled in the sky. The horses rustled in the stables, and a few guests sat on the porch, watching the fireflies.

"Savannah said she'd decided to stay through the fall. She liked the ranch. The work was easy and the guests were so happy.

"I stopped walking. Savannah looked particularly beautiful. She wore a floral sweater and a long, flowing skirt. I told her she'd miss a semester but she said she could make it up. The aspen trees were so pretty in the fall, and there was a three-day trek that was supposed to be gorgeous at that time of year.

"Colorado is stunning in the autumn. The waterfalls are a

green-blue and the leaves on the trees are burnt orange. I announced I was going back to school and she said I should stay too. If I didn't have papers to write, I could start the novel I was always talking about.

"I argued that I had to graduate. Without a degree, I might get stuck on the ranch forever.

"Savannah looked at me with those large, liquid eyes. Her mouth that I loved to kiss—turned down at the corners. She reminded me that all I wanted was to be together and write. Before I could say anything else she stalked off.

"The next day, she avoided me. She switched to another riding group and didn't come down for dinner. I did the dishes and knocked on her door. She was sitting on her bed with a towel wrapped around her head. I handed her a slim volume. It was one of my favorite books, James Baldwin's *Giovanni's Room*. It's set in Paris in the 1950s. James Baldwin moved to Paris when he was twenty-four to write his first novel. She pointed to the stack of books on her bedside table and said she might not get to it for a few months. I told her to take as long as she liked. I wasn't going anywhere without her. Then she leaned forward and kissed me. I kissed her back, and a new energy surged through my body.

"I was confident it would all work out. We'd stay together and I'd write a bestseller."

Nick stopped talking. He glanced at Caroline as if he suddenly remembered that she was there.

"Savannah became my muse. I had to prove to myself that I could write a novel." He pondered. "The first fifty pages poured out. Then she left and I stopped writing."

"In the beginning, you were afraid of how much she meant to you so you pulled back," Caroline said. "Josh feels the same when Maggie decides to stay in Colorado and keep working at the pharmacy."

Nick made some notes on the computer. He beamed at Caroline. "That's why I couldn't change the scene."

Caroline nodded. She thought about her night with Max. "Even when two people are attracted to each other, they often move at different speeds."

They revised another chapter and Caroline walked back toward the Aspen Inn. The snow had stopped falling but the clouds were still low in the sky. She watched skiers skim down the slopes and children on rubber tubes spin on damp powder.

She was reminded of the semester in college that she had planned to spend studying abroad. She and her roommate were going to share an apartment in Madrid. But the roommate broke her leg and couldn't go.

Caroline had been anxiously studying the brochures when her mother tapped on her door.

Anne set a shopping bag down on Caroline's desk.

"I bought you some clothes for Spain. It's going to be muggy when you arrive, you'll need light, cotton dresses."

The dresses were beautiful. Bright summery colors with rich embroidery.

"I'm not going to Spain," Caroline said.

"What do you mean you're not going? You've been planning it for months."

Madrid had an active literary scene, and they were going to make side trips to London and Rome. Caroline had never been to Europe without her mother and Daphne and Walter. How would she navigate a foreign country alone?

"My writing professor is teaching one of my favorite seminars this semester and I don't want to miss it." Caroline told a small white lie. "Besides, the program in Madrid runs through Christmas. We always spend Christmas as a family at the cabin."

Anne smoothed one of the new dresses so that it made a fan on the bed. She looked at Caroline pensively.

"Do you still want to be a book editor after college?"

"Of course." Caroline nodded. "I already know which publishing houses I want to apply to when I graduate."

"How are you going to edit authors with different worldviews if you don't see the world yourself?"

"I could go to Europe next summer. You and Daphne can come with me."

"Daphne is always busy and I've been asked to speak at conferences." Anne squeezed Caroline's hand. "Go now. The cabin will be here next Christmas, but you may never get this chance again."

The first month in Madrid, Caroline was lonelier than she'd ever been. All she wanted was to go home. Then she attended a literary event and met a brilliant young writer named Carmen. Carmen's family took Caroline into her home and shared their culture. Carmen's manuscript was the first novel Caroline acquired a few years later. It was translated into six languages and reviewed by *The New York Times*.

Anne lived her life fearlessly. Caroline had listened to her advice and tried to do the same. Except when it came to love. Love was precarious, and she didn't want to get her heart broken.

The lights on the Christmas tree came on. Main Street twinkled like a scene from a movie set.

That was why she didn't want to go further with Max when he was kissing her. She was falling in love with him.

She was about to go back to her room, but instead she turned around. She had to tell Max her feelings before it was too late. Her mother was right: she might never get the chance again.

Chapter Twenty

Max's mother, Pamela, answered the door of the Queen Anne mansion on Walnut Street. Caroline hadn't seen Pamela since the open house. Pamela was elegantly dressed in a beige sweater and wool skirt.

Caroline sat in the living room while Pamela went to bring them some tea. She was reminded of the beauty of Max's parents' house. A fire crackled in the fireplace, and the velvet drapes were pulled back to reveal the snow-covered garden.

Pamela reappeared. "In the spring, my garden has bluebells and primroses," she said. "Aspen at Christmas is spectacular. But spring and summer are my favorite times of year."

Caroline was about to say that her mother had adored Aspen during the summer. But she wasn't here to talk about Anne.

Pamela kept talking. "I don't usually dress up during the day. I have a meeting for next year's writers' conference." She handed Caroline a teacup. "You should be on a panel, I can put in a word."

Caroline accepted the tea. "Thank you, that's very kind. I was wondering if Max was home."

"Max took Lily sledding." Pamela gave a small smile. "Lily is one of those children who has to keep moving. Tonight, we're going to make cake pops to serve at my New Year's Eve party." She sipped her tea. "You should come to the party. It's great fun. I pull out our winery's best champagne, and everyone gets tipsy."

Caroline shifted on the sofa. "I don't know what Max would say," she said cautiously.

"Ahh, I thought there was something going on. Max came home acting like a bear who had been woken from hibernation."

Caroline didn't want to admit her feelings for Max to Pamela. She'd only met her once.

"It's nothing, Max and I just met." She waved her hand.

"I told you that Max rarely brings girls to my Christmas open house," Pamela reflected. "And he's been so happy the last few days. Like he used to be in Santa Barbara." Pamela set down her teacup. "I would never say anything to Max, my first rule is not to intrude in my children's love lives. But all relationships are tricky. When Max's father, Robert, and I got married, we were madly in love. Now, we've almost gotten divorced three times. The last time was so bad, I called an attorney. The minute the attorney's secretary answered, I put down the phone. I believe in marriage."

"What happened?" Caroline asked.

"The first time was the usual. Robert spent all his time at the winery, while I was stuck at home raising two small children. Neither of us understood how hard the other worked and we stopped communicating." She gave a little laugh. "All it took was a few weekend getaways and we were fine. The second time was more complicated, that's why they call it the seven-year itch. The last time was about Max. Robert and Max still aren't comfortable together, that's why Robert isn't here."

Max's father blamed Max for Jessica drinking half a dozen of his private reserve bottles of wine.

"Robert threatened to fire Max from the winery, and they got into a terrible fight," Pamela recalled. "They were never close. My husband is all about profit and Max has a gentler streak. He wants the distillery to be a success because he wants to show that a business can flourish and protect the environment at the same time."

"I admire that about him," Caroline said before she could stop herself.

Pamela studied Caroline curiously.

"Whatever is going on between you and Max seems real." She nursed her teacup. "Don't let it go. Love causes pain, but it's the best part of life."

They chatted for a while and then Caroline went back to the Aspen Inn. She longed to talk to Daphne, but Daphne was furious with her. These were the times when Caroline missed her mother the most. She pictured Anne sitting in the library of the town house in Manhattan. A pile of advance copies would be arranged on the coffee table, Anne would be having a predinner cocktail. They'd discuss the latest *New York Times* bestseller and Caroline would forget about men.

Caroline entered her hotel room and sank on the bed. There was an email from Nick thanking her for her suggestions. She had to find a way to distract herself. She picked up Nina's next letter and began to read.

Dear Anne,

Well, Christmas is over and New York is preparing for New Year's Eve. If I'm too old for Christmas, I'm much too old for New Year's Eve. All those crowds shivering in Times Square and waiting for the ball to drop. And it's so commercialized these days. In the 1970s, CBS covered the drop and Guy Lombardo's orchestra played "Auld Lang Syne," and that was it. Now NBC has a full day of programming. People must get so tired of watching, they turn off the television before the countdown.

It's still a wonderful time of year. I've always loved the week between Christmas and New Year's. Most offices are closed and the newspapers are filled with happy Christmas stories.

The week in Vermont was the exception. I thought it would be relaxing. I even imagined doing some writing while the contest winner pottered around the farm and Teddy snoozed in front of the fireplace. It turned out the opposite. James wasn't some housewife who delighted in trading chocolate chip cookie recipes for learning how to milk a cow. And Teddy had more energy than he ever displayed in New York. All he wanted was to stir up trouble and he was good at it. On the fourth day, everything began to go downhill.

I woke up with a crick in my neck and the worst kind of hangover. What did I expect? Teddy was right, the sofa was lumpy. I didn't bring my sleeping pills, so I drank three shots of peach brandy to fall asleep. Whoever invented peach brandy should be led straight to the guillotine. It tastes as bad as it sounds.

When I finally staggered into the kitchen, James was preparing pancakes and Teddy was sitting at the table, with a piece of paper in front of him and a pencil behind his ear.

"If James wasn't a doctor, we could hire him as our chef after we're married," Teddy said happily. "These are the best pancakes I've ever tasted."

"Barbara's Pies expanded to include other products years ago," James said, sliding a stack of pancakes onto another plate.

I wasn't hungry but I ate a pancake. Listening to myself chew was easier than hearing Teddy's peppy tone.

"The wedding is in four days." Teddy consulted his notes. "I've made a list. If we work as a team, we can get everything done in time."

"What's there to do? We'll stand in front of the fireplace and exchange rings," I said.

Teddy looked at me as if I were Custer at the Little Bighorn and had just suggested going into battle wearing our pajamas and carrying toothbrushes instead of rifles.

"Do you think I'd let my bride get married without some fanfare?" he remarked indignantly. "I'm going to drive to Burlington to buy the rings. I wanted platinum, it lasts longer. But I called and all they have is gold."

I stopped myself from rolling my eyes. As if this marriage had to last. I'd get it annulled as soon as we went back to New York.

"Then there are the flowers," Teddy continued. "The flower shop in town is closed during Christmas week. I called one of the neighbors and she told me about a friend who makes dried flower arrangements. I'm going to go there and pick them up."

"How did you know a neighbor's phone number?" I asked before I could stop myself. If I was really Laura Carter, I'd have an address book with the numbers of my neighbors, like I had in New York.

"I helped myself to your address book," Teddy said without missing a beat. "Between the flowers and the rings, I'll be busy all day and I'll need the car. So, I thought James could help you pick out the wedding dress."

There was a pitcher of orange juice on the table. If only I had a bottle of vodka. I would have drunk orange juice and vodka until all this wedding talk was over.

"James is the witness, not the maid of honor," I protested. "Besides, we're hardly going to find an open wedding shop during Christmas week."

"That's the amazing thing." Teddy beamed. "The neighbor told me about a wedding dress boutique in Stowe that's open. Apparently, the owner is French and imports the latest styles. And I can't think of anyone who'd be better at helping you than James."

This is where Teddy's conniving really came to the forefront.

"I did a little research at the town library on Barbara's Pies. James is being modest, his mother is as well known in fashion circles as she is for running the company. She's attended the fashion shows in Paris for years and she used to take James when he was a child."

I looked at James in surprise.

"My father doesn't like to travel, so she took me instead," James said. "I'd be happy to help you pick out a wedding dress."

Teddy scribbled on his list. He handed me a piece of paper.

"It's settled then. Here's the name and address of the wedding dress salon. Stowe is a forty-minute drive so you should leave after breakfast. It's supposed to snow later today."

I couldn't figure out what Teddy was doing, but I was sure he was up to no good. I had no choice but to follow his directions.

I was going to have a white wedding after all.

James and I hardly spoke on the way to Stowe. It had snowed overnight, and the scenery was spectacular. Fields covered in snow, sugar maple trees with snow-covered branches, and as we approached Stowe, Mount Mansfield, alive with skiers.

Even in the 1970s, Stowe was posher than other towns in Vermont. It attracted a European crowd, and the main street was filled with French clothing stores like Courrèges and Pierre Cardin.

The wedding shop was called Madame Eloise and it had plate-glass windows. Inside, it was modern and elegant at the same time. White wool carpet, glass cabinets filled with bridal accessories: triple-strand pearl chokers, a blue Wedgwood brooch, shoes so delicate they appeared to be made of spun sugar.

A woman in her mid-forties approached us. She glanced from me to James.

"Welcome, I am Madame Eloise. We don't often have a bride shopping for a dress with the groom."

My cheeks turned the color of Madame Eloise's lipstick. I explained that James wasn't the groom.

"A relative then?"

James stepped forward and shook her hand.

"James Stanley, a close friend." He gave a cheeky grin. "I'm here to make sure that Laura is the most beautiful bride in Vermont."

Madame Eloise brought out three dresses, each more sophisticated than the last.

I never had much interest in clothes, but I did live in New York. I had browsed through the sales racks at Bloomingdale's. So, I couldn't help falling in love with each dress. A knee-length white silk with a velvet cape. A pale pink sheath, slit up the side. And my favorite: an ivory satin gown with long bell sleeves and a sash waist.

Madame Eloise agreed with my selection, and James handed her his credit card.

"What are you doing?" I asked in alarm.

"The bride can't pay for her own wedding dress," he said easily. "Teddy will pay me back."

The sale was complete before I could argue. The mood felt different when we walked out. I had an inkling of what Teddy was up to.

Standing in front of the three-way mirrors, with Madame Eloise fussing over me, I had felt like a bride. It was the most wonderful feeling. Like standing on a mountaintop, and feeling that your whole life was ahead of you.

Something felt different between James and me too. He had seen a softer side of me. And I know that I looked beautiful in that dress. My waist was small and my legs seemed even longer.

He suggested we have lunch before we went back to the farm and I agreed.

We sat in a trendy après-ski restaurant and shared a cheeseburger and steak fries.

"You should include photos of your wedding in an upcoming column," James suggested. "I can take them, I'm a good photographer."

I almost choked on my french fry. What would happen if wedding photos of Nina Buckley and Teddy Chandler III appeared in Laura Carter's column?

"That's not a good idea. Readers form their own pictures of Laura's fiancé in their head. Teddy might not live up to their expectations."

James ate a bite of the burger. "You talk like Laura is a different person."

Where is the vodka bottle when a girl needs one!

"Sometimes she feels like another person." I gave a little laugh. "That's what comes from writing about myself for a living."

Somehow, I had to change the subject. I asked him about Rhonda in Geneva.

"Actually, we broke up last night. I called her after I went to bed and she admitted she met someone. I had a sense it was coming, we've been apart for so long."

I made a noncommittal noise and concentrated on the burger.

"It made me think about marriage. Are you sure you and Teddy are ready?"

"Of course we're ready, we've been engaged for almost two years," I blurted out.

"That's funny, I read some of your columns." James frowned. "Teddy did that surprise engagement in the snow cave last month."

I had forgotten about the snow cave! Margaret should have sent me to the farm with a page of notes.

"The engagement was unofficial for a long time, but we both knew we found the right one."

"Sometimes you don't seem sure, and you don't sleep together," James prodded. "You've been sleeping on the couch."

"Teddy snores. It's worse in the wintertime."

"I'd never sleep apart from the woman I love," James said. "And he could treat you better. He bosses you around."

That one hit home. No one bossed Nina Buckley around.

"Teddy doesn't mean any of it. He's really very sweet, he doesn't show that side of him in public."

When I looked up at James, he was gazing at me. He really was handsome. Rhonda didn't realize what she was giving up.

"You're one of the most beautiful, intelligent women I've ever met," James said. There was something odd in his voice. "If you were my fiancée, I'd wait on you hand and foot."

Before I could respond, James leaned forward and kissed me. His mouth was warm and tasted of ketchup. For one crazy moment I kissed him back. Then we pulled apart.

Thankfully we were in a booth in the back, and no one saw us. But what was I thinking! The last thing I needed was to get involved with James. He didn't even know who I really was.

"I shouldn't have done that," James apologized.

"It wasn't anything. You're upset about Rhonda."

"I wish that was the case but you're wrong," James sighed. "I've felt something for you since I arrived at the farm. You remind me of my mother and my grandmother—a career woman who is softer than she seems. Most men don't understand women like that, but I do. They're so capable, but they still want a man to take care of them."

I thought about James's words. Women at that time wanted to do everything for themselves. But James had a point. I wanted Teddy to treat me like men treated Gwendolyn Arthur. Someone to cherish and adore.

"I'm engaged," I reminded James. "Teddy and I are getting married on New Year's Eve."

James pushed away his plate.

"I'm your guest and I've only stirred up trouble," he said worriedly. "Should I tell Teddy what happened or will you?"

The last thing I had thought about was telling Teddy! But it didn't matter. The marriage would be annulled soon.

"You can tell him." I shrugged. "He'll understand it better coming from you."

That's when I understood Teddy's game. He suspected that James had a crush on me. And he wanted to prove that anyone could make a mistake in a relationship. He wasn't to blame for what happened between him and Gwendolyn.

But you see, Anne, Teddy wasn't the only clever one. I came up with a plan to pay him back.

Suddenly I was looking forward to the wedding. It was going to be the most memorable New Year's Eve I'd had in years.

Hugs and kisses,
Nina

Caroline set the paper down on the stack. Tomorrow, she'd ask the concierge if she could scan Nina's letters and email them to herself. They were so full of wisdom, she didn't want to risk losing the paper copies.

Right now, all she could think of was Max.

She thought about her mother and her lover the previous summer. Had they told each other how they felt? Perhaps Anne's lover only confessed his feelings in the letter from Santa's Little Red Mailbox and she had never known. Or he had said he was in love with her and Anne was too unsure about her future to respond?

Caroline had to tell Max how she felt about him. But what if she had already hurt him too much?

Outside, the clouds had cleared and it was a bright winter day. Christmas was the time for miracles. There had to be one saved for her.

Chapter Twenty-one

Caroline was about to go and look for Max when her phone buzzed. It was a text from Daphne.

"Are you in your room? I need to talk to you, it's urgent."

Caroline wondered what Daphne wanted. They weren't speaking to each other.

"I was about to leave but I can wait," Caroline texted back.

Daphne appeared a few minutes later. The cable-knit sweater was tied around her waist and her hair was pulled into a messy ponytail.

"Luke and I got into another fight." Daphne sank onto the bed. "It was about you."

"About me?" Caroline repeated in surprise.

Ever since Luke had sent Daphne all the roses and apologized for not telling her about his parents, everything had been going well. They spent the morning with the minister and afterward they sat in a coffee shop and wrote their vows.

"I've always been a terrible writer. But the words just flowed," Daphne said. "Luke couldn't stop writing. Every time he glanced up at me, it was as if he had discovered some precious gem."

Then Daphne told him about Daphne and Caroline's most

recent fight. Luke said they couldn't get married if Caroline wasn't the maid of honor.

"He'd rather postpone the wedding than get married without you there." Daphne twisted her diamond ring. "At first, I was furious. I said all kinds of things. That he was using our fight as an excuse to chicken out at the last minute. He and I were supposed to be a team. Nothing should come between us, not even my sister."

Daphne looked at Caroline guiltily. Her expression clouded over.

"Eventually I realized he was right. I'd never forgive myself if you weren't at my wedding."

Caroline's own eyes were wet. She felt exactly the same.

"Of course I'll be there," Caroline said. "You're the most important person to me in the world."

"Luke left the coffee shop before I admitted that I was wrong." Daphne kept talking. "I went back to our room but he wasn't there. His backpack is gone and some of his clothes. I think he plans on getting another hotel room."

It was Christmas week. All the hotels would be full.

"He wanted to give me some space," Daphne said worriedly. "But what if he rethinks the whole thing? We've been together for such a short time and we've already had fights. The problem is I'm in love with him," she sighed miserably. "Nothing changes how I feel."

"Luke is in love with you too." Caroline gave a watery smile. "I finally understand how you feel. I'm falling in love with Max, and I've pushed him away."

She told Daphne about her visit with Max's mother.

"Max thinks I only want a fling, he might not have feelings for me."

The color was coming back to Daphne's cheeks. Her eyes were bright blue. "I have an idea. Do you remember when we were kids and my new puppy chewed Mom's books? I was afraid to tell her, I knew she'd be furious," Daphne recalled. "You told her for me and explained how guilty I felt. Instead of getting angry at me, she understood. Puppies could be so mischievous and it wasn't my fault."

Caroline gave a small smile. Daphne had been nine and she'd been terrified the puppy would be taken away. Anne was upset—the books were signed first editions—but her anger subsided before she approached Daphne.

"And remember when you were in high school and had a crush on my friend Amy's older brother? You wanted to invite him to the Sadie Hawkins dance but he barely knew who you were. I asked you to take me and Amy to the movies when I knew he'd be there. We all ended up sitting together. He had a great time and went with you to the dance."

Amy's brother's name was Parker. The dance had been fun. But Parker was three years older and about to go off to college.

"What are you getting at?" Caroline prompted.

"You talk to Luke. Tell him how terrible I feel, and that he's right," Daphne suggested. "I'll talk to Max. I'll say that I've never seen you have feelings for a guy. He has to give you another chance."

Caroline turned the idea over in her mind. "I like it. But Max might not be at home, his mother said he was acting like a wounded bear. And you don't know where Luke is."

Whenever Caroline really needed to think, she went to her office at the publishing house. Being around her authors' books made her feel better. Max would most likely go to the distillery; he felt the same about the rye whiskey in its huge vats.

"And I can ask Nick to help find Luke," Caroline said. "He works at the Limelight, he knows every hotel in Aspen."

Daphne gave Caroline a hug. "We'll find them. And they'll listen to us. It's all going to work out. It has to, it's Christmas week, everything is magic."

Nick was in the middle of his shift when Caroline arrived. She waited for him in the little supply-room office.

"I told my manager I had to polish the silverware." Nick took a stack of napkins from the shelf. "Is everything all right?"

Caroline told him about Luke and Daphne.

"Most of the hotels are full, but the Hotel Jerome had a cancellation this morning. I heard the front desk direct someone there."

Caroline nodded. "I'll try it."

"Before you go, I have news," Nick said happily.

"Don't tell me you already made the changes from our notes." Caroline grinned. "I thought more about Josh after I left. I love the next chapter, where he surprises Maggie with a romantic dinner. The gesture redeems him."

She always felt better when she was discussing an author's work. Like an electric charge was shooting through her body.

"It's not about the book, it's Savannah." Nick folded a napkin. "She called a few hours ago."

"But Savannah left more than five years ago," Caroline reminded him. "You haven't even been in touch."

"She's traveled everywhere. She spent a year on an archaeological dig in Greece, and a couple of years in Croatia and Malta. She's back in the States, and she wants to come to Aspen and see me."

Caroline had an uneasy feeling. If Nick fell in love with Savannah again, she'd only hurt him.

"Are you sure that's a good idea?"

"It's nothing romantic," Nick assured her. "We were best friends too. And she's been to many places. I'll get inspiration for my next novel."

Nick had a determined look on his face. Nothing she could say would change his mind. And it really wasn't her business.

Caroline thanked him and walked down Main Street to Hotel Jerome. The lobby was filled with gingerbread houses from their gingerbread-making contest.

The winning house resembled the cottage in "Hansel and Gretel." The front door was made from gingerbread men, and the walls were red-and-white candy canes. The chimney was graham cracker with white icing, and a witch with a licorice nose peered out the window.

Caroline explained her dilemma to the front desk.

"I can't give out names or room numbers but we did have a guest check in this morning," the man said. "It was a last-minute reservation for one night."

Caroline was almost certain that it was Luke. She sat in the lobby and waited.

An hour later, Luke appeared. He wore a flannel shirt and corduroy slacks. Caroline could see why Daphne was in love with him. He was clean-cut with that thick sandy-blond hair and those deep blue eyes. He and Daphne were so alike, they looked good together.

Luke asked Caroline what she was doing there.

"I need to talk to you in private. It's very important."

He took her to his room. It was beautifully furnished in dark woods. The bed had a black walnut headboard. A birch armchair was upholstered in blue velvet, and a Christmas tree decorated with red and green ornaments stood by the fireplace.

"This was the only available room in Aspen," Luke said. "It ate up some of my honeymoon budget, but there might not be a honeymoon."

Caroline sat in the armchair. "Daphne told me everything. Of course I'll be at the wedding."

"When Daphne and I met, she talked about you all the time." Luke frowned. "I'm afraid I'm coming between you."

Caroline thought about her relationship with Daphne. All sisters fought. But it had never been like this. Daphne had always listened to her.

"It's not your fault, Daphne is a grown woman," Caroline said to Luke. "You're helping her figure out who she is."

"I don't want to be one of those couples who separate from the family," Luke said. "When we have children, you'll be their only aunt."

Caroline gave a wide smile. "I'll be the best aunt you've ever seen. I'll buy them so many Christmas presents, they'll need their own tree."

"It's not about presents, it's about being a family." Luke was still frowning. "Daphne told me dozens of stories. Christmas with your mom and her dad at the cabin. Trips to Europe, the month after you both found out your mom was sick. She put you on a pedestal but not in a bad way. We all need role models, it makes us better people. If her relationship with you changes because of me, I'd never forgive myself."

Caroline recalled her own memories of growing up. The last vacation with Walter and Anne, just before Walter died. One of his patients had a house on the Jersey Shore. Daphne was twenty, and the host's son had a crush on Daphne. He invited Daphne to a party, and Daphne and Anne spent a whole day shopping for a dress.

Caroline said she was happy reading a book at the house, but she couldn't help feeling left out. When they returned from shopping it was even worse. Daphne spent ages fixing her hair, while Anne pulled out her makeup and earrings for Daphne to wear.

Caroline was never the kind of daughter who wanted to go clothes shopping, and she didn't like to cook. She and Anne shared their love of books, that had always been enough.

"I always felt like I had to protect Daphne." Caroline stared at the ornaments on the Christmas tree. "She was one of those beautiful babies—like a porcelain doll with blue eyes and white-blond hair. People used to crowd around her stroller and I was afraid she'd get smothered. And she was always so kind—giving food to homeless people when we were teenagers.

"Later, I worried about her falling in love with the wrong guy. Neither of us had proper father figures—Walter was so reserved and I never knew my father. Now I think I got it all wrong. Mom was capable of falling in love—it just might not have been with Walter. And somehow Daphne learned all about love. No matter how the two of you fight, her feelings for you aren't going to change." Caroline took a deep breath.

She had never spoken to anyone about Daphne like that before. But Luke needed to know how special she was. "I'm the one who's terrible at love. I pushed Max away, now he's gone."

"If Max has feelings for you, nothing will keep him away," Luke counseled. "Just being apart from Daphne for one night is hard. I feel like a piece of me is missing."

"You don't have to stay here," Caroline said.

"I already paid for the room. It's much more luxurious than the Aspen Inn." He gave a sly grin. "But you're right, there's no reason to waste it on myself. I'll take Daphne to dinner at the hotel's Prospect restaurant and we'll stay here afterward." He paused. "You're pretty special, Caroline. I'm glad you're going to be my sister-in-law."

Caroline walked back to the Aspen Inn. She couldn't wait to tell Daphne about Luke.

Daphne and Luke had known each other a short time, yet they had such a strong bond. She wondered about her mother in Aspen last summer. She pictured Anne sitting at an outdoor café after listening to a panel, glancing up to see a handsome man at a nearby table. Was there an instant attraction and was it equal on both sides?

Love was so mysterious. Caroline considered the things she loved about Max. His passion for the distillery, his attachment to Lily, the closeness to his mother. And his good looks, of course. She loved the way he looked in a turtleneck, and the warm hazel of his eyes. What she loved most was his smile. When he smiled at her, she felt part of something special. It was the best feeling in the world.

Daphne was standing in front of the Aspen Inn, holding hands with a little girl. It took Caroline a moment to recognize Lily.

"Lily, what are you doing here?" Caroline asked. "Where's Max?"

Lily wore a reindeer sweater with corduroy slacks. Her dark hair was brushed smoothly under her chin.

"Uncle Max did a code three," Lily said matter-of-factly.

"A code three?" Caroline repeated, puzzled.

"Let's go for a walk. Lily will explain everything."

Daphne had gone to Max's parents' house to see if he was there. Lily and Pamela were home.

"Max took me sledding, then we went to the store to get ingredients to make cake pops. I was going to make them with Grandma tonight, but now Daphne is going to help me instead. Daphne and Luke got in a fight, so she has nothing to do."

Daphne gave Caroline a sheepish grin. "I was talking to Pamela and Lily overheard us. Lily had good advice, she's very wise for her age."

"I told Daphne to bring Luke some cake pops. Guys can't resist sweets," Lily explained.

"Max isn't at the distillery," Daphne continued. "No one knows where he went."

"That's what code three means," Lily said. "Emily's father goes code three sometimes. But he always comes back. Emily's mom says men are like puppies, they find their way home."

Caroline smiled at Daphne. "I just saw Luke. He's got a wonderful surprise for you tonight."

"He still wants to get married?" Daphne asked hopefully.

"All the buffaloes and bison in Colorado couldn't stop Luke from marrying you." Caroline gave a little laugh.

Daphne's expression was flooded with relief. She looked luminous with her cornflower-blue eyes and blond hair. Daphne was going to be a gorgeous bride, and Caroline was so happy for her.

Lily explained how a code three worked.

Code two meant that someone went to a familiar place to figure out a problem. For instance, Lily's mom drove to the yoga studio when she was upset. Lily's dad went to his medical practice, even if it was the weekend.

"Code two means the person wants to be alone. Once, my dad was worried about my mom, so he took her favorite tacos to the studio. She said she could have ordered takeout if she was hungry. All she wanted was a little peace and quiet."

Code three was more serious. That meant someone had to do heavy thinking. They went somewhere no one could find them.

"Once, Emily's father went all the way to San Francisco. Emily said he had some kind of business problem that was impossible to fix." Lily wrinkled her nose. "He must have figured it out, because he came back with a necklace for Emily's mother, and T-shirts for Emily and her sister."

"How do you know Max went code three?" Caroline asked.

"I could tell Max was upset. He's really good at sledding, but he almost tipped the sled. And at the grocery store, he didn't pay attention. I bought Tic Tacs, and I'm not allowed. My mom says they'll ruin my teeth."

"What should I do?" Caroline wondered.

"You have to wait until Max comes back," Lily counseled. "You can help me and Daphne make cake pops! If we make enough, we can take some to the women's shelter, so their kids have them on New Year's Eve."

"That's a wonderful idea." Daphne beamed. "It will be a girls' night."

Being with Daphne and Lily was just what Caroline needed. But what if Max returned and didn't want to see her? And Luke was going to take Daphne to dinner at Hotel Jerome.

"Why don't we make cake pops now?" Caroline suggested.

They walked together to the Queen Anne mansion on Walnut Street.

It was wonderful to work in the spacious, white kitchen. Pamela joined them for a while. They talked about their favorite writers, and Pamela's upcoming trip to Lisbon to visit the oldest bookstore in the world.

Afterward, Caroline and Daphne walked back to the Aspen Inn. Daphne went up to her room to take a bath and Caroline approached the front desk.

"Good afternoon, Miss Holt. How can I help you?"

"I've been out, I was wondering if there were any messages."

The man flicked through his computer screen. "I'm afraid not, were you expecting something?"

Max hadn't called or texted. She was being silly. She didn't need Max to be happy. She'd take a hot shower and order room service for dinner. There had to be some good Christmas movies on Netflix.

Then she changed her mind. She wasn't going to sit in her room. It was Christmas week in Aspen, there were so many things to do.

"I want to go out this evening. Are there any Christmas concerts or gallery openings? Afterward I'd like to eat somewhere really nice. I love Italian food and I'm a huge fan of French desserts."

The concierge told her about the activities that were part of the 12 Days of Aspen. From 7:00 to 8:00 p.m. there were free hors d'oeuvres and champagne at the Aspen Art Museum, where one could meet local artists. Hotel Jerome was hosting a variety show, and there was an electronic music concert at Belly Up. Or Caroline could attend a night of songs and storytelling at Wheeler Opera House.

The best place to eat was the Ajax Tavern at the Little Nell. Their pasta Bolognese used local Wagyu beef and they served a delicious roasted crème brûlée.

"I'll start with the art gallery, and please make me a reservation at Ajax Tavern," Caroline said when he finished.

"Party of one or two?" he asked.

Caroline gave her widest smile. "Party of one. But make sure they give me a good table."

Chapter Twenty-two

It was almost midnight and Caroline couldn't sleep.

She had had a wonderful night. She wore one of her favorite dresses, a red cashmere wrap dress she bought at a sample sale in New York, and paired it with ankle-high boots and a silver bangle. It was the same outfit she wore when she met Brad at the London Book Fair. This time she wasn't wearing it to pick up men, she wanted to feel attractive and confident for herself.

The hors d'oeuvres at the art museum had been delicious, and the artists were excited to talk about their work. She skipped the concert because the people waiting in line were in their early twenties and she refused to feel old. She sat in on the storytelling at Wheeler Opera House, and afterward had dinner at Ajax Tavern. The pasta Bolognese was perfectly cooked, and she ended up talking to a young Australian woman who encouraged her to attend the Sydney Writers' Festival.

This time when she returned to the Aspen Inn, she didn't ask the concierge if there were any messages. And she forced herself not to check her phone. Lily said there was nothing she could do about a code three. Max had to work out his feelings for himself.

Now she sat in her room and sipped a cup of warm milk and honey. Warm milk usually put her to sleep, but it wasn't working.

Nina's letters sat on the bedside table. She picked up the next letter and began to read.

Dear Anne,

I received thank-you notes from Caroline and Daphne for my Christmas presents. You brought them up so well. It's only a few days after Christmas, they must have mailed the letters the next day!

You're so lucky to have your family. People think writers are introverted and that's often true. But we all need to feel loved and part of something.

I regret not having children. The worst part of growing old is being alone. I could get a little dog like so many New Yorkers, but my place is tiny. Thank God, I have my writing. Sitting down at the laptop is like revisiting an old friend.

I wish I could blame Teddy for where I am now. But long ago I learned that we are all responsible for our own happiness.

When I think back to the week in Vermont, neither of us behaved very well. Teddy started it by asking the minister to marry us and then throwing me and James together to buy the wedding dress. But I was guilty for what happened afterward.

I had to enlist James's help to put my plan into action. I worried about what he'd think. We'd only known each other for a few days. And I was supposed to be Laura Carter, a model of moral fortitude. I broached the subject after our trip to Stowe to buy the wedding dress.

James pulled into the driveway of the farm. Teddy wasn't back yet from running errands.

"It's a marvelous idea," James said when I explained my plan. "Do you think Teddy will fall for it?"

"I'm quite a good actress. I was the star of my high school play," I said modestly. "You must think I'm terribly underhanded. What would your grandmother say if she knew what Laura Carter was planning?"

"On the contrary, I'm impressed," James answered. "I told you I don't think Teddy treats you properly. And my grandmother would approve. She couldn't have built Barbara's Pies into its huge success without behaving a little badly at times, especially when it came to men."

"Then you approve?" I breathed a sigh of relief.

For a moment I wondered what Margaret, my editor, would say if she found out. But she was the one who built the fabric of lies. What was one more?

"It's perfect except for one thing." James stepped out of the car and ran around to open my door. He gave a small smile. "I only wish it was the real thing."

I ran to my bedroom to change clothes before Teddy arrived. I put on the outfit he had given me for my birthday—a turquoise miniskirt with a matching blouse and tall boots. Then I sprayed on his favorite perfume and waited in the living room.

When Teddy arrived, his arms were laden with packages.

"Let me take those from you." I placed them on the

sideboard and handed him a cocktail. "I made you a whiskey sour. James and I picked up a bottle of malt whiskey in Smugglers' Notch."

"You stopped at Smugglers' Notch?" Teddy asked. He sniffed the glass suspiciously.

"Buying the wedding dress went faster than I thought. Afterward we had lunch in Stowe and then I asked James to stop at Smugglers' Notch. It's quite famous in Vermont, during prohibition the smugglers hid their whiskey there."

"It sounds like you had a good time," Teddy said stiffly. I smiled to myself. Teddy was already jealous.

"It was wonderful. James knows all the local history," I gushed. "And we get along so well. In fact, that's what I want to talk about."

"If you're about to tell me that James has a crush on you, I already knew that. But remember, he has a girlfriend. Whatever he says might be flattering, but it will pass."

"He and Rhonda broke up." I paused. I wanted my next words to have their full effect. "James told me that he's fallen in love with me. He asked me to marry him."

Teddy's glass fell on the rug. I bent down to mop it up.

"He did what?" Teddy exclaimed.

"When we were at the history museum in Smugglers' Notch. There was an old photo of a smuggler who proposed to his wife after knowing her for three days. The whole town thought it was only so she would hide him from the border Mounties, but they were in love. The marriage lasted forty years. And James believes in love at first sight."

"You can't be serious!" Teddy exclaimed. "Don't you see? He's only trying to sleep with you!"

"It's the 1970s, not the 1950s, women don't need a ring on their finger to have sex," I shot back. "Though he did kiss me. It was a short kiss but I liked it very much. In fact, I intend to make a habit of it. We're getting married on New Year's Eve."

This time Teddy's face turned pale. I had to avert my eyes so I didn't burst out laughing.

"You and I are getting married on New Year's Eve," he reminded me.

"That's what makes it so easy," I continued gaily. "Father Joseph won't mind if I change grooms."

Teddy's face became even paler. He sank onto the sofa.

"You can't be serious."

"I've never been more serious about anything. James is honest and charming and we have so much in common," I answered. "What do you care? We were going to get our marriage annulled anyway, it saves us a step. This time next week you'll be in Saint Kitts, sipping mai tais with your mother and Gwendolyn."

Teddy gulped his whiskey sour.

"You're the one who broke off the engagement." His voice was low.

"That's what happens when your fiancé's photo is splashed all over the *New York Times* society pages beside another woman, along with the caption that she's the reason you're not married yet."

"I told you that the photographer took pictures of everyone." Teddy sighed as if he were talking to a child. "And the only reason you and I weren't married is because we hadn't figured out the wedding details."

"You mean I wouldn't give in to your mother's demands for a large society wedding."

Teddy walked over to the sideboard. He fixed himself another whiskey sour. Then he sat next to me on the sofa and took my hand.

"If you stop this nonsense with James and marry me for keeps, we'll get married any way you like. And I'll tell my mother to behave herself or she'll never be invited to our house during the holidays. You're headstrong and stubborn, but I love you, Nina. There's never been anyone else and there never will be."

I was overcome with emotion. Teddy had never talked to me like that before. But what if he wasn't telling the truth? He would get what he wanted, and then the tug-of-war between me and his mother would begin all over again. The thing is, I did love him. And love can be blind and hopeful.

I was about to answer when the doorbell rang. I wondered whether it was a neighbor or even Father Joseph.

Instead, when I opened the door, my editor, Margaret, stood outside. She wore a fur coat with a matching muff and hat.

"Margaret!" My jaw dropped. "What are you doing here?"

"Aren't you going to invite me inside?" she demanded. "I'm a New Yorker and I don't care if I'm wearing an entire fox, I've never been so cold in my life."

I'll stop there, Anne. To be honest, writing this part of the story is exhausting. That's why love is for young people. If it's this tiring to write about it at my age, I can't imagine what it would be like to actually fall in love.

You're so lucky to have your youth and your family, Anne. Cherish all of it. It's the best time in life.

Regards,
Nina

Caroline set the letter on the stack. Then she turned off the light, and closed her eyes. Somehow, she had to tell Max how she felt about him. She was leaving in a few short days. What if she didn't get the chance?

Chapter Twenty-three

The next morning was New Year's Eve. Caroline was so excited and anxious, she woke up earlier than she had in months. She resolved to put Max out of her mind. She spent an hour rereading Nick's last revisions to make sure she hadn't missed anything. Then she grabbed a cup of coffee from the inn's restaurant and walked along Main Street. The shops were still closed; a few early-morning skiers lugged their skis to the slopes. She was tempted to share Nina's letters with Daphne. Nina had admired and respected Anne so much. Reading the letters made Caroline feel even closer to their mother. She'd finish them first, then she'd show them to Daphne.

When she arrived back at her room, Daphne was waiting at the door.

"I must have conjured you up, I was thinking about you." Caroline smiled.

It felt good not to be fighting with Daphne.

"I know it's early; Luke had some business calls with the restaurant in Hyde Park." Daphne followed her inside. "And don't start with me that a restaurateur never takes a proper vacation. I don't mind, and think of the perks. It turns out that Luke is a better cook than I am."

"You didn't know that he cooked?" Caroline asked.

"We've made lots of dishes together, but he lets me take the lead." Daphne perched on the bed. "Last night we had a wonderful dinner at Prospect. He told me about helping his parents at the restaurant in Paris during the summers. He learned to make crêpes suzette. We're going to serve them at the reception his parents are giving us next summer."

"They're going to give you a reception?" Caroline repeated.

Daphne had never looked so happy. Her cheeks glowed and her smile reached all the way to her eyes.

"We had a Zoom call with them last night," Daphne gushed. "It will only be a small reception at the farm in Wisconsin. Luke and his father are going to do the cooking."

Caroline gave Daphne a quick hug. "I'm so happy for you. You deserve to be part of a good family."

"I have a good family. I have you." Daphne hugged her back. "I also came to see if you've heard from Max."

Caroline flinched. If Daphne hadn't dared her to have a proper relationship with Max, she wouldn't have opened her heart. But Nina was right. Everyone was responsible for their own happiness. Caroline's feelings for Max had nothing to do with Daphne.

"I haven't heard from him."

"You will," Daphne said confidently. "A code three can't last forever. Max will come back."

"What if he doesn't?" Caroline felt the air leave her lungs. "Maybe I'm not really in love. It's Christmas in Aspen and it feels so romantic. But then I think about him. He's so passionate about the distillery, and he's kind and warm." She looked at

Daphne. "I didn't know I could feel like this. What if I never do again?"

Daphne squeezed her hand.

"You've made the first step, you've opened yourself up to love," Daphne reminded her. "From here it's like getting on a snow tube at the top of the mountain and simply pointing it downhill."

Caroline didn't say what she was thinking. The snow tube could spin out at the bottom and she'd go flying.

"You're much better at this than me," Caroline sighed. "I should stick to my career and being an aunt when you and Luke have children."

"You can do it all. Max would be lucky to have you." Daphne stood up. "What you need is to get drunk tonight, so you don't think about him. Zane's Tavern is doing a Western theme for New Year's Eve. Come with us. Everyone wears Western clothes and sings campfire songs."

Caroline nodded. "It sounds perfect."

Daphne left and Caroline gathered her edit notes. She walked over to the Limelight Hotel to see Nick.

Nick was in the little office, tapping at his laptop.

"I spend more time in here than I do at my apartment," he said when she entered. "I never knew editing could be fun. It was different when I edited the manuscript for Anne, I was terrified that she'd hate it. Now I know Josh and Maggie so well. I'm confident they won't let me down."

Caroline agreed with him. Authors often felt that way about their characters. The characters became so real, they carried the story by themselves.

"The section where Josh is first betrayed by Maggie needs more detail." Caroline flipped through her notes. "Until then, Josh and

Maggie are perfectly in tune. Then she does something without thinking about him. How does that make Josh feel and can he trust Maggie again?"

Nick ran his hands through his hair. He was wearing his hotel uniform and black sneakers.

"Josh is shaken, of course. But he can't blame Maggie, he hasn't given her any assurances."

"Maybe he should," Caroline suggested. "He could promise that if she stays in Colorado, he'll give her a future that doesn't include working at the pharmacy."

"How would he do that? He doesn't have money or connections."

Caroline gave it some thought. "People often do things they don't think they're capable of when they're in love. You stayed at the ranch for Savannah. How did that make you feel when she eventually left?"

Nick's face took on a pensive expression. He rubbed his chin.

"The first time I felt like it was my fault," he recalled. "I resolved to do anything to make the relationship work.

"It was September and the summer rush at the dude ranch was over. In the fall, the ranch was mainly filled with corporate groups or families celebrating birthdays. But there were long stretches without reservations. I kept busy with chores and writing my novel, but I worried that Savannah would get bored. My parents were still paying her and she had her own chores, but it was different than during the summer. Savannah was a sorority girl from Atlanta, I was afraid that she needed something more.

"I was counting out my tips from the last group. It had been a tech company, and they were quite generous. Savannah entered my room. She was wearing an elegant green dress and high boots, which surprised me. When there weren't any guests, we ate by ourselves in the kitchen.

"She couldn't have dinner, she was going in to Aspen to a gallery opening. I suggested I join her and we grab a bite afterward, but she reminded me that I planned on working on my novel.

"She was right, of course. If I put it off, the book would never get written. I leaned forward and kissed her. I loved her scent— some kind of lavender perfume. I told her I'd save some of my mother's casserole and we'd sit on the porch and eat it.

"After Savannah left, I wrote for two hours. Then my mother asked me to pick up whipped cream for her pecan pie. If she hadn't, I would have found another excuse to drive into Aspen.

"I looked in the windows of the art galleries on Main Street but Savannah wasn't inside. I had an uneasy feeling. Savannah always wanted me to do things with her, why hadn't she wanted me to attend the gallery opening?

"I bought the whipped cream and started walking back to the car. Just as I turned down Main Street, a couple entered the Little Nell. I couldn't see the woman's face but I recognized the man. His name was Oliver. He was the CFO of the tech company who had stayed at the dude ranch. I remember him telling me he had a beach house in Santa Monica and a Porsche.

"The couple entered the hotel and the woman turned. It was Savannah.

"What was Oliver still doing in Aspen? Were he and Savannah having an intimate dinner in the hotel dining room? I debated approaching them but I couldn't afford to make a scene. The Little Nell sent guests to the dude ranch for horseback-riding lessons.

"Instead, I drove back to the dude ranch. Summer had gone

by so quickly. Long days leading tour groups, followed by dinner with the other ranch hands at the kitchen table. But we had a wonderful time: evening strolls around the ranch breathing in the crisp night air, making love in my bed, manning the coffeepot together the following morning.

"Yet I hadn't promised Savannah a future. Agreeing not to go back to college was enough for me. But was it enough for Savannah? What if she needed an assurance that what we had would last? Something that would stop her from dating a guy like Oliver, who could promise her a beach house in California and a flashy car.

"I couldn't afford an engagement ring and I wasn't ready to get engaged. First, I wanted to finish my novel and get a publishing contract. But I had to do something to show Savannah my intentions. I drove back to the jewelry store on Main Street. The salesgirl helped me select a silver band set with tiny diamonds and rubies. She called it a promise ring. That sounded like something high schoolers would give to each other, but the ring was perfect.

"Savannah arrived back at the ranch as I was eating a piece of pecan pie. She cut a piece of pie and sat down beside me. I asked about the gallery opening and she said she wasn't fond of the artist, but she met some interesting people. I blurted out Oliver's name and she asked how I knew he was there. She accused me of spying on her. I had never seen her so furious. Her eyes flashed and she kept flinging her hair over her shoulders.

"I told her I wasn't spying, my mom sent me to buy whipped cream. Savannah explained that she ran into Oliver at the gallery. He was staying at the Little Nell because he had some business in Aspen, and he suggested they have dinner.

"I swallowed the rest of my pie and reached into my pocket for the jewelry box. I told her the salesgirl called it a promise ring. I didn't know what it was, but I didn't want what we had to end. She kissed me and said she felt the same. I slipped the ring on her finger and kissed her back. We both had another slice of pecan pie and went up to my bedroom."

Nick stopped. He leaned back in his chair and grinned at Caroline.

Caroline glanced up from her edit notes. "That's a wonderful story. You should add something similar to the scene where Josh sees Maggie sitting with a guy at the soda fountain next to the pharmacy."

Nick nodded his head vigorously. "I like that idea. Something that shows how serious Josh is about Maggie."

"Exactly. Even when a relationship is going well, one half of the couple often hides her feelings because she's afraid of getting hurt. But no one is a mind reader."

They talked about the next chapter, and Caroline got up to leave.

"Savannah is coming to Aspen, I want you to meet her," Nick said.

"Savannah is coming here, now?" Caroline asked.

"Just for the day," Nick said. "Her parents rented a place in Vail and she's staying with them."

"You didn't tell me her family were skiers." Caroline tried to keep her voice even. The news made her worried about Nick. It couldn't be a good idea for him to see Savannah again.

"I never met her parents and Savannah didn't ski. Apparently, she learned a couple of years ago and loves it."

"I'd love to meet her," Caroline said slowly.

"Don't have that terrified look," Nick said with a laugh. "Our relationship ended years ago. I'd never let myself fall in love with Savannah again."

Caroline wandered down Main Street. A soft snow was falling and people were returning from the slopes. Children tugged at their parents' coats, and shop windows were ablaze with Christmas lights.

She wondered where Max was and what he was doing. Nick was wrong. Once you experienced love, you couldn't decide not to be in love anymore. It took on a life of its own.

Tonight she'd join Luke and Daphne at Zane's Tavern. Then she'd drink enough whiskey that she'd stop thinking about Max altogether.

Chapter Twenty-four

Zane's Tavern advertised itself as the Aspen bar for locals. The interior was slightly cheesy, with posters on the wall, and a bar lined with unmatched glasses. There was a large-screen television and a small stage for karaoke.

The prices on the menu were lower than at the restaurants at the Aspen Inn or the Limelight, and the selections included the kinds of things tourists who were watching their weight avoided. Mozzarella sticks and mac 'n' cheese egg rolls. A Zane's burger that sounded delicious—a bacon burger with sautéed onions and mushrooms.

Caroline sat at a table in the back. Daphne sat beside her and Luke was at the bar, getting their third round of drinks. Caroline had already drunk more than she felt comfortable with—but Daphne and Luke insisted she enter the karaoke contest and she needed the alcohol for courage.

"I don't know if I can get up there," Caroline said, eyeing the stage.

"Luke and I are going to do it, you promised you would too,"

Daphne reminded her. "It will be fun. We only have a couple more nights in Aspen."

Caroline gulped. Tonight was New Year's Eve. At seven o'clock she'd meet Anne's lover in front of Santa's Little Red Mailbox. What if he didn't show up, or for some reason they missed each other? Her trip would have been for nothing. And then there was Max. He still hadn't called or texted.

"You're going to be a bride so soon." Caroline changed the subject.

Daphne's eyes sparkled in the low light of the bar.

"It feels like when we were kids, and I'd start wishing it was next Christmas as soon as Christmas was over. This time I don't have to wait a whole year, the wedding is on New Year's Day!"

"You're going to be beautiful. I can't wait for Luke to see the wedding dress."

Daphne gave a small laugh. "He keeps asking me to model it for him, I told him absolutely not. I hope he likes it." She bit her lip. "I bought him a groom's gift, a pair of Western boots to remind him of our time in Aspen."

Daphne prattled on about the wedding, and Caroline tried to listen. But her mind kept going to Max. Would he really let her go back to New York without contacting her?

"We mustn't be good company. You look too pensive for someone at a Western dive bar on New Year's Eve." Luke grinned at Caroline when he joined them. He set three glasses and a basket of chicken wings on the table.

Caroline brought her mind back to the present.

"It's Daphne's fault. She insists I do karaoke."

"That's why we're here," Luke said. "The winner gets a six-foot cheesesteak hoagie to share."

Caroline took a sip of her cocktail. It was so strong, her throat burned.

"What is this?" she asked Luke.

"The bartender recommended it. He calls it 'the Whistle Pig.' Aspen rye whiskey with orange juice and calvados syrup. The syrup is supposed to hide the potency of the whiskey."

"It's not doing a good job," Caroline groaned.

She felt slightly better. She thought about her job and the publishing house. She was confident that Claudia would love Nick's book. When Caroline returned to New York, she'd swear off love and go back to her little flings. In a few months Max would be a pleasant memory of Christmas in Aspen.

The first few singers got up onstage, and then it was Caroline's turn.

Caroline had signed up to sing Mariah Carey's "All I Want for Christmas Is You." Caroline and Daphne and Anne used to watch Mariah Carey's Christmas special together at the cabin. Anne rarely watched television, but she enjoyed doing anything with Caroline and Daphne.

The Whistle Pig calmed her nerves and she belted out the first few verses. Then the door opened and a man entered. He walked to the bar and Caroline saw his face. It was Max. He wore a suede jacket and heavy winter boots.

She glanced around for the emcee. She wanted to finish the song early and give back the microphone. But he was moving around the audience. The music finally ended. The lights came on and everyone applauded.

"You deserve another Whiskey Pig for that," Luke said when she returned to the table.

Daphne smiled at Caroline. "Luke was right, you were fantastic."

Suddenly she couldn't take it anymore. The room began to spin, and she felt dizzy. She wiped the sweat from her forehead and grabbed her jacket.

"I'm sorry, I need some air."

Outside, the air was bitter cold. A few trucks were parked in the parking lot, and snow was piled against a wall.

The bar door opened and a man walked outside. It took a moment for her to realize it was Max. She couldn't let him see how she felt.

"If you came out here to tell me I can't sing, I already know." She kept her voice light. "Luke and Daphne made me enter the karaoke contest."

"You were great." Max's easy tone matched her own. "In fact, I have secret information that you're going to win. I'm jealous. Sam makes the best cheesesteak hoagie in the Rockies."

Caroline smiled in spite of herself. Just standing beside Max made her happy.

"Is Sam the chef?" she asked.

"He's also in charge of the bar purchases," Max said. "I came tonight because he started selling my rye whiskey."

Caroline let out a moan. "Don't tell me you're responsible for the Whistle Pig. It's so strong, my mouth was on fire."

"Blame Sam, he has a heavy hand with alcohol." Max grinned. His voice dropped. "Lily made me come. I'm glad I did. It was nice to see you let your hair down."

"You saw Lily?" Caroline asked.

"I slept at the distillery last night," Max said. "But there's only so long a guy can exist without a hot shower and a fridge filled with something besides the ingredients for rye whiskey cocktail recipes."

"You'll never attract customers to the distillery if you only serve celery garnishes and olives on the end of toothpicks," Caroline agreed with a laugh.

"I was going to work on the food menu but I couldn't concentrate," Max admitted. "Today, my ankle finally felt a little better, so I went for a little walk. Then I went home and Lily said she told you that I had done a code three."

Caroline couldn't decipher Max's expression. Caroline thought about other times recently when she needed courage. When the nurse called from the hospital and told Caroline to come right away, Anne was dying. At her mother's funeral, when she had to smile and hug people. The other mourners meant well, but all Caroline wanted was to crawl into bed with Daphne and cry. Driving up to the cabin the first time after Anne died, knowing Anne wouldn't be there, waiting for her.

She needed that courage now to tell Max how she felt about him.

"Lily said I couldn't disturb a code three, you had to come back by yourself." Caroline's voice was slow and deliberate. "If I had found you, I would have apologized for asking you to leave the other night. It was my fault. The evening was going so well, and I pushed you away."

"You said you wanted a fling," Max said. "A hot Christmas romance with no strings attached. But every time we got closer to ending up in bed, you pulled away. I still don't understand."

"Is that all you wanted?" Caroline asked.

"We're not talking about me." Max's voice turned harder. "What does it matter what I wanted if you're not interested anymore?"

Caroline nodded. It made sense that Max was upset.

"I was certain I only wanted a fling. And you were the same. When we met, you said women don't understand how much effort went into running the distillery."

"But I never closed myself off to love," Max returned. "You and I are different that way. I want to be in love, it's the best part of life."

Caroline took a deep breath. This was her last chance.

"Apparently, we aren't that different. The reason I pushed you away is I discovered I didn't want a fling after all. For the first time, I wanted something with a future. I started falling in love with you and I didn't know how to tell you."

Max let out a whistle. "It's pretty easy. You say it like this: I'm falling for you, Caroline. You're beautiful and smart and kind. You put your sister before yourself, and you're warm and gracious to my mother and Lily. This might not be the right time, but it probably never is with love. The important thing is to give love a chance."

Caroline waited before she responded. Her heart beat faster and she gazed at Max.

"Is that how you feel?" she finally whispered.

"I've been trying to tell you for days. You never seemed to listen. When you pulled away it was the final straw. I knew it was time to walk away."

Caroline leaned forward and kissed him. Their kiss was long and tasted of rye whiskey.

"I didn't want you to walk away," she said when they parted. "I still don't."

Max put his arm around her. "It's not going to be easy, but we'll figure it out. You can work from Aspen part of the month, and I'll visit New York on the weekends."

"I can't work from Aspen," Caroline said without thinking. "I go into the office every day."

"Everyone works remotely these days. I'm sure your publisher will allow it." Max shrugged.

Caroline told him that her job was tenuous at the moment. If she didn't put in extra effort, Claudia would have to let her go.

"Plus, it's not just being in the office, it's being in New York," she explained. "I take agents and authors to lunch almost daily. I couldn't do that from Aspen."

"I was only thinking a few days a month," Max said. He paused and looked at Caroline. "Unless you only want to be in New York."

Caroline had always been a New Yorker. Going to the cabin to rest and recharge was fine, but working somewhere else part-time was different. New York revived her; she couldn't imagine being anywhere else.

"It's not the right time," she volunteered. "Maybe during the summer when everyone in publishing goes on vacation."

"You don't want to see each other until summer?" Max repeated incredulously.

"We'll see each other. You said you'd come to New York on the weekends. We can attend author readings and explore restaurants. You'll love the High Line, there's the best Italian food and . . ."

"I prefer Mexican food you get in California or Western burgers." Max's tone was clipped. "It's not about the food or the sightseeing. It's about having a partner who's willing to meet halfway. It's called compromise, it's the basis of any relationship."

A knot formed in Caroline's stomach. Her cheeks grew hot.

"My job is very important to me. You feel the same about the distillery."

"But I'd work on it. I'd hire a manager who can take over some of my duties while I try to sell rye whiskey in New York. You refuse to even try. Why would you tell me you were falling in love with me if you aren't willing to try?"

The knot in Caroline's stomach grew tighter.

"I wasn't thinking that far ahead."

"It's not far ahead. You're going back to New York in a couple of days."

Max was right. If their relationship stood a chance, she had to make some changes. She thought about Luke and Daphne. Caroline had told Daphne that a commuter marriage was a lot of work. A long-distance romance would be even worse.

Before she could say anything, Max stuffed his hands in his pockets.

"I think we should stop right now. You were right about yourself. You're a sophisticated New York editor who jets off to fancy ski resorts at a moment's notice, and has little flings without thinking about other people's feelings." He turned toward his car. "I have to go. Enjoy the cheesesteak hoagie."

Caroline watched him go. It was freezing, but she was too mortified to go back into the bar. Daphne would know that something was wrong and Caroline wasn't ready to tell her. Instead, she pulled out her phone and called an Uber. She waited, hugging her arms around her chest and wondering when her breathing would return to normal and the ache in her heart would subside.

When she got back to the inn there was a message from the front desk saying that Claudia called and to call her back immediately.

Caroline wondered what Claudia wanted. She was in Palm

Springs for the holidays and it was one hour earlier in California.

She called Claudia's cell phone and waited for her to pick up.

"I called your cell phone but it was off," Claudia said when she answered.

"Daphne dragged me to a karaoke bar," Caroline said.

"I hate to interrupt your holiday but this couldn't wait." Claudia kept talking. "It's been hush-hush until now but the company is in talks to merge with another publisher. I need you to send me a new manuscript within two weeks. We need to show there are exciting forthcoming titles that will be launched for the coming season."

"In two weeks?" Caroline gulped. At their meeting before Christmas, Claudia said that Caroline had until the end of winter to bring a new author onto her list.

"I need something now, and it's got to be something everyone gets excited about."

"I do have something. He's a local writer. But we're still editing it."

"Send it as soon as you can and I'll read it on the plane. Then we'd still have time to acquire it."

She and Nick weren't finished with the edits. And now Savannah was coming to Aspen. But she couldn't say no to Claudia.

"Of course. No problem. You'll have it right after New Year's."

Caroline hung up and gazed out the window. The mountain was beautiful at night. Stars lit up the slopes, and the moon was a silver ball.

Her mind went to Max, stalking away in the parking lot. She couldn't think about him now. At 7:00 p.m. she was meeting her mother's lover in front of Santa's Little Red Mailbox. The day after that, Daphne and Luke were getting married. And now she had to deliver the best manuscript Claudia ever read. All Caroline had left was her job. Without it, she wouldn't have anything at all.

Chapter Twenty-five

At 7:00 p.m., Caroline would finally get to meet the man her mother had spent her last vacation with. What if he didn't show up? And if he did, what would she say when she saw him?

She needed to distract herself. She took Nina's letter from the stack on the bedside table and started reading.

Dear Anne,

I'm afraid I don't feel very festive today. My editor at Women's World Monthly, Margaret Baker, died. When we worked together, she was so sophisticated. I always felt like she was so much older than me, but she was only eighty when she died. In five years, I'll be the same age and I have so much more to say. I suppose most writers feel that way. How many authors' books are sold posthumously? As if we're all determined to have the final word.

Margaret had a long romance with a male travel writer, but they never got married. She became editor in chief of

Women's World Monthly, and went on to be publisher of a fashion magazine based in Rome.

I visited her once and we had a fancy lunch at a restaurant at the top of the Spanish Steps. I never saw her again after that.

But her death still hits hard. If Margaret hadn't appeared in Vermont that day, my life might have turned out differently. It's odd how one small event leads to others. I can retell what happened now, but at the time I was furious with Margaret, and with Teddy. I couldn't show Margaret how I felt. She was my boss and I was a working girl. I depended on my paycheck.

I stood at the door of the farm in Vermont and closed my eyes, wishing that a Christmas miracle would whisk Margaret back to New York. When I opened my eyes, she was still there. I couldn't risk her firing me for letting her freeze to death, so I ushered her inside.

Margaret glanced around at the fire burning in the fireplace, and the two Christmas trees decorated with ornaments.

"The place looks wonderful, you're more domestic than I thought." Margaret trailed her gloved hands over the blanket draped on the sofa. I didn't explain that the blanket was there because I was sleeping on the sofa, and the extra Christmas tree was the result of the tussle between Teddy and James. Instead, I changed the subject.

"What are you doing in Vermont?" I asked. "You and Harry were going to Palm Beach."

"Harry got a last-minute assignment covering New

Year's Day in Sydney. I didn't want to travel thirty-six hours just to see the first New Year's Eve across the world." She took off her fur coat. "I was going to go skiing in the Adirondacks while Harry was away, but then Teddy called with the invitation."

"The invitation?" I repeated, puzzled.

"To your wedding." Margaret pulled off her gloves. "What a splendid idea! Laura's fans will love that you got married on New Year's Eve. You'll have to write about it in a column, and we'll add some recipes. Perhaps a special wedding cocktail. The Laura and Teddy Love Potion."

My stomach lurched.

"Teddy invited you to our wedding?"

"He called this morning. Father Joseph is going to be the officiant and James will be his best man. I'm happy to be your maid of honor."

Teddy was clever. Having Margaret at the wedding would make sure I went through with it.

I cleared my throat. "The thing is that I'm not marrying Teddy. James and I have fallen in love, and we're getting married instead."

Margaret looked at me as if I'd told her that I had walked on the moon.

"You're marrying the contest winner?" Her eyebrows shot up.

"James is handsome and kind and intelligent," I said enthusiastically. I had to make Margaret believe me. "His grandmother started Barbara's Pies, and James is a successful pediatric oncologist. We have so much in common. He loves reading and history . . ."

"I don't care if his grandmother is the CEO of Sara Lee and James's the head of NewYork-Presbyterian Hospital, you can't marry him. Laura's fans would be furious. Laura can't ditch her fiancé for a man she's known for a few days."

"Her fans don't have to know," I said.

"Of course they'll know! If Father Joseph is officiating, people in town will talk. It's out of the question. And marrying Teddy on New Year's Eve will be so romantic, Laura's readership will go through the roof."

"I can't marry Teddy to please Laura's readership."

"Of course you can. You're going to marry him anyway," Margaret said patiently.

"But I'm not Laura Carter. I'm Nina."

"That's the wonderful thing. Betty has kept Laura's fiancé so private, her readers don't know anything about him."

I glanced at the scotch bottle on the sideboard. If this charade kept up much longer, I'd develop a serious drinking problem.

"You and Teddy can get married again properly when you get back to New York. I'll even get you a good deal at the Waldorf Astoria, they're big advertisers of the magazine. It will take a bit of work to get Laura's name changed to yours on the marriage certificate, but I know someone at City Hall."

I tried one more time. "Things between Teddy and me have been strained for a while. James and I really are in love. Wait until you meet him."

Margaret gave me the same look she used on a copy editor who was late on a deadline.

"I told you, it's out of the question." Then her expression softened. "All couples go through difficult times. You and Teddy have been together for so long, you'll work it out."

Before I could answer, James entered the room. He had changed for dinner and looked particularly handsome in a V-neck sweater and gray slacks.

"This is James Stanley, the contest winner," I said, introducing him. "This is Margaret Baker, lifestyle editor at *Women's World Monthly*."

Margaret let out a slow whistle.

"You really are handsome, we'll have to get a photo of you. Laura's readers will love it."

"Delighted to meet you." James shook her hand. "My grandmother is a huge fan of the magazine." He shot me a smile. "And Laura has been the perfect hostess. I'm having a wonderful time."

Margaret's fawning expression faded.

"Laura filled me in on recent events. You can't marry Laura. It's a ridiculous idea, and I could lose my job. I'm the one who set this all up."

I hadn't thought of that. I glanced at James beseechingly.

"I don't want to get anyone in trouble," James said. "The thing is, Laura and I fell in love and . . ."

Teddy took that moment to enter the living room. It was almost as if he had been listening at the door. He wore an apron over a wool sweater.

"Margaret! You made it." He beamed. "I'm cooking beef Stroganoff. The beef comes from a local farm."

"I love Stroganoff, but we have to settle something first," Margaret said. "There seems to be some confusion on who is the groom. You invited me to your and Laura's wedding. That's the one I plan to attend."

Teddy walked over to me and placed his arm around me.

"We already talked about it, of course we're getting married." He kissed me on the cheek. "Lots of brides get cold feet before the big day. What we all need is a round of drinks."

Teddy fixed scotch and sodas for everyone. He and Margaret talked about Palmolive's advertising budget for the new year.

Teddy refilled Margaret's glass. "The farm is getting crowded, so I reserved a room for you at the Mountain Inn. It's not quite the Ritz, but you'll be comfortable."

"As long as there's central heating." Margaret nodded. She glared at me. "Now about this wedding. Are we clear on who's marrying whom?"

I had known Margaret long enough to recognize when it was time to wave the white flag.

"I'll marry Teddy," I said glumly.

Teddy leaned over and kissed me. "That's my girl. Why don't you help me with the beef Stroganoff. Give James and Margaret time to get to know each other."

Dinner was more pleasant than I expected. Teddy was his most charming self. I resigned myself to marrying him. I'd get it annulled when I returned to New York. By the same time the following week, I'd be Nina Buckley again. I even resolved to stop putting off writing my next novel.

James and Margaret got along so well, they flirted with each other. I didn't blame Margaret. James was polite and good-looking, and Harry had been stringing her along for ages. Margaret deserved a man who treated her properly.

It was the next morning that all hell broke loose. Father Joseph was going to arrive at noon; the ceremony would be at 1:00 p.m., followed by a light lunch and wedding cake.

When I entered the kitchen, the house was quiet. James was out and Teddy must have gone to the inn to pick up Margaret.

I was making coffee when there was a knock at the door. A man in a bulky lumberjack jacket stood outside.

I opened the front door. "Can I help you?"

"I'm Jack Arnold, a friend of Father Joseph's," he said. "I wonder if I could come in for a minute."

I ushered him inside.

"I was making coffee, would you like some?"

The man sat on the sofa. He nodded. "I've lived here all my life, but I still get cold without my morning coffee."

I brought his cup into the living room and sat opposite him.

"My wife ran into Father Joseph's wife at the general store, you know how women love to gossip. Father Joseph's wife mentioned that Laura Carter is getting married today, the whole town is excited." He nursed his cup. "I write a column for the local newspaper. I'd be honored if you give me a quick interview, just a few quotes about the wedding."

I put down my coffee cup.

"I'm afraid that's out of the question. My fiancé is very private, you might say he's reclusive."

"You don't have to mention his name," Jack pleaded. "It

would mean so much to all of us. You helped put this town on the map, and tourists bring in money."

If the whole town was gossiping about the wedding anyway, it wouldn't hurt to give him a few quotes.

"There's not much to tell," I began. "Teddy and I have known each other for ages. We both love Vermont, it's so invigorating."

At that moment the kitchen door swung open. James entered; he was carrying an armful of logs.

The man jumped up and held out his hand. "Jack Arnold. Nice to meet you, Teddy."

"I'm not Teddy." James moved the logs so he could shake Jack's hand. "James Stanley, contest winner."

Jack looked puzzled. I was about to explain about the magazine contest when the kitchen door opened again. This time it was Teddy and Margaret. Margaret wore her fox fur coat and matching muff.

I introduced everyone.

"Jack writes a column in the local newspaper. He wants to write a short piece about the wedding."

Margaret was looking intently at Jack. And Jack was staring at Teddy.

"That's not Jack Arnold, that's Jack Gold, page six photographer for the *New York Post*," Margaret announced. "What are you doing here?"

A smirk crossed Jack's face. "A little bird tipped me off that Teddy Chandler the Third was getting married today. Except the bride isn't Laura Carter." He turned to me. "I recognize you from that women's lib event in

New York. You're that author who hates men, Nina Buckley."

"I do not hate men," I said before I could stop myself. "I simply believe that women have rights too."

At that moment, Jack took a camera from under his jacket and pointed it at our little group.

"Page six readers won't care about that. They'll be more interested in why you're pulling the wool over thousands of readers' eyes and pretending to be Laura Carter."

Then he clicked his camera.

Dearest Anne, I have to stop there. I'm going to donate some money to the animal shelter in Margaret's honor. She loved animals, especially stray dogs.

I promise I'll finish the story in my next letter. I know that even the best writer loses her audience when a book drags on for too long.

Thank you for listening to me. Writing these letters has been the best therapy I could imagine.

Regards,
Nina

When Caroline arrived at the Limelight Hotel, Nick wasn't in the little office. She found him in the lobby. She almost didn't recognize him. His hair was neatly combed and he wore a collared shirt and loafers instead of his usual black sneakers.

He jumped up when he saw her.

"Savannah will be here any minute."

Caroline was about to tell him about her conversation with Claudia when a woman in her late twenties entered the lobby. She was strikingly beautiful, with green eyes and wavy strawberry-blond hair. She looked extremely chic in a cream sweater and beige cashmere slacks.

Caroline glanced at Nick's almost dazed expression and knew immediately that this was Savannah.

Savannah walked up to them and kissed Nick on the cheek.

"You haven't aged a bit in five years," she said.

"This is Caroline," Nick said. "She's my editor."

"I couldn't believe it when you told me over the phone," Savannah gushed. "You sold your novel! I feel so proud." She turned to Caroline. "I encouraged Nick to write, I knew he could do it if he tried."

"The book hasn't sold yet," Caroline said. "But I know it will, as long as we do the work."

"Well, I want to hear all about it." Savannah took Nick's arm. "Just think, I know a famous author."

Caroline glanced at Savannah curiously. There was something about her tone that was almost cloying. But Nick was like a kitten lapping up a bowl of milk.

They went to a coffee shop on Main Street. Caroline and Nick had hot chocolates and Savannah ordered avocado toast and chai tea. Caroline was surprised when Savannah asked Nick to pay for hers.

"My parents have me on an allowance." Savannah rolled her eyes. "And their condo in Vail only has rich, fried Southern food. I've spent the last five years in Europe, I'm not going to eat unhealthy fried eggs and grits."

Savannah told them everything she had done since she left the ranch. First, she spent the year on an archaeological dig in Greece, followed by a few months in Croatia and Malta. But she found that the sun on archaeological digs was usually too hot, and everyone slept in tents.

"All I wanted was to sleep in a proper bed, so I took a job for the winter working at a ski resort in the German Alps. Then, last spring I went to Spain. I love Spain," she said dreamily. "I worked at a resort on the Mediterranean. Everyone takes long siestas during the day and stays out late at night." She beamed at Nick. "I even taught horseback riding. I was going to stay forever, but then something happened."

Savannah fell in love with a dashing older Spaniard named Antonio. She swore she didn't know he was married. One day, his wife appeared at the resort. She made a terrible scene in front of everyone. Savannah was fired; she couldn't find another job and ran out of money.

"I had to ask my parents for the plane ticket home." She gave a heavy sigh. "Now they have me practically under house arrest. They're insisting I spend a year in Atlanta at home. I don't know what I'll do for work. It's easy to find work in Europe without a college degree, but it's different here. And everyone in Atlanta knows what happened. I won't be able to show my face anywhere."

Savannah went to the restroom. Caroline and Nick sat together at the table.

"Poor Savannah." Nick stirred his hot chocolate. "She's had a hard time."

Caroline wanted to say that spending five years in Greece and Croatia and Spain didn't sound that hard. But she could tell by Nick's expression that he wouldn't hear her.

"There's something I need to talk to you about," Caroline said instead. "I had a call with Claudia today."

Nick looked up from his cup.

"Can it wait?" he asked. "I'm going to drive Savannah back to Vail. She took the bus here, her parents wouldn't lend her their car."

Savannah returned and gave Caroline a quick hug.

"I'm so glad to have met you." She linked her arm through Nick's.

When Caroline arrived back at the inn, Daphne was standing outside her room.

"I thought you would be with Luke all day," Caroline said, opening the door.

"He went to the airport to pick up Eric, his best man," Daphne answered. "I wanted to see you. You left Zane's and didn't come back."

Caroline took off her jacket and sat on an armchair.

"Max came outside, we had a long talk." She remembered how he looked so handsome in a suede jacket.

Caroline told Daphne the whole story.

"Max is right, I could work remotely from Aspen some of the time. But part of my job is taking authors and agents to lunch. And I couldn't live without the throb of New York."

"You're living without it now," Daphne reasoned.

"It's Christmas week in Aspen. Anyone can live in a fairyland for a while."

Caroline expected Daphne to keep arguing.

"I'm proud of you for opening your heart," Daphne said instead.

"I'm proud of me too," Caroline laughed. She realized she did feel better. Falling for Max had opened something inside her. She felt freer, and almost happy.

"I'm so anxious. I hope Mom's lover will be there."

"That's the other reason I came," Daphne replied. "I can go with you if you like."

Caroline shook her head. "What if Mom didn't tell him about us? It will be overwhelming for him to meet both of us at the same time."

"I guess you're right," Daphne agreed. "I'm going to take my last, long bath as a single woman. Luke and I promised to save on hot water. It will reduce our monthly bill and it's good for the environment."

As Daphne was about to leave, she turned from the door.

"Even if you and Max aren't together, I'm still going to throw you the bridal bouquet. You tried and that's a good start."

Caroline stood across the street from Santa's Little Red Mailbox. Main Street was quieter than Caroline had seen it. Most people were at their hotels, getting ready to celebrate New Year's Eve.

She had arrived ten minutes early. Now it was exactly seven o'clock and the other things on her mind—Daphne and Luke's wedding, her phone call with Claudia, the reappearance of Savannah in Nick's life after all these years, even her feelings for Max— faded. What would her mother's lover be like and what would she say to him? Would she know who he was when she saw him?

Another twenty minutes passed. Caroline's nervousness and excitement turned into disappointment. He couldn't have written such a heartfelt letter begging Anne to come, and then not show up himself.

At seven thirty she was about to leave when a man rushed up to the mailbox. He glanced at his phone and then peered up and down the street.

The man was very tall, with dark brown hair and a longish face. He wore a calf-length wool coat and leather gloves.

Caroline took a deep breath and strode across the street.

"I'm Caroline," she said, introducing herself.

He pulled his gaze toward her.

"Caroline Holt," she said. "Anne Holt's daughter."

The man paused, then held out his hand.

"I'm Michael. Where is Anne?" His eyes were bright. "I can't wait to see her."

Caroline shook her head. She dug her hands into her pockets. "She didn't come."

She waited, not quite knowing what to say next.

He frowned, puzzled. "So, she sent you to tell me?"

"Not exactly. You see, my mother died two months ago. I found the letter in a pile of mail, so I . . ."

"Anne is dead?" he asked, heartbroken.

Caroline could tell from his expression that he never knew Anne had cancer.

"She had cancer. Last summer, she was in remission. The cancer returned in September and she died a month later."

"Cancer," he breathed. He looked at Caroline intently. "So, you're Caroline. Did she mention me to you?"

"She didn't say anything. I came because I didn't want you to think that she stood you up." Caroline gulped. She didn't know why she felt like she had to explain, but the words kept rushing out. "She wasn't like that. She never kept anyone waiting, and she was so giving. I'm sure if she got your letter, she would have gone out of her way to meet you. She was a very special person, I miss her every day."

"I'm glad you came." He nodded. His eyes were kind and gentle. "Why don't we get coffee? I don't know about you, but I wouldn't mind a warm place to sit and talk."

They sat in a booth at Paradise Bakery and ordered coffee and orange-iced muffins.

"Tell me about the cancer," Michael said, eating a bite of muffin.

Caroline told him how her mother kept it secret in the beginning. After she finished the treatment, she seemed so confident that she would stay in remission.

"My sister, Daphne, and I were shocked when she went back to the hospital. She had asked us to come to the Aspen writers' conference and we both said no. Now I wonder if she knew that it would be her last summer. She did some other odd things too, things she hadn't done before." Caroline sipped the cider. "She bought herself a pair of earrings simply because she thought they were pretty. My mother loved jewelry but she only bought pieces when one of her authors had a big success. It was one of her traditions."

"I would have liked you and your sister to have come." Michael nodded. "She never told you anything about me? How we met or what happened afterward?"

"I don't even know your last name," Caroline said. "All I had was your letter asking her to show up at Santa's Little Red Mailbox."

Michael picked up his cup and told her the whole story. They met during college, while they were studying abroad. Michael was an architecture major and spent the spring and summer in the South of France. They became serious and for a while they were inseparable. They traveled together on the weekends, and they spent countless hours sitting at cafés and talking about what they wanted out of life.

"A few weeks before we were supposed to go home, Anne just left," Michael said. "It was a different time. We didn't have cell phones or emails. And we hadn't given each other our home addresses or phone numbers. Why should we? We saw each other every day. I couldn't understand why she left without saying goodbye or even without leaving a note, but I blamed myself. I was young and scared, I never told Anne that I was falling in love with her. She probably thought it was a college romance and it was better to end it quickly than for it to drag on when we got back to the States.

"I graduated and got a good job at an architectural firm. I traveled the world designing buildings and became quite successful. I didn't see Anne again for thirty years. Then last year, I ran into her in New York. She looked more beautiful than ever: she was so poised and sophisticated. I insisted we have coffee and we filled each other in on our lives. She told me she was a successful literary agent. She had been married and had two daughters. Her husband died a few years earlier. This time, we exchanged phone numbers. But when I called the number I realized it was her office. I left messages but she never returned my calls.

"Then, in June, she called and asked if I wanted to attend the writers' conference in Aspen. I said yes and we had a magical time. I admitted my old feelings for her and told her they hadn't changed. She never said 'I love you,' but I felt confident she felt the same. So, on the last day, I wrote her the letter from Santa's Little Red Mailbox." He pulled a small box out of his pocket and opened it. "I was trying to think of the most special way to propose. I decided to ask her to marry me on New Year's Eve."

Caroline gasped. The engagement ring was beautiful, a square diamond on a platinum band. Her mother would have loved it. Tears formed in Caroline's eyes. She looked at Michael.

"I'm so sorry, she never said anything."

"She didn't tell you anything about me and you?" Michael questioned.

"Me and you?" Caroline repeated, puzzled.

Michael set the jewelry box on the table.

"The reason she went back to New York without telling me was that she was pregnant. She was afraid that if she told me, I'd do the honorable thing and insist we get married."

A chill ran through Caroline. Of course, she hadn't been thinking clearly. Michael's last name must be Palmer. He lived in Philadelphia and he was her father.

"She told me everything last summer, but she made me promise not to contact you. She wanted to tell you herself first."

"I guess there wasn't time," Caroline said. Tears welled in her eyes. She bit her lip and pushed them away. If she let them start, they'd never stop. "She went into the hospital a couple of months after she came home."

Michael touched Caroline's hand.

"She was terrified you wouldn't forgive her. She felt terrible for depriving you of a father and me of a daughter. Times were different then. She was afraid she'd end up as a housewife. Her future and her career were so important to her, she couldn't just let them go."

"I don't know what to say," Caroline stammered. The whole world seemed different. The room tipped and she was afraid she might faint. It was impossible to know how to feel. She wanted to ask her mother so many questions. Why hadn't she told Michael that he had a daughter? What would it have been like if Caroline had known him as a child? Would she have spent Christmases with him, or visited him for a month in the summer?

For a moment, Caroline was furious. A father/daughter bond was so important; Caroline had missed out on something she could never get back. But at the same time she could understand Anne's reasoning. Caroline had Walter as a father. Anne didn't want to separate the family or create any distance between Caroline and Daphne. Perhaps she was even afraid that Caroline would want to go live with Michael. Nothing was more important to Anne than her daughters.

Caroline pulled her mind back to the present. Michael was still talking.

"You don't have to say anything," Michael assured her. "I never married. I told myself it was because I was busy traveling for work, but the truth was that I never met anyone like your mother. And I always wanted a daughter. I'm sure you have a full life, but I'd love to spend time together." His own eyes clouded over. "You had Anne for a mother, you must be very special."

Michael was right, her mother was very special. And whatever reasons she kept Caroline and Michael apart didn't matter anymore. Her mother was dead, and Caroline and Michael had found each other.

Caroline swallowed the lump in her throat. She blinked away the tears and suggested he come to Daphne and Luke's wedding.

"Daphne would love to meet you. She wanted to come to the mailbox but I wanted to go alone."

"Are you sure it won't be an imposition?" Michael asked. "I don't want to interfere with the most important day of her life."

Caroline promised it would be perfect. As if part of their

mother—the young Anne whom neither of them had known—would be there.

They talked about Michael's life in Philadelphia, and Caroline's job at the publishing house. Michael was staying at Hotel Jerome, and they walked together down Main Street.

Then Caroline went back to her room and sent Daphne a text saying she had a headache and wasn't going to stay up until midnight. She wanted to feel her best for the wedding.

Meeting her father in front of Santa's Little Red Mailbox was a Christmas miracle. If only her mother had been there too.

Chapter Twenty-six

Caroline woke up the next morning, full of energy. The ceremony was at five o'clock and she had so much to do. First, she wanted to read Nina's last letter to Anne. She ordered scrambled eggs from room service and took a quick shower. Then she got dressed and sat down to read.

My dearest Anne,

It is finally January! Macy's and Saks have taken down their Christmas windows and replaced them with sales on coats and sweaters. I have a closet full of winter clothes so I don't need anything. I promised I'd make this my final letter and tell you the rest of the story.

At first, I was furious with Teddy. But what happened wasn't his fault. He had no idea that a photographer had followed Margaret to Vermont. There was nothing any of us could do. The photos ran with a feature in the *New York Post*. Teddy's mother was so embarrassed, she fled New York and didn't return for months. I admit, the turn of events made me secretly happy. I had nothing against Dolly as a person, but her interference almost ruined our relationship. Teddy and I stayed in Vermont. I was fired from *Women's World Monthly* and Teddy resigned from Palmolive. Margaret's job was on the line too, but I swore that it was all my idea and she didn't know my true identity. There was no point in us all being out of work.

Teddy and I didn't get the marriage annulled. At first, we were going to do it when we returned to Manhattan. But the longer we were together, the more I realized I loved him. Yes, he had made mistakes, but none of us were perfect. And he made me happy.

Vermont that spring was glorious. We rented a cottage near to town. The trees blossomed, and the grass was a bright emerald green. One day, Teddy mentioned that the farm a few doors down was for sale and we should buy it. I thought it was a crazy idea, but the more I thought about it, the more I liked it. I could write anywhere, and Teddy loved having cows and sheep.

We pooled our savings and bought the farm. In the beginning, the locals were leery of us and about what I had done. But I guess they thought that all New Yorkers were a bit crazy. And we made sure to give back to the community. I mentored girls at the high school who were interested in journalism, and Teddy taught a class in business and advertising. We hosted an annual Christmas party and donated our milk and cheeses to local charities.

We tried to have children, but they never came. I didn't

mind too much. Teddy and I had each other, and that was enough.

My agent tried selling my next book, but I had been backlisted in the publishing world. So, I wrote romances under a pseudonym. They didn't pay much, but they satisfied my creative outlet. Over the years, the romance field changed, and my publisher eventually dropped me.

A few years ago, Teddy got sick, and last year he died. I knew it was time to come back to New York. It would have been too difficult to live on the farm without him. And I was lonely.

That's how I ended up in your office, Anne. I'm so glad you agreed to represent me. Now, I'll hunker down and write the novel that I promised you.

I know the question you'll ask, when you read these letters. I am a writer after all, my job is imagining people's reactions to things. And I can give you my answer.

No, I don't regret any of it. I may not have had the brilliant literary career I imagined for myself, but for over forty years I had love. And I made someone else happy. If we can improve even just two people's lives—our own and the person's we love—that's a successful life.

You have so much in your life—your wonderful career, a lovely home, those beautiful daughters. You're very lucky, cherish all of it.

Happy New Year, dear Anne! I'm putting the seal on this envelope and I'm getting to work.

Regards,
Nina

Caroline put the letter on top of the stack. She thought she understood why her mother had kept the letters. Nina had been the opposite of Anne. She had given up her career for love. Did that mean that Anne regretted her own choices? Did she wish she had stayed with Michael all those years ago?

Caroline wished she could ask her. But there was nothing she could do. And it didn't matter now. Caroline had to figure out her own future by herself.

She took the letters to the front desk and asked the man behind the counter to scan them and send them to her email. Then she went to the Limelight Hotel to see Nick. She had to tell him that she needed the manuscript sooner than they had planned.

Nick wasn't in the little office. His laptop was gone and the coffee cup that usually stood beside it was missing. Instead, there was an envelope with Caroline's name.

Caroline opened it and read the letter.

Dear Caroline,

There's something I have to tell you. I could have just sent an email but I didn't want you to get it and try to stop me.

Savannah and I are eloping. Then we're driving to Lake Tahoe in California. Savannah knows someone there who runs a ski resort. We'll work there during the winter and then we'll figure out what to do next.

I promise I'll finish the revisions once we get settled. It might take a couple of weeks longer, but I won't let you down.

I'm sure you think I'm crazy. Savannah left before,

*what's to stop her from disappearing again? I could
say that we're both older and wiser, but I don't know
if that's true. All I know is that I'm in love with her.
When Savannah is around, I feel differently about
everything, I can't let that feeling go.*

*I'm grateful for your belief in me and my book.
It changed the way I see myself. I have a lot to give
Savannah and I have a lot to offer the world. You're not
only a great editor, you're a good person. You made me
a better man.*

*I'll email you the pages as soon as they're done.
Happy New Year, Caroline!*

*Sincerely,
Nick*

Caroline folded the letter and slipped it back in the envelope.
How would she explain to Claudia that she wouldn't have the
manuscript until the end of January?

She pulled out her cell phone to call Nick, but then she put it
back. There was no point in telling him Claudia's ultimatum. Her
career was not his responsibility. Nick was a talented writer. If Claudia didn't buy the book, another publisher would. And she couldn't
stop him because she thought he might get hurt. He was in love with
Savannah, nothing was going to change his mind.

Caroline walked down Main Street to the Aspen Inn. She saw
Lily entering the souvenir shop behind Santa's Little Red Mailbox.
Caroline ran in after her.

"Caroline?" Lily turned around. "What are you doing here?"

"I saw you walk inside," Caroline said. "We're leaving tomorrow.

I wanted to come and say goodbye, but I was afraid Max would be there."

"Uncle Max and I are leaving too. Uncle Max is coming to stay in California. He said it's because he needs a week of sunshine at the beach, but it's because he got into a fight with Grandma. I heard them arguing in the kitchen."

"Arguing about what?" Caroline asked.

Lily glanced around, as if she was afraid someone was listening. She moved closer.

"I didn't mean to eavesdrop. I came downstairs to get some pumpkin bread," she said. "Grandma was saying that if you love someone you don't let them go. Uncle Max argued that you'd made yourself perfectly clear. Then he said it was none of Grandma's business and he was going to California to hang out with me when my mom is working."

"They were arguing about me?" Caroline said in surprise.

"I told you that code three is extreme. Sometimes when people come out of a code three, they don't know what they're saying," Lily said anxiously. "I'm sure Uncle Max isn't really angry at you."

"He should be," Caroline sighed. "I said some things that were unforgivable."

"Almost everything can be forgiven. That's why there's Christmas," Lily offered logically. "You have to give things time."

"Max is leaving tomorrow and so am I," Caroline said. "We might not see each other again."

"Do you want to see Uncle Max again?"

Caroline glanced around the store at the Christmas trees decorated with colored ornaments. At the toys and boxes of candy. Christmas was about forgiveness, but it was also about miracles. It was a miracle that she had met her father. It was a miracle that she found Nick's manuscript and that it made her excited about her career again. And it was a miracle that she had met and fallen in love with Max in such a short amount of time.

She thought about the courage it had taken her mother to face her cancer, and the courage that Daphne needed to marry Luke so soon after they met. Caroline needed that kind of courage now.

"I guess I do." Caroline nodded. "Perhaps I can come back to the house with you."

Lily picked out four envelopes.

"That's a great idea. I just need to buy these envelopes to put in Santa's Little Red Mailbox." Lily took out a little purse.

"I'll buy them for you and get some of my own." Caroline added a few more envelopes to the pile. "Then we'll walk together."

Max was sitting at the kitchen counter when they arrived. He looked up from the list he was writing.

"What are you doing here?" he asked. There were circles under his eyes, but he still looked handsome. He wore a gray V-neck sweater and blue jeans.

"I ran into Lily at the souvenir shop," Caroline said nervously. Her hands were clammy and it was hard to swallow. "Lily said you were going to California tomorrow."

Max grunted a reply. He stood up and poured a cup of coffee from the coffeepot. "I didn't think I'd see you again."

"I wasn't going to try to see you," Caroline began. "You made yourself pretty clear, but the thing is . . ." She took a deep breath. "You were right about everything."

Max was about to say something but Caroline didn't let him

interrupt her. This was her only chance and she had to say exactly what she was feeling.

"Yesterday I waited in front of Santa's Little Red Mailbox for my mother's lover to show up. He was half an hour late and I was about to leave when he appeared. I'm so glad I waited. Not only was he the love of my mother's life, he's my father. Thirty years ago, she didn't have the courage to make the relationship work, she was too afraid of missing out on having a career. I know her career brought her joy, and I can't ask her if she felt that she had made a mistake. But I spent the last twenty-four hours asking myself what I wanted. I do want to be successful at my job, but it isn't the only thing I want. I'm falling for you and I don't want to give that up. I'm willing to work part-time from Aspen if that's what it takes."

Max didn't say anything. Caroline glanced anxiously at her hands. It was too late. Max had already made up his mind about her and he wasn't interested in a relationship anymore.

Finally, he walked over to her and kissed her. It was a long, sweet kiss.

"I'm falling in love with you too, Caroline," Max said. "I wouldn't have let you go."

"You wouldn't?" Caroline said in surprise.

Max picked up the piece of paper.

"I was writing out a list of reasons we should be together," he said with a smile. "The writers' conference in Aspen is looking for speakers for next summer, my mother put your name up to be on a panel. And Luke's going to start selling my rye whiskey at his restaurant in Hudson. So, I already have a reason to come to New York. I was going to leave the list with the concierge."

Caroline gulped away a tear.

"You should bring Lily to New York. We can take her to the New York Public Library and the Museum of Natural History," she suggested.

Max kissed her again and Caroline kissed him back.

"I have to get ready for the wedding!" she exclaimed. Her eyes were moist with tears. "My father is going to be there. I can't wait for you to meet him."

When Caroline arrived at the little church, Daphne was sitting in the anteroom. Her veil was spread out on the desk, next to a box containing their mother's turquoise earrings.

"I left a note with the concierge," Daphne said. She wore a striped turtleneck sweater and white jeans. "I was afraid something happened to you."

"I feel terrible that I'm late," Caroline apologized. "I had some things to take care of that couldn't wait."

"Did one of them involve Max?" Daphne asked.

Caroline flushed. "How did you know?"

"You have that glow." Daphne stood up and hugged her.

"It's not just Max," Caroline said. She told Daphne about Santa's Little Red Mailbox and finding her father.

"I asked him to come to the wedding, I hope that's all right."

"It's the best thing I've ever heard." Daphne's eyes were round with disbelief. "I can't wait to meet him. And I know Luke will be thrilled."

Caroline walked over to where Daphne's wedding dress hung by the window.

"Last Christmas I never would have believed that this year

we'd be in Aspen and you'd be getting married." Caroline ran her fingers over the pink crepe.

"Mom would have loved it, Christmas was her favorite time of the year." Daphne joined her. She grinned impishly. "The only thing she would have liked better would have been a double wedding."

"I've only just started this relationship thing," Caroline laughed. "First I intend to be thoroughly spoiled with trips together and romantic dinner dates."

"And make sure Max celebrates all the important events." Daphne ticked them off on her fingers. "Valentine's Day and your birthday and the anniversary of the day you met."

"I intend to spoil him too." Caroline nodded emphatically. "I've never done things for a guy before. Maybe you can teach me how to cook."

"I'd be happy to." Daphne beamed.

There was the sound of footsteps in the church.

Caroline peered out. Luke stood at the altar, looking handsome in a navy-blue tuxedo and yellow tie. Eric, his best man, stood beside him.

Max and Lily were in the front row, and a tall man sat in the back. It was Michael, Caroline's father.

"Everyone is here." Caroline turned back to Daphne. She took the dress from the hanger. "It's time to dress the bride."

Chapter Twenty-seven

The next morning, Caroline folded sweaters into her suitcase.

Daphne and Luke's wedding had been straight out of a storybook. Daphne was the most beautiful bride, and Luke was so handsome and serious. For one awful moment, Eric couldn't find the wedding rings. Then Luke realized he had been so nervous he forgot to give them to him.

After the ceremony, the whole wedding party, including Max and Lily and Michael, walked down Main Street. The wedding dinner was held in the private dining room of Hotel Jerome. Michael insisted on buying champagne for everyone, and Luke gave a toast saying that not only was he marrying the love of his life, he had the good fortune of marrying into a wonderful family.

Max kept his hand firmly on Caroline's during dinner, and Caroline almost burst with happiness. Afterward, they danced at the hotel's bar, and then they all walked back to the Aspen Inn. Lily was so tired that Max had to carry her, and it was the best night that Caroline could remember.

Now, her phone rang and she saw that it was Claudia calling.

"Happy New Year," Claudia said. "I received the manuscript, I read it in one night. It's one of the best things I've ever read."

"The manuscript?" Caroline repeated, puzzled. She hadn't sent Nick's novel. She wanted to wait until it was perfect.

"Nina Buckley's letters," Claudia prompted. "I don't know where you dug them up, but they're mesmerizing. I read her obituary in *The New York Times*. She was a real talent in the 1970s. Then she disappeared, and now we know why."

Caroline tried to think. When she asked the business center to scan Nina's letters, she must have given the man Claudia's email instead of her own by accident.

Claudia was still talking. "You know how much I love a book written in letters, and it's a wonderful Christmas story," she said. "I think we could make this a huge bestseller for next fall."

"I have another manuscript for next winter's catalog," Caroline said anxiously. "It won't be ready for a couple of weeks."

"I'll save a space for it," Claudia said easily. "Nina's letters are proof that the old Caroline Holt is back—the Caroline who can spot a bestseller the minute it hits her desk. I'm confident you won't let me down."

They talked more about Nina's letters, and then Caroline hung up.

There was a knock at the door. Caroline thought it was Max, but it was Michael.

"My flight leaves in an hour. I wanted to come and say good-bye," Michael said.

Caroline ushered him inside. She told him about Claudia, and Nina's letters.

"Anne was always so proud of you," Michael said. "She said you have a golden future."

"A few days ago, I wasn't sure I'd have a job," Caroline admitted. "When you come to New York, I'll give you a tour of the publishing house, and of the literary agency where she worked."

Caroline and her father had already agreed to get together in New York. And she was going to visit him in Philadelphia.

"I'm in the market for a puppy. Maybe you can help me find one at an animal shelter in Philadelphia," Michael suggested.

"I'd love to," Caroline agreed happily. "I'll take you to my mother's favorite places in New York. She loved fancy restaurants but she had a soft spot for the pizza at Lombardi's. She'd walk ten blocks after work for a slice of their white pizza with ricotta and mozzarella cheese."

After Michael left, Caroline zipped up her suitcase and set it by the door. There was another knock. It was Max.

"Are you ready?" he asked.

"You don't have to take us to the airport. Daphne and Luke and I can take a taxi."

Max kissed her. "I want every minute with you until we see each other again. Besides, I got out of taking down the ornaments on the Christmas tree. My mom and Lily are going to do it while I'm gone."

Caroline and Max had already worked out a tentative schedule. Max was coming to New York for a few days after he returned from California. Caroline would spend a week in Aspen during March, and Max was going to visit New York again in April. Beyond that, they would play it by ear. But it felt good to have dates down on paper.

Caroline gathered some envelopes from the desk.

"First, I need to drop these in Santa's Little Red Mailbox." She held up the envelopes. "I wrote them last night to the important people in my life."

Max took her suitcase and Caroline followed him to the lobby. Outside the window, the sky was pale blue and the aspen trees were covered with fresh powder. It was going to be an exciting year. Nick would finish his revisions. And next December, Nina's letters would be published as a book. Daphne and Luke were going to open a second restaurant, and Caroline was thinking of selling her mother's town house and buying a place of her own.

And there was her relationship with Max. She didn't know where she and Max would be next Christmas. But she felt certain that they would be together.

Acknowledgments

Thank you to my wonderful agent, Johanna Castillo, for always making me a better writer, and thank you to my terrific editor, Sallie Lotz, for bringing so much to this story. Thank you to the whole team at St. Martin's Press, including Jennifer Enderlin, and Alexis Neuville in marketing.

Thank you to my children, Alex, Andrew, Heather, Madeleine, and Thomas; my daughter-in-law, Sarah; and my two Christmas miracles, my granddaughters, Lily and Emma.

About the Author

David Perry

Anita Hughes is the author of *Rome in Love* (adapted into a Hallmark movie in 2019) and *Christmas in Vermont* (adapted into a Lifetime movie in 2019). She is also the author of *Market Street, Lake Como, Santorini Sunsets, Christmas in Paris, Monarch Beach,* and other titles. She attended UC Berkeley's Master's in Creative Writing Program and lives in Dana Point, California.